Advance Acclaim

"Delightful at every turn, *A Bride for All Seasons* gives the
'mail-o   wist.
I could   nder-
hearted

er,

?r

"Four   eking
happin   t any
better

nd
e
Grove

"Four   :ollec-
tion w   essing
to del   otions
aroun   ride,
with e

ugh,
award-winning
author of 27 books
and novellas,
including the Pioneer
Promises series

"Grab a glass of sweet tea and settle in for a spell because you won't be able to put this wonderful book down! Penned by some of the best western romance writers in Christian fiction, this collection will become an instant, page-turning treasure."

— Lorna Seilstad, author of the Lake Manawa Series and *When Love Calls*

"Great mail-order bride stories! They're funny. They're poignant. A round-up of wonderful authors that you won't want to miss."

— Janet Tronstad, *USA Today* best-selling author

A BRIDE
FOR ALL
SEASONS

Other novels by these authors include:

Margaret Brownley

Gunpowder Tea
(available Fall 2013)

Waiting for Morning

Dawn Comes Early

A Vision of Lucy

A Suitor for Jenny

A Lady Like Sarah

Log Cabin Christmas Collection

Robin Lee Hatcher

Beloved

Betrayal

Belonging

Heart of Gold

A Matter of Character

Fit to Be Tied

A Vote of Confidence

Debra Clopton

Her Unforgettable Cowboy

Her Homecoming Cowboy

Her Lone Star Cowboy

Her Rodeo Cowboy

Her Forever Cowboy

His Cowgirl Bride

The Trouble with Lacy Brown

Mary Connealy

Swept Away

Kincaid Brides series

Petticoat Ranch

Lassoed in Texas trilogy

Married in Montana trilogy

Sophie's Daughters trilogy

Cowboy Christmas

A BRIDE FOR ALL SEASONS

A MAIL-ORDER BRIDE COLLECTION

MARGARET BROWNLEY
DEBRA CLOPTON, MARY CONNEALY
ROBIN LEE HATCHER

THOMAS NELSON
Since 1798

NASHVILLE   DALLAS   MEXICO CITY   RIO DE JANEIRO

Published in Nashville, Tennessee, by Thomas Nelson. Thomas Nelson is a registered trademark of Thomas Nelson, Inc.

Thomas Nelson, Inc., titles may be purchased in bulk for educational, business, fund-raising, or sales promotional use. For information, please e-mail SpecialMarkets@ThomasNelson.com.

Scripture quotations are taken from the King James Version of the Bible. THE NEW KING JAMES VERSION. © 1982 by Thomas Nelson, Inc. Used by permission. All rights reserved. The *Holy Bible*, New Living Translation. © 1996, 2004, 2007 by Tyndale House Foundation. Used by permission of Tyndale House Publishers, Inc., Carol Stream, Illinois 60188. All rights reserved. The Holy Bible, New International Version®, niv®. Copyright © 1973, 1978, 1984, 2011 by Biblica, Inc.™ Used by permission of Zondervan. All rights reserved worldwide. www. zondervan.com.

Publisher's Note: This novel is a work of fiction. Names, characters, places, and incidents are either products of the author's imagination or used fictitiously. All characters are fictional, and any similarity to people living or dead is purely coincidental.

Library of Congress Cataloging-in-Publication Data

[Novellas. Selections]
A bride for all seasons : a mail order bride collection / by Margaret Brownley, Debra Clopton, Robin Lee Hatcher, and Mary Connealy.
    pages cm
    ISBN 978-1-4016-8853-0 (alk. paper)
    1. Mail order brides—Fiction. 2. Christian fiction, American. 3. Love stories, American. I. Brownley, Margaret. And Then Came Spring. II. Clopton, Debra. An Ever After Summer. III. Hatcher, Robin Lee. Autumn's Angel. IV. Connealy, Mary. Winter Wedding Bells.
    PS648.L6B753 2013
    813'.08508—dc23   2013000168

Printed in the United States of America

13 14 15 16 17 18 RRD 6 5 4 3 2 1

To Natasha Kern, literary agent extraordinaire!

Margaret Brownley: *Natasha is my guardian
angel. I'll always be grateful to her for
believing in me—and leading the way.*

Debra Clopton: *Natasha, working with you has
been a blessing from the beginning—I'm looking
forward to where we shall go from here!*

Mary Connealy: *Deciding to work with Natasha Kern
was the best decision of my professional life. And
without her,* A Bride for All Seasons *would not exist.*

Robin Lee Hatcher: *Thanks, Natasha, for twenty-
four great years. I value our professional relationship,
and I treasure our personal friendship.*

Contents

And Then Came Spring

Margaret Brownley

The lot is cast into the lap,
But its every decision is from the Lord.

PROVERBS 16:33 NKJV

THE HITCHING POST

A mail-order bride catalogue for the
discerning, lonely, or desperate . . .

WHAT IN THE NAME OF BETSY WAS SHE THINKING?

Melvin Hitchcock reread the letter from one Miss Mary-Jo Parker and shook his grizzled head. Not only was her spelling atrocious but she also expressed interest in a "fine Christian man," then carelessly described herself as a *gambler's* daughter!

No, no, no, that would never do. As owner and editor of the *Hitching Post Mail-Order Bride Catalogue* it was Melvin's duty to present clients in the best possible light. To that end, he had no qualms about rewriting clients' ads or editing letters exchanged between couples wishing matrimony. In his not-so-humble opinion, his clients were fortunate to have him looking out for them.

Men often described themselves in glowing, even mythical, terms. The more a man lacked in height, hair, or bank account, the more exaggerated his pen. If Melvin didn't know better, he would think the Wild West was populated by rich, tall, and handsome men with an abundance of head fur and charm.

And the women . . . ah, they were a different story. The

fair sex tended to be so disarmingly honest that he wondered if they really wanted husbands at all. Or perhaps worried or overbearing mothers were pushing their daughters into the realm of holy wedlock. That would certainly explain Miss Parker's disregard for propriety.

No matter. Melvin had a reputation to uphold. Following the War Between the States, mail-order bride catalogues had sprung up like mushrooms, though none could claim as many successful marriages as the *Hitching Post*. That was because Melvin, with a swipe of his pen, turned a "chunky" figure into "charming," "homely" to "comely," and "undomesticated" into a "willingness to learn." Melvin would have no trouble making the gambler's daughter sound like a pillar of virtue and innocence.

He wasn't dishonest—heavens no. He was simply looking out for his clients' best interests. If that charitable action benefited him and his company, what possible harm could it do to the soon-to-be happily wed?

CHAPTER ONE

Colton, Kansas
1870

SURE AS GOD MADE LITTLE GREEN APPLES, MR. DANIEL Garrett would rue this day. Mary-Jo Parker would make it her business to see that he did. For two solid hours he'd kept her waiting at the train station. He didn't even have the courtesy to leave a message or arrange for someone to pick her up.

"Well, Mr. Garrett, I've got news for you. You'd better have a good explanation for keeping me waiting or the wedding is off!" Now she was talking to herself, but that was the least of her problems. She was cold and tired and hungry and . . .

She hated admitting it, but she was also scared. What if she'd traveled all the way from Georgia for nothing? Her aunt thought her crazy to marry a man she'd never met, but his kind letters convinced Mary-Jo that she was doing the right thing. *Don't let me be wrong about that, God.*

She dug in her purse for her watch. Two hours and twenty-two minutes she'd been waiting! If her errant fiancé bothered showing up at all, it better be on hands and knees.

She slipped the watch back into her drawstring bag and reread the dog-eared telegram. All correspondence was screened by the proprietor of the *Hitching Post Mail-Order Bride Catalogue,* so the telegram was signed by Mr. Hitchcock. It clearly stated that her fiancé would meet her train. They would then drive to the church to be married posthaste by a preacher.

She stuffed the telegram into her bag and marched back into the telegraph and baggage office for perhaps the eleventh or twelfth time. Her high-button boots pounded the wooden plank floor like two angry woodpeckers. Nearly tripping over the threshold, she froze.

The last time her foot had caught in a doorway, a tornado blew the roof off her aunt's house. Mary-Jo gave the wood panel wall three quiet knocks. Warding off bad luck was a full-time job, but no matter how hard she tried not to tempt fate, misfortune seemed to follow her wherever she went.

Careful not to step on any cracks, she paced the length of the counter, waiting for the youthful operator to finish tapping the gilded telegraph key.

After a while, he swung around on his stool and peered at her from beneath the visor of his cap. He was probably no more than eighteen or nineteen. "Like I told you before, ma'am, no one left a message for you."

"Yes, you made that perfectly clear." She hadn't mentioned her fiancé by name. She was humiliated enough without the whole town knowing that she had been left not only at the train station but quite possibly at the altar as well.

"Could you please direct me to the nearest hotel?" After a hot bath and change of clothes, she was bound to feel more like herself. Maybe then she could figure out what to do.

Relief crossed the youth's face, but whether it was because she was about to leave or had finally asked a question he could answer, it was hard to tell.

"Just go straight up that street." He pointed in an easterly direction. "The hotel's on the right, opposite the church."

"Thank you."

She stepped outside. Brr, it was cold. She pulled her shawl tight and straightened her bustle, but the more she tried brushing train cinders off her yellow skirt, the more they smeared. Giving up, she reached beneath the narrow brim of her straw bonnet to fluff her curly bangs and then patted down the sausage curls in back. Perhaps things would work out for the best. At least now she wouldn't have to meet her future husband looking like a ragbag.

Gathering the carpetbag that held her carefully sewn trousseau in one hand and her Singer Fiddle Base sewing machine in the other, she started on her way.

In his letters, her betrothed had described the town as thriving and he hadn't exaggerated. Wagons raced back and forth along the dirt road leading through town. Dust flew in every direction and her already dry throat prickled.

The buildings were mostly brick, though some were faced with what looked like marble or limestone. Between taking in her surroundings and trying not to step on a crack, she failed to notice the young boy until he plowed into her.

"Oomph!" she cried. Her carpetbag flew out of her hand, but she managed to regain her balance and hold on to her precious sewing machine. The boy, however, was facedown on the boardwalk.

"Oh dear." She dropped to her knees, setting the Singer by her side. "Are you hurt?"

He shook his head and climbed to his feet. He reached for his slouch cap and plopped it haphazardly atop stringy brown hair that hadn't seen a comb for a month of Sundays. Face flushed, he looked like he was trying his hardest not to give way to tears. She guessed his age at seven, maybe eight.

"Are you sure you're not hurt?" she persisted. He regarded her solemnly, and she tried again. "What's your name?"

"They call me Fast Eddie."

"I do declare, you can talk. Fast Eddie, eh? I guess I know how you came by that name." She pulled off a glove and held out her hand. The boy's eyes widened before taking it. "You can call me Miss Parker. I'm new in town and I'm mighty pleased to meet you."

The boy frowned as if he didn't know what to make of her. Still, she couldn't help but feel sorry for him. Never had she seen a sorrier-looking child. His trousers were at least two inches too short and his shirt had more wrinkles than a rotten apple. Where were his parents? And why wasn't he in school?

She didn't have the heart to lecture him or even demand an apology for nearly knocking her off her feet. Instead, she lowered her voice so as not to alarm him any further.

"Perhaps you could help me." Helping adults always made children feel important. "I'm looking for Mr. Daniel Garrett. He's a lawyer. Do you know him?" Though he'd never mentioned it in his letters, surely he had an office somewhere, perhaps even nearby.

The boy regarded her with eyes blue as the bright Kansas sky. Finally he nodded. "I . . . know him."

"Praise the Lord." It was the first piece of good news she'd heard since arriving in town. Maybe her luck was about to change.

"He's my pa."

Had Fast Eddie punched her in the stomach, she wouldn't have been more shocked. Dumbfounded, she stared at him and felt sick.

"Did . . . did you say . . . he's your pa?" she managed at last. Again the boy nodded.

Hand on her chest, she tried to catch her breath. Her fiancé never mentioned children. There had to be a logical explanation. Yes, yes, of course. There must be *two* Daniel Garretts in town, odd as that seemed.

"Are you his cantaloupe bride?" Eddie asked.

Her breath caught. "Do . . . do you mean catalogue bride?"

With a nod of the head, the boy effectively wiped out any hope of there being two men with the same name.

Her body stiffened. Feeling suddenly light-headed, she

9

forced air into her lungs. If the boy was telling the truth, that meant Daniel Garrett had a serious memory problem. Not only had he failed to meet her train, but he also had a son he'd forgotten to mention.

She stood and glanced up and down the street. This day was turning out to be a nightmare. She should have known better than to leave Georgia last week on a Friday. Everyone knew that traveling on a Friday was bad luck.

"Where might I find your"—she narrowed her eyes and ground out the last word—"pa?"

The boy's face clouded and she felt a surge of guilt. She didn't mean to take it out on him. None of this was the child's fault. She swallowed hard and tried again. "Do you know where I might find him?"

The boy pointed to the high-steepled brick church across the street from the hotel. He then tore away as if being chased.

She started after him, waving. "Wait! Come back!"

Eddie darted in front of an oncoming horse and wagon. "Watch out!" she gasped.

The irate wagon driver managed to stop in time, but he wasn't finished with the boy. He pumped his fist and railed against irresponsible youth in general and Eddie in particular.

Mary-Jo hated to see the child being yelled at, but a good tongue-lashing would probably do him a world of good. He could have been killed. As for his father . . . not only had Daniel Garrett lied by way of omission, he also appeared to be a neglectful parent, and she had no tolerance for either.

She grabbed her sewing machine with one hand and her

carpetbag with the other. Teeth clenched and bosom heaving, she marched across the street. She was so incensed she forgot to watch for cracks.

"You better be in that church praying, Daniel Garrett," she muttered. "Because when I get through with you, you'll wish you never heard of me!"

CHAPTER TWO

MARY-JO CHARGED INSIDE THE CHURCH. THE DOOR slammed shut behind her with a loud bang that made her jump. After setting her sewing machine and carpetbag in a corner of the narthex, she straightened her attire. Not a sound filtered through the thick walls or the doors leading to the sanctuary.

Having no idea what to say or do upon coming face-to-face with her errant fiancé, she plunged through the double doors. Expecting the church to be empty or near empty, she was shocked to discover the pews filled to capacity—on a Wednesday, no less. Every head turned in her direction, but no one said a word.

A man rose from several pews away and rushed up the aisle to greet her. It wasn't until he reached her side that she noticed the sheriff's badge on his vest.

"May I help you, ma'am?" he asked in a hushed voice.

Towering over her five-foot-eight-inch height by a good six inches, he had a rugged square face, a neatly trimmed mustache, and short brown hair. He regarded her with eyes so blue and intense that for a moment she forgot her reason for being there.

Gathering her wits about her, she spoke in a quiet but urgent voice. "I wish to speak with Mr. Garrett."

"I'm Sheriff Tom Garrett."

"Sher—" Now that she thought about it, Daniel did mention something in one of his early letters about his brother being a lawman.

"Mr. *Daniel* Garrett." She glanced at the nearby faces turned toward her and wished she'd changed at the hotel before barging in. Everyone else was dressed in black, and she stuck out like a sore thumb in her yellow outfit. She shifted her gaze back to the sheriff.

His brow creased. "Who might you be?"

"I'm Mary-Jo Parker." When the sheriff made no response, she added, "I'm Daniel's fiancée." Or was.

Sharp and assessing eyes studied her from beneath the shadow of his wide-brimmed hat, and her cheeks flared. Was that surprise on his dark, muted face or something else? Disapproval, perhaps?

"Tell him I'll wait outside."

"I'm afraid that telling him anything at this point would be . . . impossible."

"And why is that, Sheriff?"

He stepped aside and inclined his head toward the distant altar.

A previously unnoticed pine coffin rested on a stand surrounded by wreaths of flowers.

She sucked in her breath. "That can't be—" She swayed and the sheriff grabbed her by the arm.

"Perhaps you should sit down, ma'am. Can I get you some water?"

Shaking her head, she regained her balance. "I-I'm all right. Thank you."

He released her. "Did you say you were Dan's . . . fiancée?"

She nodded mutely and stumbled down the aisle toward the altar. Nothing seemed real. She had to see for herself.

"Ma'am," the sheriff called to her, but she kept going, ignoring the curious eyes that followed her down the aisle.

Daniel was dead? *Not again, dear God. This can't be happening again. Please let this be a dream. Let me wake up and . . .*

She stopped in front of the coffin and stared in horror at the stranger she'd promised to marry. Daniel had the same sandy hair color as his brother and son. Two silver coins covered his eyes so she had no way of knowing if they were the same intense blue.

Suddenly the reality of her situation struck her—she was in the middle of who knew where, and her whole future, all her plans, had evaporated with the death of this man. The walls of the church started closing in, and it was hard to breathe. Whirling about, she picked up her skirts and raced up the aisle toward the door. The sheriff tried to stop her, but she ran past him and kept going. She grabbed her sewing machine and carpetbag and bounded from the church.

Moving as quickly as the weight of the Singer allowed, she didn't know she'd walked under a ladder until the man on top yelled, "Hey, watch it!"

Oh no! Now she'd done it! More bad luck. Hadn't she had enough already? "Sorry," she mumbled.

Blinded by tears, she ducked into an alley. Setting her sewing machine and carpetbag down, she slumped to the ground and bawled.

❀

County sheriff Tom Garrett chased after the distressed woman in yellow. The bright sun nearly blinded him as he dashed out of the church and ran down the steps to the boardwalk. He looked both ways but the lady had vanished.

He wished now he'd been better informed as to his brother's plans, but the two were never close. Dan had moved back to town less than a year ago following the death of his wife, but even then they hadn't spent much time together.

He and his brother argued the last time they spoke, and Tom regretted that more than words could say. He was against Dan's crazy plan to send for a mail-order bride from the start. Not only did the idea strike him as distasteful, he considered it beneath a man's dignity to order a bride sight unseen like purchasing one's under-riggings.

And what was wrong with a woman who couldn't find a husband without the help of a marriage broker? Either she was lacking in looks or personality, maybe both.

Not that anything was wrong with this lady's looks. With

her honey-blond hair, delicate features, and big blue eyes, she looked quite fetching. That could only mean one thing: she lacked something personality-wise.

Perhaps integrity. Old man Whitcomb's mail-order bride robbed him blind before taking off, never to be heard from again. A lawyer like Dan should have been more cautious, but once he got something into his fool head, there was no changing his mind.

The church door opened and Mrs. Hoffmann stepped outside, her huge black hat shaped like a ship. She owned the boardinghouse where Tom lived.

"Do you know if Barnes found the boy?" he asked. Eddie had taken one look at his father's coffin and taken off. His deputy sheriff chased after him. Garrett grimaced at the memory; the boy was like a wild mustang.

"*Nein.*" Mrs. Hoffmann shook her head. "Not that I know of." She spoke in a thick German accent. "Who vas that woman?" She said something else in her native tongue, but Garrett didn't bother asking for a translation. "Imagine. Coming to a funeral dressed like a harlot!"

The woman's tendency to be judgmental irked him at times but he kept his annoyance at bay. With all her faults, she meant well and she was the only one willing to watch the boy.

Still, recalling the shocked look on the young woman's face, Garrett felt a need to protect her. He didn't approve of her reasons for coming to Kansas, but none of what happened to Dan was her fault.

"I don't think she expected to attend a funeral." Neither, for that matter, did he.

"Then she had no business barging into a church, of all places." The woman stabbed the ground with her cane and vanished back inside, the door slamming shut in her wake.

Garrett was about to follow her when he noticed his deputy sheriff walking toward him, shaking his head. Barnes was at least six inches shorter than Garrett and, at age forty-five, ten years older.

"Sorry, Tom. No sign of Eddie."

Garrett blew out his breath and, after scanning the street one last time, followed his deputy back into the church. Right now his top priority was to bury his brother. He'd deal with the boy—and the mail-order bride—later.

CHAPTER THREE

The note beneath the door of Mary-Jo's hotel room read:

We need to talk. Meet me in the hotel dining room at seven a.m. for breakfast. Sincerely, Sheriff T. Garrett

The bold script made it seem more like a command than an invitation. She swallowed her irritation. She couldn't imagine what the sheriff wanted to talk about, but he was Daniel's brother and she owed him a hearing, if nothing else.

A seamstress by trade, she normally had little time to fuss with her own clothes, though she had made a couple of new outfits to start wedded life. Today she chose the most conservative of the three, a pretty blue skirt and matching shirtwaist. Multiple rows of ruches circled the skirt and the delicate puffed sleeves complemented the carefully draped bustle in back.

Her aunt heartily disapproved of such frills, but Mary-Jo couldn't help herself. Sewing was a breeze with her recently purchased Singer. Once she got started on an outfit, she couldn't seem to stop adding embellishments. Fancy dresses required fancy hairstyles and she took special pains to smooth each carefully rolled ringlet in place. A quick pinch of her cheeks and she was ready except for her shoes.

She put the right shoe on first so as to prevent a headache or more bad luck. Then she braced herself with a quick prayer, for all the good it would do her. She had more faith in knocking on wood than she had in God.

She reached the hotel dining room before the appointed hour, but already the sheriff was seated at a table in front of the window overlooking Main Street. He rose when she approached and she was reminded once again how tall he was. He sure enough was pleasing to the eye and given the early morning hour, that was saying something.

"Thank you for meeting with me," he said, as if he doubted she would. His gaze lingered on her a moment too long, bringing a blush to her face. Seeming to catch himself, he hastened to pull out a chair for her. He then took his seat opposite. He'd removed his hat and a strand of sandy-brown hair fell across his forehead from a side part. Without his hat he looked younger, but no less commanding. He also looked tired, as if sleep had been as elusive for him as it had been for her.

"I apologize for yesterday," he said. "I had no idea you

were arriving in town. Had I known, I would have arranged for someone to meet your train."

"It's me who should do the apologizing. I had no call to barge into church like I did." She should have known something was seriously wrong when her fiancé didn't show up as promised, but as usual she had jumped to all the wrong conclusions. She pressed her hands in her lap. "I'm sorry for your loss."

A muscle tightened in his jaw. "I'm sorry you had to find out the way you did." And as if there could be any question as to what he meant, he added, "About Dan."

"His son, Eddie?" The boy had been so upset he almost got himself run over. "Is he all right?"

The sheriff rubbed his chin. "Far as I can tell he hasn't been all right since his mother died two years ago."

Poor child. Had she known he was running away from his pa's funeral, she would have chased after him.

She glanced around and, following the lead of another diner, shook out the folded linen napkin and laid it on her lap. "Oh my. All this silverware," she said, examining a knife previously hidden by her napkin. She could see her face in the blade. "How do they get it so shiny, I wonder?"

The sheriff stared at her, his thoughts hidden behind a closed expression.

She set the knife down. "Your brother said nothing? About us getting hitched, I mean?"

"He said something."

Something. Sensing the sheriff's disapproval, she shifted in her chair. "Daniel insisted we tie the knot soon as I arrived."

"Did he now?" He opened his bill of fare, but she sensed that its main purpose was to put a wall between them.

"He wanted to protect my virtue, but I told him it wasn't necessary." Oh no, here she went again, talking up a blue streak. Somehow she couldn't seem to help herself, although she did manage to use her best Sunday-go-to-meeting grammar.

"I figured that if my virtue had lasted this long, a couple more days wasn't gonna make a difference, but he insisted." Ignoring the startled look on the sheriff's face, she opened her own bill of fare. "Oh my. All these choices and not a grit to be found."

He frowned. "I had no idea Dan meant to marry so soon."

She closed the menu. "Looks like we were both kept in the dark."

He arched his brows. "I'm not sure what you mean."

The waiter came to take their order. Everything on the menu looked a bit rich for both the pocketbook and the appetite, so she simply ordered coffee.

"I'll have the flapjacks," the sheriff said. "And bring the same for the lady."

She opened her mouth to decline but thought better of it. Food on the train was expensive and her fare home would practically take her last penny. Better eat now while she could.

After the waiter left, the sheriff picked up the conversation. "You were saying? About being kept in the dark?"

"Your brother and I exchanged dozens of letters, but he never mentioned his son. Or even that he had been hitched before. That might not be a hanging offense, but it sure enough is wrong."

The sheriff's dark brows practically met. "I can't believe he kept that from you. It doesn't sound like Dan."

"Hmm." She paused to study him. "Perhaps you didn't know him as well as you thought."

He narrowed his eyes. "My brother had many faults, Miss Parker, but I can assure you dishonesty was not one of them."

She bit back the retort that flew to her tongue. The man had lost a family member and it didn't seem right to argue with him or speak ill of the dead.

The silence that followed lasted so long that she wasn't able to take an honest breath until the waiter arrived with their orders. Having not eaten since getting off the train, she slathered her flapjacks with butter and dived into her meal with relish.

In reaching for the syrup, the sheriff knocked over the saltshaker. Little white grains spilled across the table.

"Don't move!" she exclaimed. She grabbed the saltshaker, meaning to toss a few grains over his left shoulder. Instead, the top flew off and white granules landed all over his shirt and vest.

He looked down and brushed off his vest with a flick of his wrist.

"F-For good luck," she stammered.

He frowned and afforded her a frosty look. "I don't believe in luck," he said. "Good, bad, or otherwise."

She set the shaker down and silence hung between them thick as wool. He concentrated on his flapjacks and she stared into her coffee. She forced herself to eat, but now it felt like she was swallowing lead. After a while she gave up.

"How . . . did he die?" she asked.

He swirled more syrup on his flapjacks before responding. "He was in court defending a man accused of murder. The jury had just brought in a verdict to acquit when someone burst through the courtroom doors and shot him."

She grimaced.

He took a bite and chased it down with coffee before adding, "The killer got away."

"Do you know who it was?" she asked.

"The victim's brother, Link. I was out of town when it happened."

His voice was thick with sorrow and regret. Without thinking she moved her hand to his. Fortunately, she caught herself just in time and stopped short of touching him. She might not always get her nouns and verbs right, but she knew her p's and q's.

She dropped her hand to her lap. "Blaming yourself won't bring him back."

Another awkward silence followed while she stirred coffee that didn't need stirring and he poured yet more syrup on his flapjacks.

She glanced around the restaurant. Today was to have been her first full day of married life. Nothing seemed real. Not the couples who spoke in low voices or the businessmen seated at the other tables, and certainly not the sheriff stabbing at his food.

Her knee accidentally rubbed against his and he looked

up in surprise. To hide her embarrassment she took a quick sip of coffee.

He pushed his plate away and pulled something from his vest pocket. It was a check.

"What's that for?" she asked.

"Your train fare. Since you came all the way here for nothing, I want you to have it."

The check was more than generous, but it didn't seem right to take it. The sheriff owed her nothing.

"That's very kind of you, but I can't." In light of Daniel's deceit, she would never have married him anyway. The one thing she was adamant about was honesty.

"Take it. Dan would have wanted you to have it."

"I don't want your money."

He reached for his napkin and dabbed his mouth. "What *do* you want?"

"I want to go home and forget any of this ever happened." Calling her aunt's tumbledown shack in Georgia a home was a bit generous, but it was the closest thing to a home she'd ever known. "I most certainly don't want anything to remind me of your brother."

"None of what happened is his fault."

"He lied to me. He never mentioned a son. That *is* his fault."

He glared at her. "He was a fine Christian and an upright citizen." He stabbed the table with his finger. "He would never lie about anything, especially about his son."

"You call it what you want, but that don't change nothing," she shot back, giving no mind to her grammar.

"And what do you call what you did?" he asked, his voice harsh.

That knocked the wind out of her sails, or at least rendered her momentarily silent. "What do you mean?" she managed at last. "What did I do?"

"Dan was under the impression that you were—" He hesitated momentarily. "A well-educated and accomplished woman."

"I am accomplished," she sniffed. "You won't find a finer seamstress anywhere. As for *well educated*, I'm not sure what to say. I can read and write, though I'm not much good at spelling." She brightened. "But I can pick out the States from the atlas and even recite the alphabet frontward and backward though I've never had occasion to do so. I also know all the books of the Bible and I've never broken a single commandment." *At least not knowingly.* She folded her arms with a nod. Let him find fault with that!

Astonishment suffused his face, as well it should. Let him find anyone more accomplished and she would eat her hat.

"Somehow, I think he expected . . . someone with different qualifications," he said, clearing his throat. Was it scratchy? He seemed to be having some sort of throat trouble.

"I can play a tune on a penny whistle," she added. "And I can cook. No one cooks possum as good as mine. The trick is to feed them corn and—"

He cleared his throat—again! "Miss Parker—"

"I can also whip up something for your throat trouble," she added. "You can't beat hot peppers and—"

He held up the palms of his hands. "Stop!"

She gaped at him.

"He wanted someone who could straighten out the boy. Teach him manners. He thought that since your father is a preacher—"

She sat back in her seat. "Daniel told you my father was a preacher?"

"Not in those precise words. He said your father was in the profession of hope and faith. I just assumed—"

She burst out laughing. "I never heard it put that way, but I guess you could say that. My father lives on hope and faith, all right. He's a high roller."

You could have cut the silence that followed with a knife. He took a quick swallow of coffee and dabbed at his mouth. "Are . . . you saying he's a *gambler*?" He made gambling sound like a hanging offense.

She nodded. "He'd rather win a quarter on a bet than earn ten." For all his winnings, after her mother died she might have starved to death had it not been for her aunt.

When she saw the disapproval on the sheriff's face, something snapped inside her. She was sick and tired of being judged as lacking because she was a gambler's daughter. As if she had a choice in the matter.

She tossed her napkin on the table and reached for her reticule. "Obviously you didn't know your brother as well as you thought." She dug for her money and a deck of cards dropped to the floor.

He leaned over to retrieve it, handing her the small

rectangular pack. He didn't say a word; he didn't have to. His tight face and narrow eyes said it all.

She stuffed the pack back into her small fabric purse without explanation. They were her pa's lucky cards and the only thing he ever gave her. She wasn't about to apologize to the sheriff or anyone else for carrying them. She tossed two coins on the table.

He pushed the coins toward her. "I'll take care of it."

Leaving the money on the table, she stood so abruptly her chair flew backward.

He stood too. They stared at each other like two hostile animals at a watering hole, before she turned and walked away.

CHAPTER FOUR

SHAKING FROM BOTH HER MEETING WITH DANIEL'S brother at the restaurant and the cold morning air, Mary-Jo arrived at the train station. She was surprised to find it deserted and the ticket booth closed. She walked into the telegraph and baggage office. The same youth from the day before greeted her with a nod.

"Did you find the person you were looking for?" he asked.

"Yes, as a matter of fact I did." She cleared her voice. "I would like to purchase a ticket to St. Louis." From there she would have to transfer trains.

"Train left already," he said.

"Left? But it's only eight thirty. The schedule says the train doesn't leave until nine o'clock."

"It's after nine," he said, pointing to the clock. "The train runs on railroad time."

She stared at him in dismay. After everything that

happened, she'd completely forgotten about railroad time, which seldom corresponded with local time. "Then the train I heard earlier . . ." She forced herself to breathe. "Isn't there another one today?"

He shook his head. "Not eastbound. Sorry. Do you want a ticket or don't you?"

She hesitated. "Yes, please." After purchasing her ticket, she had little money left. She could afford a meal or two but not a hotel room.

She considered storing her sewing machine at the station but decided against it. Should something happen to it she'd be in a fine fix. Dressmaking was the only trade she knew. She turned away and, not knowing what else to do, headed back to town.

On the way, she stopped beneath a windmill and stared down a well built from rocks. She set her baggage down and dug a penny from her purse to toss it into the watery depths. The problem was, she didn't know what to wish for. She once hoped to find true love, but that was when she still believed that God cared for her. She now had two very good reasons to believe that He didn't give a whit about her—she had *two* dead fiancés.

Loud voices caught her attention. A crowd stood in front of the general store. Curious, she gathered her belongings and crossed the dirt road. Stepping up to the boardwalk, she carefully avoided walking on a crack.

A half-bald man stood shaking his fist, his red suspenders stretched to the limit by a protruding stomach. "I'm telling you somethin's got to be done with the boy. If the sheriff won't do it, I will."

"Come on, Pete," someone shouted from the crowd. "The boy just lost his pa."

"That don't give him no right to go stealing from me."

Mary-Jo rose on tiptoes to peer over the crowd. Just as she suspected, the boy in question was Eddie. He held a half-eaten apple in one hand. The man named Pete held him by the ear.

Her temper flared. Of all the—

Pushing through the crowd, she worked her way to the front. "Let him go." Everyone was talking at once, so she repeated herself, this time louder. "I said let him go!"

This got everyone's attention or at least drew silence.

The shopkeeper glared at her. "I don't take no guff from strangers."

"That makes two of us." She turned, so incensed she accidentally dropped her sewing machine on his foot.

The shopkeeper yelled, "Ow!" He let go of the boy and hopped around, holding on to his sore foot, cursing a blue streak.

"Oh, I'm so sorry. I didn't mean—"

Eddie pushed past her and took off like a cat with his tail afire. All he left in his wake was an overturned barrel of nails.

Pete shook his finger in her face. "Now look what you've gone and done." He stalked into the store and slammed the door, rattling the windows and causing a display of shovels to topple over.

The crowd quickly dispersed, but some glared at her before

taking their leave. Mary-Jo picked up her Singer, surprised to find the penny meant for the wishing well still in her palm.

Standing in the middle of the deserted boardwalk surrounded by scattered nails, she held her sewing machine in one hand and lost dreams in the other.

The sun sank below the horizon and Mary-Jo's spirits sank with it; it would soon be dark. Cold air blew from the north and she shivered. She pulled her shawl tight, but it offered little warmth against the cutting wind.

It had been a long and tiring day, and her arm and shoulder hurt from lugging her sewing machine around town. It was too cold for the park bench and the hotel proprietor had pointed to a No Loitering sign and chased her out of the lobby. With no money for a room she headed for the train station. At least she could rest there.

The telegraph operator had left for the day and the station was deserted. Feeling as homeless as a poker chip, she finally walked back to town, just to be around people.

The lamplighter whistled as he made his way up Main with his long pole. The sound of a tuneless piano drifted from a nearby saloon. Laughter rolled out of another.

She looked around for a place to spend the night. A stoop-shouldered woman walked out of the church and that gave Mary-Jo an idea.

Much to her relief, the church door was still unlocked. The rusty hinges creaked as she slipped into the narthex.

It was dark inside the sanctuary except for a couple of burning candles. The flickering flames cast a golden glow upon the stained glass windows. It was still cold, but at least she was out of the brisk north wind.

She picked a middle row and set her sewing machine down on the pew before taking her seat. Her carpetbag made an adequate pillow. Though the pew was hard, she soon fell asleep.

Something woke her. For a moment she didn't know where she was. It all came back in a flash. The coffin. *Two* coffins. The sheriff's disapproving look. She blinked the memories away. The candles were still burning so she hadn't been asleep for long.

Footsteps on the slate floor made her heart thump. "Hello." She peered over the top of the pew. "Eddie!"

The boy looked startled and poised to run. Obviously, he hadn't expected to find anyone inside the church.

"Don't go. Remember me? I'm Miss Parker. I won't hurt you." She sat up. "What are you doin' here? Why aren't you home in bed?" Why, for that matter, wasn't she?

"I—I was lookin' for Pa."

At first she didn't know what he meant. "But your pa—" Of course. Eddie last saw his father here. He didn't realize his father had been taken to the cemetery.

"Come and sit down," she said. She moved her sewing machine from the pew to the floor, leaving a space by her side.

The boy walked slowly down the aisle clutching his hat. Finally he slid onto the polished pew next to her.

"Your pa's not here," she said gently.

"Is he in the ground?" Eddie asked. "Like Ma?"

Something in his voice tugged at her heart. "His body is, yes, but not his soul." Someone had said those exact words to her after she lost her ma. As a child they had comforted her and she hoped they comforted him. She pointed at the stained glass window that depicted the Lord holding out His arms. "Both your pa and ma are in heaven."

Eddie didn't say anything but his gaze was riveted to the altar. The memory of Daniel's coffin was very much on her mind and she imagined it was on Eddie's mind too.

"I'm sorry 'bout your pa," she said.

He continued to stare dry-eyed at the spot where the coffin had been. She wondered if he held back his tears on purpose or simply had none to shed.

"It's okay to feel sad." She heaved a sigh. "I feel sad too." She studied the boy's pale face.

Eddie sniffed but still no tears. "I didn't say good-bye," he said.

She swallowed hard. "I didn't either." Saying good-bye had been the last thing on her mind. For several moments neither spoke. Finally she asked, "Does your uncle know you're here?"

"He's gone. Out looking for the man who killed Pa."

It was all she could do to keep her temper. What was the matter with the man, leaving his young nephew to fend for himself? "Don't you have other relatives? Someone to care for you?"

He slid a glance in her direction. "I don't need a nursemaid."

"No, I don't reckon you do." She pushed a strand of hair out of his eyes. "But surely you have family."

"Just my uncle."

"I see."

One of the candles sputtered and went out. Soon they would be left in darkness.

"I know why Pa didn't tell you about me," he said.

She arched a brow. "How do you know he didn't tell me?"

"I heard my uncle tell Deputy Barnes."

"Eavesdropping, eh?" She studied the boy. "So why do you think he didn't tell me?"

"'Cause he hates me."

Hates. Not *hated*. He still hadn't accepted his father's death. That would explain the lack of tears. Not that she blamed him. She was having trouble believing it herself.

"I don't know why your pa didn't tell me, but I know he didn't hate you."

"Did too!" he said. "He hates me for what I did to Ma."

His sudden outburst surprised her. "What . . . did you do?"

"I gave her smallpox. I got sick and gave it to her."

"Oh, Eddie." She laid a hand on the side of his face. "You poor sweet boy. Don't you know it was an accident? You weren't to blame. No one was. It wasn't your fault."

"Dad blames me."

She drew her hand away. "Did . . . did he say that?"

"Nope, but I know that's what he thinks. That's why he won't . . ."

"Won't what?" she prodded gently.

"He won't take me fishing no more."

She moistened her lips. "I'll tell you what I think. I think your pa stopped taking you fishing 'cause he was sad. When adults are sad they stop doing fun things." She certainly had after her first fiancé died. She took the boy's hand. It felt like ice. "You're cold." She pulled off her shawl and wrapped it around his thin shoulders. "It's late. You better go home."

"I don't want to. I'm . . ."

"You're what?" she urged.

"Nothing." He hesitated. "I don't want to leave you here all alone. There are bad men out there. One of them shot Pa."

Scared. The boy was scared. Maybe for her, but mostly for himself. "Your uncle will protect you," she said.

"He won't be home till tomorrow."

She chewed on her bottom lip. "Do you think he would mind if I spent the night at your house?" She couldn't think of any other way to make the boy go home.

Eddie brightened. "You can sleep on the couch."

"Well then." Compared to the church pew, the couch sounded like heaven. She stood and gathered her carpetbag and sewing machine. "Lead the way, young man. Lead the way."

CHAPTER FIVE

I<small>T WAS WELL AFTER MIDNIGHT BY THE TIME</small> T<small>OM</small> Garrett reached Mrs. Hoffmann's Boarding House, a two-story brick building just outside of town. A headwind not only slowed his journey but chilled him to the bone. April sure had come in like a lion.

Normally he would have flopped down in an out-of-town hotel for the night, but he didn't want to leave the boy any longer than necessary. It was good of his landlady to agree to watch him, but she had a bad back and was no match for an active eight-year-old. Especially one as wild as Eddie.

He still didn't know what to do about his brother's house. Would living in the home he shared with his pa make things better or worse for Eddie? Maybe it would be better to sell the house and buy another; one that wasn't a constant reminder of all that they'd lost.

After settling his horse in the stable for the night, he

climbed the stairs of the wraparound porch and let himself in the front door. The smell of cooked cabbage, no doubt left over from supper, mingled with the kerosene odor of the still-burning lamp in the front parlor.

He lit a candle and took the stairs two at a time, careful to make as little noise as possible so as not to disturb the other boarders.

His room was at the end of the hall, the door ajar. Mrs. Hoffmann must have left it open so she could hear the boy. He entered quietly and stopped. The light from his candle revealed an empty bed. A quick glance around confirmed it; Eddie was gone!

No longer concerned about waking the other boarders, he stomped down the hall and pounded on the widow Hoffmann's door. The light at his feet told him she was still awake. It seemed to take forever but the door sprang open. Wearing a white dressing gown, the boardinghouse owner's gray hair hung to her shoulders.

"Where's Eddie?"

She looked startled and said something in German before switching to English. "I thought he was in your room."

Drat! He whirled around and rushed down the stairs.

Dan's house was a little over a mile away from the boardinghouse. Tom didn't bother saddling his horse. Instead, he ran most of the way, reaching Dan's place in little more than ten minutes.

The house was dark and looked desolate even in the full moon. He'd only been here a couple of times since his brother moved back to town. Guilt cut through him every bit as much as the icy wind. Would things have turned out differently if he'd been a better brother? A more involved uncle? Likely not.

It wasn't until he reached the porch that he noticed the curtains moving. Had Eddie opened the window? Or had someone else?

He pushed the door open and the hinges creaked. Moonlight streamed through the open window. If something happened to his brother's son, he would never forgive himself. At the sight of the mound on the sofa, relief flooded through him.

But why was Eddie sleeping out here and not in his own bed? Garrett tiptoed across the room. The boy had kicked off his covers. He bent to pick the blanket up off the floor and caught an unexpected whiff of lavender. That was odd.

Straightening, he leaned forward to cover the boy and froze.

He would recognize the blond hair feathered across the pillow anywhere. Miss Parker . . .

But what was she doing here?

Her creamy complexion glowed softly in the moonlight. Long lashes shadowed delicate cheeks. A memory of blue eyes and proud turn of her head came to mind.

Could she have been telling the truth about Dan? Had his brother really neglected to tell her about Eddie? It didn't seem likely, but what reason would she have to lie?

He covered her with the blanket, careful not to wake her. He straightened and when she didn't stir, he tiptoed to Eddie's room.

The boy was sound asleep. Thank God for that. Perhaps he owed the lady an apology.

He blew out his breath and pinched his brow. He'd fought in the war and chased down some of the meanest, most ornery criminals in the county. But he hadn't the foggiest idea how to care for an eight-year-old boy, especially one who wanted nothing to do with him.

Satisfied that Eddie was all right, at least for tonight, Garrett let himself quietly out of the house.

A picnic basket in one hand and a blanket in the other, Mary-Jo waited for Eddie to open the iron gate leading to the church cemetery. By now, she expected to be on her way home, but she couldn't leave town until Eddie's uncle returned.

White fluffy clouds chased across the sky, playing peek-a-boo with the sun.

Yellow flowers grew in wild abandon along the fence, lifting brown-bonneted faces to the sky.

Daniel's grave wasn't yet marked with a headstone, but the mound of fresh dirt made it easy to find. Someone had stuck a small wooden cross in the center of the soft soil.

Mary-Jo spread the blanket on the ground next to the grave and set the picnic basket on it. She dropped to her knees.

Eddie's gaze was cast down, the toe of his shoe digging

into the dirt. Her heart went out to him. He was trying so hard to be brave.

His trousers were still too short, but today his shirt was pressed and his hair neatly combed. She had even trimmed his bangs so they were no longer in his eyes.

"Do you want to go first?" she asked. When he failed to respond, she gave him a nod of encouragement. "Say good-bye to your pa."

He stared down at the mound. "This is dumb. You can't talk to someone you can't see."

She straightened the little wooden cross. "Don't you talk to God?"

"That's different. God can see and hear everything. Pa can't."

"I reckon, then, you're gonna have to ask God to give your pa a message."

The frown on his face made him look older than his eight years. "Do you think He would do that?"

She shrugged. "Why not ask Him?" *If that don't beat all.* She sounded like she was an expert on God or something. Some expert.

Eddie dropped down on his knees and pulled off his cap. Head lowered, he began. "God, tell Pa I'm sorry I didn't say good-bye."

"Go on," she coaxed after a long silence. "Tell your pa everything you want him to know."

Eddie rubbed his nose with the back of his hand. "Tell Pa it's okay that he didn't take me fishing. I don't like fishing that much anyway. Amen." He replaced his hat. After a long silence he glanced up at her. "It's your turn."

She hadn't planned on talking to the Lord herself. She had no idea what to say, but since Eddie was waiting she clasped her hands and closed her eyes. Maybe something would come to her. She wanted to do this right, for the boy's sake.

"God, tell Daniel . . ." Words caught in her throat. It seemed strange to say good-bye when she hadn't even had a chance to say hello.

She swallowed, but the lump remained and everything hit her at once. The coffin—*two* coffins. The lies, the unfairness of it all.

"I . . . I am so angry I could scream." She lifted her voice until she practically shouted to the heavens. "How could you do this to me, God? First Charles and now Daniel—" Words spouted out of her like water from a primed pump.

But after a while she fell silent. And she felt as though an awful weight had been lifted.

A hand on her arm startled her and she opened her eyes. Eddie stared up at her, his peepers round as wagon wheels.

Oh dear, what had she done? "I'm s-sorry," she stammered. She felt terrible for making the poor child witness her shouting at the Lord. "Sometimes . . . it helps to tell God how you feel."

Eddie pulled his hand away. "I reckon He knows now. Pa too."

She sucked in her breath. "Yes, I reckon they do."

"Who's Charles?" he asked.

Hearing the name fall from Eddie's lips made her wince. "He was a . . . friend. He died during the war."

"My uncle fought in the war too," he said.

"Did he now?"

Eddie gave an earnest nod. "Maybe he knew your friend."

She didn't have the heart to tell him that his uncle and her fiancé probably fought on opposite sides. "Maybe." She reached for the picnic basket. "Time to eat." She pulled out bread and cheese and slices of sausage. For a man without a wife, Dan's kitchen was well stocked.

They ate in silence for several moments before Eddie spoke. "What's gonna happen to me?"

She took her time answering, hoping to find the right words. "I guess you'll live with your uncle and go back to school and grow up to be . . . someone really special. Maybe a lawyer like your pa."

"I hate school."

"I don't believe that. A bright boy like you?"

"I got a four on my math test. That's 'cause it takes me too long to figure out the answers. Miss Madison says I have to take it again."

She knew precious little about school, but she did know that a four meant he'd flunked. "Addition?"

He shook his head. "Multiplying."

"I have an idea." She reached into her reticule for the deck of playing cards. "I may not be good at spelling or grammar, but I know 'rithmetic."

Eddie watched her separate the jokers and face cards from

the numerical ones, a doubtful look on his face. "My teacher says that playing cards are sinful."

"Did she now?" She separated the cards into two piles. "It's not the cards that are sinful, it's what you do with them. And right now they're going to help you turn that four into a one."

For the next hour or so they worked on multiplying numbers. Eddie was a fast learner and was soon shouting out answers almost before she turned over the cards.

"Sixty-four!" he yelled when she held up two eights.

"Okay, now times these . . ." Just then a gust of wind swept across the prairie and through the cemetery, blowing a whirlwind of dust and leaves and scattering cards in every direction.

"Oh no." Her lucky cards! "Quick." She jumped to her feet and Eddie lunged for an ace. Together they chased the cards around the cemetery, dodging in and out of headstones.

"Get that king," she yelled.

"There's a card over there," he yelled back.

She tripped over a gravestone and fell facedown in the grass. Eddie hurried over to help her up and soon they were laughing hysterically. It was as if someone had pulled a cork and all the tension of the last twenty-four hours poured out of them.

"Miss Parker!"

The male voice thundered across the graveyard, followed by its marching owner. Sheriff Garrett stormed up to them and scowled at the playing cards in their hands.

"Why, Sheriff Garrett . . . Are you trying to raise the dead?"

He glared at her, his face dark as a thunderhead. "And are

you trying to corrupt my nephew?" He snatched the cards out of Eddie's hand and shoved them into hers.

Without giving her time to explain, he turned to Eddie. "Why aren't you in school?"

Eddie stared at his feet and said nothing, and so she answered for him. "He just lost his pa."

"Yes, he did, Miss Parker. That's why I'm having a hard time understanding what the two of you found so . . . funny. In the vicinity of my brother's grave, no less."

The boy turned pale, and Mary-Jo felt a maternal need to protect him. "It was my fault. We had . . . something important to do."

"Important?" He glanced at the cards in her hands. "The boy doesn't need anyone helping him get in trouble. He's quite capable of managing that himself. Right now, the best thing for everyone is for you to leave town." He motioned to the boy to follow and stalked away.

Eddie's gaze clung to hers and the pleading expression he gave her stabbed at her heart.

"It'll be all right," she said softly, giving him a gentle shove in the sheriff's direction. Clutching his cap, he took one last glance at her before following his uncle through the cemetery and out the gate.

Eddie had to run to catch up with the sheriff's long strides. Fists at her sides, Mary-Jo watched with gritted teeth. The sheriff was cold as a fish on ice. Just like Pa.

Her father wasn't a family man in any sense of the word, and he often said he ended up with one through no fault of his own. Loving Pa was like knocking on a door when no one was home.

She hated to compare the sheriff to her gambling father, but Tom treated his nephew in much the same way Pa treated her. Eddie wasn't just running to catch up; he was knocking on the door of an empty house.

CHAPTER SIX

DREADING ANOTHER NIGHT IN TOWN, MARY-JO WENT back to Daniel's house. Eddie was staying with his uncle at the boardinghouse, so she knew it would be vacant. Since Daniel went and got himself killed, the least he owed her was another night's shelter.

Still, she felt like an intruder. She moved from room to room, imagining how her life might've been different if Daniel were still alive when she saw a torn pair of Eddie's trousers. Just opening the top drawer of the desk in search of a writing implement to mark the fabric made her feel guilty. So anxious was she to close the drawer she almost missed the letters with the *Hitching Post*'s return address.

She lifted the stack from the drawer. It touched her to know that Daniel had kept all her letters just as she'd kept his. She couldn't decide whether to toss these or keep them. All she knew was that she didn't want anyone else reading them.

She threw the stack into the wastebasket to burn later, but the string broke and one letter drifted to the floor.

She stooped to pick it up and frowned; the handwriting was not her own and yet it looked somehow familiar. Curious, her gaze followed the fine script across the page. The writer gave a glowing account of her many accomplishments. Mary-Jo's lips puckered. What a braggart! Whoever this woman was, she didn't have a modest bone in her body.

She frowned. Obviously Daniel had considered another mail-order applicant, but why would he choose her over a woman nothing short of a human dynamo?

She glanced at the signature on the second page and froze. The letter was signed *Mary-Jo Parker* clear as day. Falling to her knees, she retrieved the letters from the wastebasket and quickly riffled through them. Her name was on every last one.

She now knew why the handwriting looked familiar. Whoever wrote these letters to Daniel was the same person who wrote Daniel's letters to her. And unless she missed her guess, that person was Mr. Hitchcock himself.

Horrid realization swept over her, and it all began to make sense. The owner of the mail-order catalogue edited and, in some cases, rewrote the letters she and Daniel exchanged.

Fury rushed through her and her body shook. She thought Daniel had lied in failing to tell her about his son and previous marriage, but she was wrong. It was that deceitful Mr. Hitchcock who had done the lying. She had a good mind to give him what-for. While she was at it, she just might wring his dishonest neck!

❈

The day went from bad to worse. Garrett knew nothing about taking care of an eight-year-old and even less about taking care of a problem child like Eddie. After leaving the cemetery, he realized it was too late to take the boy to school. Instead, Garrett stopped to pay the shopkeeper for the stolen apple and made Eddie apologize. After heading back to the office, he ordered Eddie to sit while he finished paperwork.

It would have been easier to tame a bronco. Eddie wiggled back and forth and swung his legs. He finally occupied himself by tossing his rabbit foot in the air and catching it with his cap. Eventually he fell off the chair altogether.

Garrett grimaced with irritation. "Put that thing away!"

Eddie stuffed the rabbit foot in his pocket and tried to catch a fly that was buzzing around his face.

Deputy Sheriff Barnes finally offered to take the boy to the ice-cream parlor, but Garrett still couldn't concentrate. Thoughts of Miss Parker kept interrupting, making it impossible to have a clear thought. He tossed his pen down and rested his head in his hands. What had he been thinking, yelling at her like that? On church property, no less.

That morning he and Barnes had to deal with one problem after another. Between them, they'd made three arrests before eleven a.m., mostly for fighting. Barnes blamed it on the full moon. It was either that or spring fever.

By the time Garrett was able to stop at the house and thank Miss Parker for staying with Eddie the night before, she wasn't there. Worried, he headed for the schoolhouse, hoping to find his nephew there. It was only by chance that he happened to spot the two of them in the cemetery. Relief was soon followed by anger.

It didn't seem right for the boy to be laughing so soon after his father's death—not just laughing, but running around with playing cards in his hands.

That memory was followed by another. He remembered how Miss Parker looked with the boy, a lacy petticoat showing beneath the hem of her skirt. She sure did look pretty when she smiled and the thought made him grimace. He had no right thinking such thoughts of his brother's fiancée with Dan not even cold in the grave.

He buried his face in his hands. Still, he shouldn't have yelled.

Dan wouldn't have. He fought injustice with quiet, firm resolve in the hallowed rooms of the courthouse. That was where he and his brother differed. Most of Garrett's fights had been in ditches and cotton fields, behind blaring guns and cannons.

Dan knew how to save a client from the gallows, but he didn't know how to raise a child like Eddie. That was one area Garrett had in common with his brother.

The door sprang open and Garrett's thoughts scattered. Miss Parker stormed into his office looking madder than a newly plucked hen. She flung a pile of letters onto his desk. Never had he seen so much rage pour out of such a pretty package.

"Of all the low-down, despicable . . ." On and on she railed.

He tried to make heads or tails out of her rants. "Are you saying that this . . . uh . . . Mr. Hitchcock wrote these letters to Dan?" he asked when he could get a word in edgewise.

Her pretty blue eyes flashed with indignation. "That's exactly what I'm saying!"

He scratched his head. "But why would he do such a thing?"

"Obviously, he wanted to make me sound better. Not only did he hide my lack of learning and Pa's gambling, I have no doubt he deleted any mention of Eddie in Daniel's letters to me."

Garrett rubbed his chin. "So then Dan didn't lie to you."

She lifted her chin. "And I didn't lie to him."

"I guess it's settled then," he said.

She stared at him, incredulous. "Settled? Nothing is settled. I want you to arrest Mr. Hitchcock for fraud."

"I'm afraid I can't do that." He glanced down at the return mailing address in New York. "It's out of my jurisdiction. You'll have to contact the district attorney in his home state."

She rose to her full height and whirled about. "That's exactly what I intend to do! I'm leaving on the morning train, but you can be sure I'll write the district attorney the first chance I get!"

With that she stomped out of his office, slamming the door behind her.

Guilt rushed through him for having misjudged her. Had she given him half a chance, he would have apologized.

He had just about decided to chase after her when Barnes returned with Eddie. The deputy sheriff took one look at the letters scattered across Garrett's desk and frowned.

"What's all this?"

"Long story." Garrett gathered up the letters and stuffed them in his drawer. He had no desire to work and decided he might as well call it a day. He motioned to Eddie. "Come on, let's go."

Eddie folded his arms across his chest. "I don't want to go with you. I want to go with Miss Parker."

Barnes shrugged and sat at his own desk. "Looks like you got your work cut out for you, boss."

Garrett grunted and studied the boy. He was the spitting image of his father, not just in appearance but in mannerisms. Dan had the same jutting-jaw look when defending a client, the same way of narrowing his eyes.

"You know Miss Parker is leaving town."

"Only because you're forcing her to," Eddie said, pushing his bottom lip out farther.

"I'm not forcing her." Okay, so he hadn't exactly made her feel welcome. He tried to put the memory of flashing blue eyes and unleashed rage out of his mind. The woman was a regular wildcat, that was for sure. But he'd also seen those same eyes soften when she looked at Eddie.

"I can't make her stay, but I'll tell you what. If you come back to the boardinghouse with me and mind your manners, we'll go to the train station tomorrow morning and bid her good-bye. How's that?" That would also give him a chance to apologize.

"Promise?"

"Promise."

CHAPTER SEVEN

MARY-JO ARRIVED AT THE TRAIN STATION EARLY. HAD it only been forty hours since she first arrived in town? Hard to believe. In some ways it seemed like a lifetime ago.

Everywhere she looked, families stood around in secure little knots. One man perched a small boy on his shoulders and she couldn't take her eyes off the two of them. Loneliness cut through her. If God was good enough to ever bless her with children, that was the kind of father she hoped they would have, knock on wood.

"Miss Parker!"

Hearing her name, she turned and smiled. Never did she think she'd seen a more welcome sight. "Eddie! What are you doing here?"

"We came to say good-bye," he said.

"Who's *we*?" she asked.

"That would be me." Sheriff Garrett stepped from behind

a post and laid a hand on Eddie's shoulder. "I . . ." He cleared his throat.

"You really ought to do something for that throat of yours, Sheriff."

Today his eyes matched the color of bluebells growing along the station fence. "I want to . . . apologize for my behavior yesterday in the cemetery. Eddie explained you were helping him with schoolwork and saying good-bye to his pa."

The sound of a whistle announced the arrival of the train. The platform vibrated beneath her feet. "And he was helping me collect my lucky playing cards."

The train screeched to a stop with a hissing sound. All around them, people started to scurry.

"I'm sorry we met under such trying circumstances," the sheriff offered. They stared at each other for several moments before he broke eye contact to glance at the train. "We won't keep you. We just came to say good-bye."

"Good-bye." She smiled and added, "Good luck." The sheriff might not believe in luck, but judging by the dark look on Eddie's face, he sure was going to need it.

"I don't want you to go," Eddie cried out.

The sheriff frowned. "Miss Parker has to leave."

Eddie glared up at his uncle. "She's only leaving because you're making her."

"That's not true." Garrett reached for Eddie's arm, but the boy pulled back and took off at a run, disappearing into the milling crowd.

Mary-Jo felt terrible. She never meant to cause the sheriff

trouble. "I'm sorry," she said, then without thinking she laid her hand on his arm.

He glanced at her hand before lifting his gaze to hers.

She pulled her hand away. "I never meant—"

"You better hurry," he said, his voice taut. "You don't want to miss your train." With that, he spun around and hurried away. Tearing her gaze from his retreating back, Mary-Jo walked toward the train on lead feet.

❀

That night Mary-Jo walked up the boardinghouse steps to the dark porch and knocked on the door. A light shone in the window and that was a good sign.

The door opened a crack and a nose as long as a crow's beak was all she could make out. "May I help you?" It was a woman's voice and even her thick guttural accent couldn't hide the disapproving tone.

"Yes, I wish to speak with the sheriff," she said. "I was told he lived here."

The door opened all the way, revealing a gray-haired woman in a lace cap and a long dressing gown. Sharp gray eyes assessed her. "You're the woman who wore the yellow dress to Mr. Garrett's funeral." Without allowing Mary-Jo time to confirm or deny it, she added, "It's late."

It was a little after eight, but the woman made it sound like the wee hours of the morn. "It's important that I speak with him."

The woman hesitated a moment, then invited Mary-Jo

into the house with a nod of her head. She pointed to the parlor and waited for Mary-Jo to sit before climbing the stairs.

Mary-Jo straightened her skirt and folded her hands on her lap.

Footsteps on the stairs almost made her lose her composure. She debated whether to stand or stay seated. In the end the choice wasn't hers to make. The moment the sheriff's tall form filled the doorway, she jumped to her feet without thinking.

"I didn't mean to disturb you, but I was worried about Eddie," she said in one breathless sentence.

Surprise suffused his face. "I thought you'd left town."

"I couldn't leave without knowing he was all right." He was, after all, Daniel's son. "I stopped by your office and your deputy said you were still looking for him. I thought he might have gone to the cemetery, but he wasn't there and . . . I couldn't find him anywhere. I looked for him all day . . . all over town. And he never returned to the house."

"He's fine. He's asleep."

Relief rushed through her. "Praise the Lord."

They stood staring at each other. The dainty furniture and delicate knickknacks looked absurd in contrast to his height and powerful build. The only sounds were the steady tick-tock of the long case clock and the pounding of her heart.

"I . . . I won't keep you," she stammered. She reached for her reticule.

He reached out his hand. "Stay."

Her eyes widened. "You . . . want me to stay?"

"It's not all that late. Please have a seat." He strode into the room.

She sat on the edge of the floral-print settee to accommodate her bustle, and he sat in a nearby wingback chair.

"I'm so happy to hear that Eddie is . . . where he belongs," she said, filling in the rather uncomfortable silence that stretched between them.

"He doesn't think he belongs here with me." He rubbed his chin. "I didn't expect to have to raise a child, at least not under these circumstances."

"He . . . said you're his only family."

The sheriff nodded. He talked about his deceased parents and growing up in Kansas; she told him about her amazing sewing machine.

"I planned to start my own business once Daniel and I were married."

"The town could use a dressmaker." He studied her. "Eddie told me you lost a friend during the war."

She lowered her lashes, not sure how much or little to say. "My fiancé," she said at last.

His eyebrows shot up. "I'm sorry . . ."

"So am I." She took a deep breath. "What do you call a woman like me?"

"I don't understand what you mean."

"When a woman loses a husband, we call her a widow. What do you call a woman who loses a fiancé? Who loses *two* fiancés?"

"I have no idea," he said, and the sympathy in his eyes unnerved her.

She quickly changed the subject. "Eddie told me you fought in the war too."

He looked surprised, then pleased. "I didn't know Eddie knew that about me."

"I reckon we'd both be surprised at how much Eddie knows."

"Maybe so." He studied her. "I shouldn't have mentioned the war. It must bring back painful memories."

"The war's over," she said.

"But the memories remain." Raw pain shimmered in the depth of his eyes, but whether from memories of the war or grief for his brother, she didn't know. Probably both.

"You and Eddie are very much alike," she said.

"How so?"

"You both have strong feelings about what you believe in. The only difference is, Eddie hasn't yet found a cause."

"Never thought Eddie and I shared anything but a slight family resemblance," he said.

"Not so slight."

He gazed at her with an intensity that made her blush. For the first time she noticed the intriguing cleft in his chin.

The clock began to gong, reminding her of the lateness of the hour. "I . . . I better go." She slipped the chain of her reticule over her wrist. "I have an early train to catch."

"Let me take you back to my brother's house."

She hesitated. She still felt like an intruder whenever she

entered Daniel's house and yet what choice did she have? "I hope you don't mind, but I left my belongings there earlier."

"I don't mind and Dan wouldn't either. And I'll sleep a lot better knowing you have a place to stay."

His concern for her welfare made her feel all cozy and warm inside. The emotion left the moment the chimes began to slow.

She jumped to her feet. "You better wind the clock." Her voice was edged in panic, but it couldn't be helped. If he didn't hurry, the clock would stop, and that meant death.

He gave her an odd look but said nothing as he rose. He opened the clock's glass door and turned the key. "There," he said, closing the cabinet. He frowned. "Are you all right?"

With an uneasy glance at the clock, she nodded. The chimes continued all the way to nine. "I'm just tired, is all. It's been . . . a hard week."

A big yellow moon hung in a star-studded sky as they walked to Daniel's place. The wind that had swept through town the day before had stopped, leaving the air cool and delicately scented with sweet verbena.

"Tell me about Eddie's father," she said as they walked along streets lined with shuttered establishments.

"What can I tell you? Things always came easy for Dan." They walked past a sleepy farmhouse and newly tilled fields before he continued, "He could read by the time he was three, and he was successful at everything he did."

"Must run in the family," she said. "A war veteran and sheriff. That's pretty impressive. I say you've both gone and done your parents proud."

"My parents were pacifists." His voice was without bitterness or rancor, but she detected a strain of resignation. "My way was never their way."

"But your brother's way was," she said, reading between the lines. "I reckon they never figured out that every family needs a warrior."

He flashed a smile and his teeth gleamed in the moonlight. "After what I saw in my office yesterday, I venture to guess you're the warrior in your family."

She smiled too. It seemed like she had been fighting all her life just to survive. "I guess that makes us two of a kind."

"I don't think you and my brother would have made a good match," he said.

She turned her shoulder, trying not to let on how much his words hurt. Finally she found her voice. "I guess he needed someone with more learning."

There was a long pause. "I . . . uh," he began. "That's not what I meant. I don't think he'd know what to do with a wife who wasn't afraid to speak her mind."

She glanced at his face, but it was too dark to read his expression. "Guess we'll never know, will we?"

"Guess not."

They arrived at Daniel's house. Not even the moonlight penetrated the dark, and he insisted on going in first.

"Be careful of my sewing—"

A thud and groan met her words.

"Are . . . are you all right?" she cried.

For an answer the light came on. He seemed all right and relief rushed through her. "Sorry. I shouldn't have left it there."

He stood her machine upright. "No problem." He hesitated, and she had the strangest feeling he was reluctant to say good night or perhaps that was only wishful thinking on her part. "Are . . . are you still planning on leaving town?"

She nodded. "In the morning."

"I'll pick you up and take you to the train station."

"That's not necessary."

"I'd feel better knowing you made the train safely," he said.

"Thank you, that's very kind."

They gazed at each other for a moment and a warm glow rushed through her.

As if to catch himself from staring, he blinked and quickly headed for the door. "I . . . I better let you get some sleep. Good night."

"Good night." She stood at the threshold, not wanting to see him go. "Unlucky," she called after him.

He swung around to face her. "I'm sorry?"

"That's what you call a woman who loses two fiancés. Unlucky." And with that she closed the door.

CHAPTER EIGHT

MOVING A MOUNTAIN HAD TO BE EASIER THAN GETTING
Eddie out of bed and ready for school. Garrett was sure of it.

"Should have called you Mule," he muttered as he coaxed
the boy downstairs and into the dining room for breakfast.
Most of the other boarders had already left for the day, so it
was just the two of them.

Garrett scooped flapjacks and sausage onto a plate from
the buffet and set it on the table. He pointed to a chair. "Hurry
or you'll be late."

Eddie sat and pushed the plate away. "I'm not going. I hate
school."

Mrs. Hoffmann walked in with a pot of coffee in her
hands. "*Huch!* In my day, talking back to my *vater* . . . my
pa . . . would have gotten me a whupping."

"He's not my pa."

Mrs. Hoffmann opened her mouth to say something but Garrett stopped her with a shake of his head.

She snapped her mouth shut, set the coffeepot on the buffet, and walked back into the kitchen, clucking with disapproval.

Eddie stared at his untouched plate. His lips stuck out like a buggy seat. Garrett filled a cup with coffee and sat opposite him.

Sipping the hot brew, he watched the boy over the rim of his cup. Invisible walls were always the hardest to penetrate, but somehow he had to find a way. He owed his brother that much, at least.

"Eddie, I'm sorry about your pa." He set his cup down and rubbed his forehead with both hands. "I'm also sorry I yelled at you. I don't know much about kids. I'll need your help in figuring out what I'm supposed to do."

Neither his apology nor his plea for help made Eddie lower his hostile glare. "You're not supposed to be mean."

"I'll keep that in mind."

Eddie narrowed his eyes. "Or be mean to my friends."

"If you're talking about Miss Parker, I apologized to her. I even offered to take her to the train today."

Doubt flickered in Eddie's eyes. "She's still here?"

"Yes, she is. Instead of leaving town yesterday, she stayed and looked for you."

Eddie jumped up from his chair. "You have to make Miss Parker stay. You gotta! Pleeeeeeeeease."

Make her stay?

"I can't *make* her do anything." He certainly couldn't

make her stay, but the shining hope on Eddie's face made him want to try. That and the memory of her moonlit eyes.

"I can . . . I can ask." What in blazes was he thinking? Why would she even think about staying? There was nothing here for her now that Dan was gone.

"You . . . you will?"

Garrett blew out his breath. Now look what he'd done— given the boy false hope. Still, he didn't want to spoil the sudden rapport between them, however tentative. "I guess it wouldn't hurt to ask. But if you don't hurry, you'll make me late and there won't be time to ask her anything."

Eddie picked up a sausage and shoved it in his mouth. Garrett was tempted to reprimand him but decided there would be time enough later for teaching proper table manners. First, he had to earn the boy's trust.

He thought of something Miss Parker said. *"You and Eddie are very much alike, you know. You both have strong feelings about what you believe in."*

"I might get her to postpone her journey for a day or two," he said. "But it's going to take a lot more to get her to stay longer."

Eddie grabbed his hat and coat and the strap that held his schoolbooks together and raced for the door.

"Why the sudden hurry?" Garrett called.

"Maybe if I go to school and get a one on my 'rithmetic test, Miss Parker will stay for good!"

Garrett grimaced. If he couldn't talk Miss Parker into staying, Eddie wouldn't believe another word he said. But what could he possibly say to keep her in town?

※

Not wanting to be late for her train, Mary-Jo stood in front of Daniel's house to save time, her sewing machine and carpet-bag by her side. It was cold and she walked back and forth to stay warm.

The sheriff arrived promptly at eight as promised. He set the brake on his wagon and hopped to the ground.

She greeted him with a smile. "Morning."

He returned the favor. Their breaths formed white plumes in the cold air, but his crooked smile brought a warm flush to her cheeks. As quickly as it came, the smile left his face and he looked so serious she feared that perhaps Eddie had run off again. He picked up her sewing machine, but instead of placing it in the wagon he stood holding it.

"Do you mind if we talk for a moment?" he asked.

"I suppose. Is Eddie—?"

"He's fine. He's at school. Determined to get a good grade for you."

She clasped her gloved hands together. "That sure is good to know."

He shifted his weight between the heels and balls of his feet and seemingly made no effort to fill in the silence that stretched between them.

"What do you wish to talk about, Sheriff?" When he still hesitated, she added, "Please feel free to speak your mind." She didn't mean to be impatient, but she did have a train to catch.

He set the Singer down and pulled off his hat. "I was wondering if . . ."

"Yes? Go on."

He clutched his hat to his chest. "I was wondering if . . ." He cleared his throat, made a face, and looked as helpless as a man about to face a firing squad.

She tapped her foot. He really did need to do something about that throat of his. "Yes, you were wondering?"

"I was wondering if you'd marry me?" He said it so quickly that at first she thought she'd misunderstood.

Realizing he was serious, her mouth dropped open. Had he suddenly sprouted two heads she wouldn't have been more surprised. "I—I . . . don't know what to say. We don't even know each other."

"Yes, I realize it's sudden, but you didn't know Dan either."

"Yes, but we wrote for several months." For all the good it did, since that no-good, lying catalogue owner took it upon himself to edit their letters.

"I don't expect you to marry me right away. We can take our time getting to know each other."

"You mean you want us to write to each other?"

He grimaced as if the very thought was distasteful. "I thought it would be easier . . . if you stay here." When she made no response, he continued, "I'll be a good husband to you, and I know you'll make a great mother."

Mother! "Bless my soul, that's what this is about. You want me to take care of Eddie."

He put his hat on and adjusted the brim as if biding for time. "I admit my first consideration is Eddie, but if I wanted just a nursemaid I would hire someone. The boy needs a real home. With a ma and a pa."

"Aren't you forgetting something? My pa's a gambler and I don't have much learning."

"You have what the boy needs."

She was still puzzling over what he meant by that when he continued, "All I'm asking is that you consider it. We'll know in a couple of weeks if it'll work out." He paused for a moment. "A month at the most."

She chewed on a nail. It wasn't like she had a lot of options. "I . . . I don't know what to say."

"Say you'll stay. If by the end of a month you decide the thought of marriage appeals to you, we'll have a proper courting."

What he offered was tempting. On the other hand . . . "What if it doesn't work out?"

"Then you can go home as planned."

It was a startling offer, no question, and if the plan failed, she'd be in a heap of trouble, money-wise. She had a train ticket, nothing more.

"I don't know—" It wasn't just mothering someone else's child that worried her; she couldn't imagine herself a lawman's wife.

"Miss Parker, all I'm asking is that we get to know each other . . . see if there's anything we can build on."

"Well, I—"

"One month," he persisted. "Thirty days. Please. I'll pay

your expenses. What could it hurt? If nothing else, it will allow me time to figure out how best to care for the boy."

She might have been able to withstand those blue eyes, but his crooked smile—she didn't have the heart to resist that.

On Sunday, Garrett and Eddie picked her up for church. Eddie looked as bright as a shiny new penny with his pressed clothes, neatly combed hair, and polished boots.

The whispers started even before the three of them took their places on the hard wooden pews. Though she couldn't make out the words, Mary-Jo could well guess what was being said: *Daniel Garrett isn't even cold in his grave and already his fiancée has taken up with his brother.*

For shame.

She glanced at Garrett but he seemed oblivious to the stares and whispers around them. Eddie sat between them and was as restless as a litter of playful kittens. He wiggled and squirmed and twice dropped his Bible. She took his hand in hers and it seemed to have a calming effect on him, at least until the sermon was over.

They stood to sing the closing hymn. Seeming to sense her gaze on him, Garrett's eyes met hers. The searching blue depths made her cheeks flare and she quickly turned away.

Her soprano and the sheriff's baritone encircled Eddie's youthful tenor as if to give the boy a musical hug. The organ stopped and she closed her eyes, trying to imagine the three of them a family. Surprisingly, it wasn't that hard.

"Turn to hymn two-thirteen," the preacher said.

Her mouth went dry. Unlucky thirteen . . . She glanced at Garrett and recalled his words. *"I don't believe in luck. Good, bad, or otherwise."*

Voices rose all around her. "Rock of Ages, cleft for me . . ."

She closed her eyes and tried to concentrate on the words of the hymn.

"Let me hide myself in Thee . . ."

If only I could, God. If only I could . . .

CHAPTER NINE

DURING THE FOLLOWING WEEK SHE MADE HERSELF useful by cleaning the house and mending Eddie's clothes. Though the home was modest by Kansas standards, it was the grandest house she'd ever lived in. She still couldn't get over the shiny forks and knives, and she was equally impressed with the drinking glasses. Back home they drank out of canning jars or simply held their mouths to the water pump. Equally amazing, the dishes all matched, without a single chip or crack!

Still, the house could use a woman's touch. Some pretty curtains and a picture or two on the walls and fresh flowers would make a world of difference.

As much as she liked thinking up ways to make things homier, she liked the domestic routine even more. Eddie stayed with her and the sheriff stopped by every day after work.

Garrett was always polite to her and handled Eddie with the same caution one might use with a firearm. Sometimes she wondered if he tried too hard.

It was a week before she gained courage enough to open the door to Daniel's bedroom. Her gaze lit on the black felt hat atop the quilt. Alarm rushed through her. She dashed across the room and flung the bowler to the floor. Didn't Daniel know that it was bad luck to put a hat on a bed? Was that what led to his early demise?

Shivering at the thought, she glanced around. This was the room Daniel intended to share with her. If things worked out as the sheriff suggested, it might also be the room she and Tom would share as husband and wife.

She felt all tingly inside. Mrs. Tom Garrett. Hmm. Not bad.

She had just finished beating the bedroom rug and polishing the furniture when Eddie burst in the front door.

"Look, Miss Parker, I got a two on my 'rithmetic test."

"Why, Eddie, that's wonderful." She took the paper from him and marveled aloud. "Why, look at that. You only missed one!"

"I ran out of time," he said. "But next time I'll get them all right."

It was then that she noticed the sheriff standing on the porch. She beckoned him inside. "Do come in, Sheriff." She wasn't yet ready to call him Tom as he asked or even Garrett. "This calls for a celebration. I made gingersnap cookies."

She still had trouble figuring out how to work the unfamiliar stove and the cookies were hard and burned on the bottom, but no one seemed to mind.

Later, after a meal of roasted chicken, Eddie asked his uncle to tell him a story.

The sheriff ran a finger around his collar. "I'm not much for storytelling," he said. "But I'll be happy to read from the Good Book."

"That sounds like a mighty fine idea," Mary-Jo said.

He reached for the Bible on the mantel and chose the story of Jonah and the big fish. Eddie settled by his side and listened attentively.

The story seemed so real, Mary-Jo could almost feel the storm's fury and Jonah's horror. As she listened to the sheriff's mesmerizing voice, she realized she had truly misjudged him. He did want to do right by the boy.

"And that's the story of Jonah," he said, closing the leather-bound Bible.

"Jonah was mighty lucky to be saved by a fish," she said.

The sheriff frowned. "Luck had nothing to do with it. It was God's grace that saved him."

Her cheeks flared with embarrassment and she quickly turned to Eddie. "Time for bed, young man."

By the time she finished tucking Eddie in bed and turned off his light, the sheriff had finished cleaning the kitchen. Where she came from, washing dishes was considered women's work.

She sat at the table, watching him. Domestic chores seemed as natural to him as sitting behind the sheriff's desk. "Thank you."

He shrugged, then hung the flour sack towel on a hook and joined her. "Everything okay?"

"I'm worried about Eddie," she said. "He won't talk about his pa and he hasn't shed a single tear. That's not good."

He rubbed his chin. "Give him time, Mary-Jo."

It was the first time he'd used her front name and it startled her. As if he thought things were more settled between them than they actually were.

"Sometimes it takes awhile to find the hurt," he added.

"He's going to need you when it happens," she said.

"I'm not good at things like that," he admitted, then paused, adding quietly, "I hope you'll help me."

His questioning eyes made her draw in her breath. "I don't know that this is a good idea, my staying. I don't want Eddie getting too attached to me should things not work out between us."

"You don't think this is working?" He sat back, his gaze prolonging the moment. "Is it . . . something I've done?"

She shook her head. "I don't think I have what it takes to be a sheriff's wife."

He rubbed the back of his neck. "I don't think it takes anything special."

"You have a dangerous job." She'd already lost two men she promised to marry.

"Not that dangerous," he said. "Colton isn't like other places you may have read about. Granted, we had a bunch of trouble with the railroad workers, but now that the track is laid they're gone. The town's not perfect, but the citizens here are mostly farmers and good churchgoing folks."

"And one of them killed Daniel."

His face turned dark. "It should never have happened. I knew Link was a hothead. I shouldn't have left town until after the jury verdict." He paused to shake his head. "I promise. Nothing like it will ever happen again. Trust me."

"I do trust you," she said; it was others she didn't trust. Last night she had a horrible nightmare and the memory of it still plagued her. In her dream she stood looking into a coffin, but it wasn't Charles's or even Daniel's face she saw. It was Tom's.

No matter how hard she tried, she couldn't shake away the fear of losing him.

On the following Wednesday, Eddie sat at the kitchen table after school doing his homework while she prepared supper. Garrett was due at any time and she wanted everything to be perfect.

Eddie looked up. "We're having parents' night in May and I want you and Uncle Tom to come." He seemed to hold his breath waiting for an answer, all the while wiggling his pencil back and forth.

May was still a couple of weeks away. She wiped her hands on her apron and sat on the chair opposite him. "I don't know if I'll still be here then," she said.

His pencil stilled. "Why not?"

She sighed. So many reasons came to mind but none that an eight-year-old would understand.

She finally settled on a noncommittal, "I might have to go home to Georgia."

He frowned. "Don't you like my uncle?"

The question surprised her. "We don't know each other all that well, but yes, I like him just fine." The truth was she liked him a lot. If it wasn't for the persistent nightmares, she would consider herself the luckiest girl alive that such a man asked her to marry him.

"When Bobby Watkins and Henry Hill got into a fight, my teacher made them stay after school until they got to know each other better. Now they're the bestest friends."

She smiled at his meaning. She didn't want to promise anything, but neither did she want to worry him. "Perhaps once your uncle and I get to know each other better, we'll be *bestest* friends too."

Garrett arrived and his presence seemed to fill every nook and cranny. He lifted the lid off the pot on the stove and sniffed. "That's not possum, is it?" he teased.

"It's beef stew," she said. "But I can fix possum if you like."

He replaced the lid. "Stew's fine," he said, winking at Eddie.

After they ate, Eddie was excused from the table to go and feed his pa's horse. She and Garrett lingered over coffee. While reaching for the sugar, he knocked over the salt.

She held her breath and clenched her hands together. Garrett had made it clear that he didn't believe in luck and she didn't want to do anything to earn his disfavor. Not while things were so fragile between them. And yet the urge was so strong.

He set the saltshaker upright. She tried to ignore the

white grains that dotted the table. It would have been easier to ignore a herd of cattle moving through the room.

She chewed on a fingernail. She imagined the white grains of salt dancing across the table, mocking her. She thought of the nightmares that plagued her and she felt sick to her stomach.

"I've been thinking," she began.

He raised a dark eyebrow. "And?"

She tried to recall the speech she'd rehearsed, but none of it came to mind. "Maybe . . . it would be best if I returned home."

He set his cup down. "It's only been two weeks," he said. "You promised you'd take at least a month to think about it."

"Yes, well, I have thought about it. I've also prayed about it but . . ." Much to her dismay, tears welled in her eyes. For more than six years she'd grieved for Charles. She didn't know how to grieve for Daniel. What little she thought she knew about him turned out to be lies from Mr. Hitchcock's pen. That explained some of the tears but not all.

He handed her a clean handkerchief and she dabbed her cheeks. "I don't think God means for me to get married." There, she said it.

He reared back in his chair, his face suffused with astonishment. "Did you come to this conclusion because of what happened to Dan?"

"And Charles." She still didn't want to tell him about her nightmares.

He blew out his breath and scratched his temple. "I don't

think God has anything to do with your losses," he said. "Bad things happen and—"

Before he could complete his sentence, Eddie ran into the house, shouting, "Fire, fire!"

"Oh no!" She jumped up from her chair.

The sheriff was on his feet and out the door in a flash. Mary-Jo started after him, then stopped. She grabbed the salt shaker and shook it over her left shoulder before bounding out the door.

* * *

Dark, thick smoke poured out of the barn. Garrett pulled a bucket of water from the well and dashed inside. Mary-Jo grabbed a second bucket and followed, water sloshing over the sides.

The air was hazy with smoke, but by the time she entered the barn, the fire appeared to be out. She set the bucket down.

"What is that awful smell?" She wrinkled her nose. "It smells like rotten eggs."

Garrett turned, his face dark with anger. "Where's Eddie?"

"I don't know. I—"

Just then the barn door slammed shut. Garrett bolted forward but the door was locked from the outside. "Eddie, open this door. Do you hear me? Open it at once!"

Nothing, not a peep came from outside.

"Drat!" Garrett kicked the door with his boot. "The boy is out of control."

"What do you mean? Are you saying he set the fire?"

"Not a fire, a smoke bomb." He lifted his voice. "Eddie!"

His raised voice made her flinch. "I'll say one thing. They sure do know how to build strong barns out here."

"You won't be so calm if he burns down the house."

"I reckon I know why he locked us in here." The more she thought about it, the more certain she was. "He wants us to get to know each other better." She quickly explained about Eddie's two schoolmates. "That must be what gave him the idea."

Garrett threw up his hands. "Now, isn't this just dandy?" He gave the door a whack with his fist. "We're locked in here and he's running free out there. God only knows what mischief he'll get into next."

She sat on a bale of hay and twisted her hands on her lap. "Perhaps if you stop yelling he'll open the door. Right now all you're doing is scaring him." He was scaring her too, though she sensed he was more frustrated than angry. He was also worried about Eddie.

"That's not all I'll do when I get hold of him." He plunked down on a hay bale opposite her.

She chewed on her lip. "He didn't mean no real harm. He just wants us to be friends."

Head buried in his hands, Garrett said nothing, but at least he'd stopped yelling.

"Did your brother have a temper like yours?" she asked after a while.

The mention of Daniel seemed to have a sobering effect on him. Elbows resting on his thighs, he rubbed his hands together. "Dan was the quiet one, except when he was arguing a case."

"Was he a good lawyer?" she asked.

"He was better at getting criminals out of jail than I am at putting them there, if that's what you mean."

She supposed he was still blaming himself for not having captured his brother's killer. To divert his thoughts, she asked, "And your pa? Was he in law too?"

"He was a banker. He dealt in faith and hope, just like your father."

She laughed. "Well now, I reckon you have a sense of humor after all." He didn't smile, but she'd sensed a thawing in his voice.

He studied her. "I know about your father, but you never said anything about your mother."

She drew in her breath. "Ma died in an accident when I was five. That left just me and Pa. I slept in gambling halls, under the tables while he gambled."

A shadow touched his forehead. "It must have been a hard life."

"It was. One night when I was twelve, my pa was losing real bad and for a joke, he let me play a hand. You don't spend the better part of seven years in a gambling hall without knowing how to gamble and—wouldn't you know?—I won."

"No!" He studied her. "You were so . . . young."

At the time she'd felt anything but young. "I guess I had what they call beginner's luck. I didn't win much. Less than three dollars. Pa thought I would give it to him, but I refused. Instead, I walked out of that gambling hall and took the first stage to my aunt's house." Surprised to find herself sharing something she'd not shared with anyone but her aunt, she added, "It was the best thing I ever did."

No more sleeping on casino floors or going to bed hungry. No more putting up with her pa's drinking during losing streaks. "My aunt taught me to read and write and how to mind my p's and q's. She's a seamstress and she taught me to sew. She also took me to church."

Judging by the dim light filtering through the cracks, the sun had set and, just as rapidly, the temperature dropped. Mary-Jo rubbed her hands up and down her arms for warmth.

"You're cold," he said, standing. He grabbed a horse blanket from an empty stall and shook away the straw. He then wrapped it around her shoulders, his hands lingering a bit longer than necessary. The blanket smelled of hay and dust and horseflesh, but it was warm despite its rough texture.

"Much obliged," she said.

Instead of taking his place on the opposite hay bale, he sat next to her. His arm brushed against hers and an unwelcome surge of excitement flooded through her.

"May I ask why you signed up to become a mail-order bride?" In the fast-fading light he looked serious, but no less pleasing to the eye.

"I'm from Helen, Georgia. We suffered heavy casualties during the war. Every man living there now is either old, married, or in jail. If a gal wants to get married, she best set her sights elsewhere."

She heard his intake of breath and it was awhile before he

spoke. "I guess I owe you an apology. I told Dan he was a fool to order a bride out of a catalogue."

"But if he'd listened to you, I wouldn't have come to Kansas and we wouldn't be in this pickle."

He pulled a piece of straw from her hair. "Actually, it's not a bad pickle to be in," he said, adding a smile.

Something in his voice sent gooseflesh racing up her arms. "You . . . you once said I had what the boy needs."

He nodded. "You're the only one able to reach him and see past his childish pranks."

His words touched her deeply. "Don't be angry with Eddie. He's scared. I know how it feels to be scared, not knowing what's gonna happen to you."

He ran his fingers gently down her cheek. "If . . . if you agree to be my wife, I'll make sure you're never scared again."

His promise washed over her like warm sunshine. He nudged her chin up and gazed into her eyes. It was all she could do to breathe. He covered her parted lips with his own and the gentle impact of his mouth sent warm tremors rushing through her. The sweet tenderness of his kiss made her emotions swirl, and she lost all sense of time and place as she happily kissed him back.

"Uncle Tom?" The tentative voice floated toward them, followed by a sob.

They pulled apart and Tom jumped up. "Eddie? What's wrong?"

Eddie flew into his uncle's arms. "It's . . . it's getting dark out here. I want my pa." Tears flowed down his cheeks and sobs wracked his thin, small body. Holding the boy in his arms, Tom met Mary-Jo's gaze and they exchanged a knowing look.

The boy had found his hurt.

Tom lifted Eddie tenderly in his arms and carried him out of the barn. Mary-Jo had to run to catch up.

Inside the house, he set Eddie ever so gently on the couch while she lit a lamp. Eddie's body shook with sobs and the tears streaming down his face nearly broke her heart.

It took awhile, but Eddie finally stopped crying. "I'm sorry I locked you in the . . . the b-b-barn."

Tom ran his mouth across the boy's forehead. "It's okay, buddy." He brushed hair from Eddie's wet face.

Eddie made a sobbing sound. "You're . . . you're n-not mad?"

"I'm not mad." Tom glanced back at her. "Actually, you did us a favor locking us in the barn. You helped me persuade Miss Parker to stay awhile longer."

Eddie knuckled away his tears. "I did?"

She smiled. She couldn't help herself. "You did."

Tom straightened. "Does this mean what I think it means, Miss Parker? That I can begin to properly court you?"

At that moment she felt as if her heart would burst with joy. "I believe that's exactly what it means, Tom."

No sooner were the words out of her mouth than a shiver ran down her spine, filling her with dismay. According to her aunt, such a shiver meant someone had just walked over her grave.

❀

Garrett and Barnes were just about to check on a disturbance at Buck's Saloon when old man Walters walked into the office.

"What can I do for you, Chuck?" Garrett asked. A farmer by trade, Walters seldom came to town except to haul his produce to the general store. Appearance-wise, he was a man of extremes. A long white beard hung from a prune-like face and a barrel-shaped torso sat upon matchstick legs.

Walters pushed his chewing tobacco from the inside of one cheek to the other and thumbed his suspenders. "Just thought you should know I saw Link's paint out at the old Coldwell cabin."

Garrett's hands tightened into fists. It was the break he'd been waiting for, hoping for, praying for. He wouldn't rest until he put his brother's killer behind bars, and it was all he could do to contain the rage building inside.

He plucked his hat off the wall peg and slapped it on his head. Barnes looked at him for direction. "You check out the problem at Buck's and meet me at Coldwell's."

Barnes looked about to argue, but Garrett stormed outside and raced for his horse.

CHAPTER TEN

GARRETT HID BEHIND A WATER TANK, HIS GAZE FOCUSED on the sod house some thirty feet away. The abode had a windmill, barn, and an assortment of rusty farm equipment. Old man Walters was right; it was Link's paint, all right. No question. Garrett would recognize the brown-and-white horse anywhere.

The only sign of life was smoke curling from the pipe sticking out like an afterthought on the thatched roof. Garrett pulled out his watch. Where was Barnes? His deputy sheriff should have been here by now. What was taking so long?

The cabin had only one door and one window and Garrett had them both covered. Link wasn't going anywhere except to jail.

Minutes passed and still no sign of Barnes. Suddenly, the cabin door flew open and Link walked out and headed for his horse.

Garrett stood. "Drop your weapon."

Link spun around and reached for his gun.

Garrett moved forward. "I said drop it!" he yelled.

"I didn't mean to kill your b-brother," Link stammered. "I—I was out of my mind."

"I said drop your weapon."

Finally Link did what he was told. His gun hit the ground, stirring up a cloud of dust. "Come on, Garrett." He shook his hands in the air. "We've known each other a long time. I got a family. You put me away, what's gonna happen to them?"

"You should have thought of that before you entered the courtroom with a loaded gun."

"I wasn't thinkin' clearly. All that was goin' through my head was that my sister's killer was goin' free. I didn't mean to kill Dan. You know I've always had bad aim. I couldn't shoot my way out of a chicken coop."

Garrett pulled out his handcuffs with his free hand. "Well, unfortunately, your aim wasn't bad enough."

He stepped closer. With lightning speed Link grabbed his gun and they struggled. The handcuffs went flying. Link matched Garrett in height but he was a good fifty pounds heavier. The gun went off with a deafening blast and Garrett reeled back. Time stood still. Vision blurred, he slowly sank to his knees before his head hit the ground.

Mayhem. Confusion . . .

Someone spoke but the words made no sense. Two blue eyes stared at him. How did she get here? "Mary-Jo?" She smiled and faded away. He tried to call her back but his lips wouldn't move. He blinked but this time it was Deputy Barnes who came into view.

"We got him." Barnes's voice sounded muffled. "He tried to get away but I got here just in time."

Garrett tried to speak, but everything went black.

✤

Mary-Jo sat at her sewing machine smiling to herself as she repaired a rip in Eddie's shirt. Honestly, she didn't know what the boy did to his clothes that they were in constant need of repair. Turning the hand crank with her right hand, she guided the fabric beneath the needle with the other. After sewing the seam, she snipped the thread with scissors.

Turning the scissors over, she slipped her finger through one of the gold-handled rings. Turning it to collect the light, she envisioned a gold band instead of the humble tool.

"Does this mean what I think it means, Miss Parker? That I can begin to properly court you?"

The memory made her smile, but thinking about his kiss filled her with unspeakable pleasure. Maybe the third time would be a charm. *Oh, God,* she prayed. *Please don't let anything happen to Tom!*

She laid the shears down and knocked on wood before reaching for another shirt. But just as she started the machine, Eddie burst through the door. Startled, she jumped and the scissors flew to the floor. More bad luck.

"Heavens to Betsy, you near scared me to death." She

reached down, but seeing Eddie's pale face she promptly forgot the scissors. "Eddie, what is it?"

"Uncle Tom's been sh-shot."

"No!" For a moment she sat there, stunned, then she jumped to her feet. *Oh, God, please! Not again, not again.* At last she found her voice. "Where is he?"

"At Doc Haggerty's place. Hurry!"

The doctor lived in a two-story brick house just outside of town. Mary-Jo frantically pounded on the door and a round-figured woman quickly ushered them inside. "I'm Mrs. Haggerty. The doctor's removing the bullet now."

"Is h-he g-going to die?" Eddie, white-faced and trembling, stammered the words.

His question sent chills down Mary-Jo's spine. It was bad enough to think the unthinkable without hearing the words aloud. "Your uncle's very strong." She spoke to Eddie but she kept her gaze fastened upon the woman's face, looking for some sign of hope.

Too young to know that death showed no favoritism between the strong and the weak, Eddie accepted her answer as only a child could.

Mrs. Haggerty laid a hand on the boy's shoulder. "I just made some gingerbread. Come with me. You can be the official taster."

Eddie hesitated, but Mary-Jo gave him a gentle shove. "Go along. I'll stay here."

The doctor's wife tucked Eddie's hand in her own. "You'll find the sheriff right through that door." She then led Eddie down the hall.

No sooner had the two vanished from sight than Mary-Jo whirled about and reached for the doorknob. With a bracing breath, she charged into the room.

Tom was stretched out on a table, the doctor standing over him. She rushed to his side. He looked pale, his bare chest covered in blood. Nevertheless, he managed a wan smile.

"Oh, Tom . . ." She lifted his hand and held it tight, biting back tears.

"Don't worry." His voice sounded strained. "It'll take more than a little lead ball to keep me down."

"You're just lucky you took it in the shoulder," the doctor said. A bespectacled man with a balding head, he applied gauze to the wound and wrapped a strip of cotton around Tom's upper torso. "You lost a lot of blood."

"Will he be all right?" Mary-Jo asked.

"Should be." After the doctor finished bandaging the wound, he held up a pair of tongs to show her the bullet. "Far as I know, it didn't do any major damage."

"Thank God," she whispered.

"We still have to watch for infection." The doctor dropped the bullet back into a bowl and set the tongs down. "Lots of rest and some good home cooking and he'll be good as new." The doctor washed his hands in a basin and left the room.

She pushed a lock of hair away from Tom's forehead. "Jumping catfish, you nearly scared the life out of me."

He squeezed her hand. "Mary-Jo . . . we got him. We got the man who killed Dan."

She tried to be happy for him. "I'm glad," she said. It didn't bring Daniel back, but maybe now Tom would know peace of mind. Maybe they all would.

"If anything happened to you . . . ," she whispered.

"I'm fine. Can't you see?"

She laid her head on his good shoulder and closed her eyes. He was fine now, but what about next time? And the time after that?

The door flew open and Eddie ran into the room. "Uncle Tom!"

Not even the joy on Eddie's face upon seeing his uncle could chase away her worry.

※

For the next two days, Mary-Jo took care of Tom. He slept on the couch and she plied him with homemade soup and stew. Every morning she cleaned his wound and changed his bandage.

It did her heart good to watch him and Eddie grow close. He helped Eddie with his schoolwork and the two spent hours playing draughts and dominoes.

Deputy Sheriff Barnes stopped by daily to report on the latest town happenings. After one such visit she walked into the parlor to find Tom up and dressed.

"Where do you think you're going?"

"To work."

"But the doctor said—"

"Someone stole a bunch of horses from the Dobson farm. I've got to check it out."

With dismay, she watched him buckle his holster. "It's so soon. You hardly have your strength back."

"I'll take it easy."

"But . . ."

His eyes narrowed. "It's my job." Without another word, he left.

It was late by the time he arrived home and Eddie was already asleep. Tom walked into the house, took one look at her carpetbag and sewing machine by the door, and stopped.

"What's this?" His gaze sharpened. "Mary-Jo?"

Mary-Jo lifted her chin and forced herself to say the well-rehearsed words. "I'm going back to Georgia."

CHAPTER ELEVEN

FOR THE LONGEST MOMENT HE STARED AT HER. "IS IT something I did?" he asked at last.

"No."

He glanced at Eddie's bedroom door. "I know he can be a handful but—"

She shook her head and moved away from him. It was the only way she could keep her wits about her. "My decision has nothing to do with Eddie." Actually, she had grown quite fond of the boy and would miss him terribly.

A muscle tightened in his jaw. "Then why? I thought . . . we'd made headway."

She swallowed hard. No doubt he was referring to the kiss in the barn. Her cheeks burned with the memory. "I can't be a sheriff's wife. I'm sorry. I just can't."

"Because of Dan and your other fiancé?" He didn't wait for an answer. "And you're afraid something will happen to me."

"Something *did* happen to you." Tears burned her eyes and she blinked to hold them back. "You were nearly killed."

"But I wasn't."

She hugged herself to ward off a sudden chill. "I'm just not lucky where men are concerned." She wasn't lucky at all.

Anger flashed in his eyes and his face grew dark. "I don't believe in luck. I only believe in God."

"I believe in God too."

"But you don't trust Him," he said.

"Do you blame me?" she lashed out. This time there was no holding back the tears. "If He's so trustworthy, why does He let bad things happen? Answer me that!"

"I can't," he said quietly. "I don't think anyone can. Dan's death is about as bad as it gets, but God can take something like that and turn it into something good. That's what I believe He's trying to do here."

"I—I wish I could believe that." She swallowed the lump in her throat. "But I can't."

He beckoned her with his one good arm. "Mary-Jo, please, we'll work this out. We'll find a way."

She shook her head and her heart squeezed in anguish. Why was this so hard? It wasn't as if she loved him. She'd only known him for a short time. What she felt wasn't love, couldn't be love. And yet, in some ways it felt as if she'd known him all her life.

"Nothing you say can make me change my mind. I'm leaving on the morning train." He started to say something, but she cut him off. "Don't try to stop me."

A look of despair spread over his face. "At least let me drive you to the station."

"It's better if you don't." The harsh reality of a future without him hit her full force and she fled the room in tears.

❀

It was a good mile-and-a-half hike to the train station and Mary-Jo had to keep stopping to rest her arm. It was hard to know what was heavier: her sewing machine or her heart. Still, she arrived nearly an hour early. She cried most of the way. Whenever she was tempted to turn back, she deliberately stepped on a crack. While passing through town she walked under a ladder and then she chased a black cat until at last it crossed her path.

She did everything possible that morning to tempt fate so as not to turn back; it was only a matter of time before something awful happened. To go back now would only subject Tom and Eddie to the bad luck that was surely heading her way, and that she would never do.

Tom. Just thinking his name nearly shattered what little control she had left. If only she could have his faith. She wanted to put her trust in God but she didn't know how.

For as far back as she could remember, everything, from the roof over her head to the food on the table, was the result of her father's luck at the gambling tables. He even blamed her mother's death on an unlucky roll of dice.

How much easier life would be if she could leave everything to God and not have to worry about every little wayward grain of salt. If only . . .

Ticket in hand, she lowered her sewing machine next to the wooden bench and sat.

She tried not to think of Tom. Better to concentrate on the people around her. A woman walked by holding two small boys by the hand. A man with a walrus mustache and a cane sat on the other end of the bench.

A boy around Eddie's age ran past her and she closed her eyes to block him from view, but that only brought back memories of Tom and how much she had hurt him.

She shook her thoughts away and chewed a fingernail. Tom's voice came back to haunt her. *"God can take something bad and turn it into something good . . ."*

What if Tom was right? She wanted so much to believe that was true, but it wasn't. She knew it wasn't. It was only a matter of time before her reckless stepping on cracks and walking under ladders that morning caused something awful to happen. *Let's see what God will do then!*

And so she waited.

Nothing fell from the sky.

The station didn't collapse.

The world didn't end.

She opened her reticule and pulled out her father's lucky playing cards. Holding them in her hand, she hesitated. Finally she flung the pack into the trash receptacle behind the bench.

She waited some more. Still nothing bad happened.

The train pulled into the station in a cloud of hissing steam and came to a screeching stop. Passengers filed off in orderly fashion. People called to each other and hugged. Minutes passed and no one fell or suffered a mishap. She turned to retrieve the playing cards, but something stopped her.

The deck of cards was the only gift her father ever gave her. That was why she'd held on to them all these years. Now they only reminded her that gambling had ruined his life and pretty near ruined hers too. It might not be possible to throw away unhappy memories, but leaving the cards in the trash might well be a start.

"All aboard," shouted the dark-skinned conductor hanging from a handrail.

She reached for her sewing machine, but all that greeted her grasping hand was empty space. She looked down. Oh no! Her Singer was gone!

Jumping to her feet, she quickly glanced around. No, no, no! Don't let this be happening!

She stopped a woman cradling an infant in her arms. "Excuse me, ma'am. Did you see anyone carrying a wooden case this size?" She indicated the length with her hands. "It was a sewing—"

The woman shook her head and kept going.

At her wit's end, Mary-Jo ran toward the train, her sweeping gaze checking each passenger's baggage.

"Sir!" she called to the conductor. "Someone stole my sewing machine."

"Report it to the stationmaster." He tossed a nod to the ticket booth and vanished inside the passenger car.

The train whistle sounded and the train began to move. It was taking off without her, but she couldn't leave without her precious sewing machine. She knew it! She knew something awful would happen.

She should never have stepped on all those cracks or thrown away her father's lucky playing cards. Or chased the cat or . . .

Let's see you make something good out of this, God!

Wiping tears away with a gloved hand, she rushed toward the ticket booth. A large crowd stood waving good-bye as the train pulled out of the station and she elbowed her way through. "Excuse me, excuse me . . ."

Was that her sewing machine in the distance? On the platform? Heart pounding, she bobbed up and down trying to see over the mass of hat-covered heads.

The crowd finally thinned and she worked herself free. In an instant she forgot about luck, good or bad. She forgot about everything but the two people standing on either side of her Singer.

"What . . . what are you doing here?" Her temper flared. "I told you not to come!"

Tom's gaze pierced the distance between them. His arm was still in a sling, but he looked no less strong and vibrant. "I know what you said." His eyes darkened with emotion. "But I suddenly realized I couldn't let you go without a fight." He gave her a sheepish grin. "You said it yourself—I'm a warrior."

Her heart had been broken many times, but this was the first time she felt it melt. No one had ever cared enough to fight for her, and she didn't know what to say.

Tom continued, "Actually, you can blame Eddie. He said you wouldn't get on the train without your sewing machine."

"Oh, did he now?"

Eddie stepped forward, an eager look on his face. "I have a gift for you."

"A gift?"

He nodded and placed a rabbit's foot in her palm. "It's supposed to bring good luck. Uncle Tom said it would make you feel better and maybe even convince you to stay."

Fighting back tears, she gazed at the lump of fur in her hand. Making such a concession couldn't have come easy.

"Thank you," she whispered.

She was touched, but more than that, she saw the rabbit foot for what it was—a sham. She now realized how foolish it was to put one's trust in something as random as luck. She'd done everything possible that morning to tempt fate, but nothing awful had happened.

Tom said God could take something bad and turn it into something good, and she wanted to believe it was true. Gazing into his loving eyes, she *did* believe it. She believed it with all her heart. For once in her life her anxiety about the future was gone, melted away like a winter thaw followed by the warmth and promise of spring.

"I don't think I'll be needing this rabbit's foot." She pressed the furry paw into Eddie's palm. "I'd rather put my trust in God."

Tom's eyes softened with gentle understanding. "Does that mean I can resume a proper courtship?"

She smiled. Not only was he the most handsome man she ever set eyes on, but he wore his new family status so well. "Not *too* proper, I hope."

With a happy whoop, Tom wrapped his one good arm around her waist and pulled her so close their hearts beat as one. He then gave her one very improper kiss.

"Does that mean you're going to be Uncle Tom's cantaloupe bride?" Eddie asked.

Mary-Jo laughed and ruffled Eddie's hair. "Only if you let me be your cantaloupe ma."

Eddie flung his arms around her waist.

Blinking back tears of joy, she was just about to say that she was the luckiest girl alive, but stopped herself just in time. This wasn't luck; this was a blessing from God and for that she gave a silent prayer of thanksgiving.

As if to read her mind, Tom lifted his gaze to heaven as if he too said a silent prayer. He then smiled at his new family. "Come on, you two. All this talk about cantaloupes is making me hungry."

Glossary of Mail-Order Bride Advertising Terms

(*And What They Really Mean*)

Eager to learn—can't cook; can't sew; can't clean

Accomplished—can ride, shoot, and spit like a man

Modest dowry—poor as a church mouse

Independent means—mean face and mean disposition

Loving nature—keep her away from the ranch hands

Traditionally built—you may wish to reinforce the floors

Matrimonially inclined—working on husband number three

Maternal—has six children and one on the way

Possesses natural beauty—don't let the false hair, cosmetic paints, or bolstered bosom scare you

Industrious—give her a dollar and she'll figure out how to spend ten

Young looking—doesn't look a day over sixty

And they lived happily ever after—AND THEY LIVED HAPPILY EVER AFTER.

An Ever After Summer

Debra Clopton

"For I know the plans I have for you," declares
the Lord. *"Plans to prosper you and not to harm
you, plans to give you a hope and a future."*

JEREMIAH 29:11 NIV

Widowed rancher looking for practical woman to keep
house and be a mother to his two-year-old baby girl.
Bible believers need not apply. Mathew McConnell,
Honey Springs, Texas.

SITTING AT HIS DESK IN THE OFFICE OF THE *HITCHING*
Post Mail-Order Bride Catalogue, Melvin Hitchcock scowled
at the letter.

"The man is wasting his time. *And* his money," Melvin
grumbled, shaking his head. The ad had been in the catalogue
for weeks with no response—other than a few letters from
candidates of ill repute whom Melvin quickly disqualified,
after all, there was a child's welfare at stake!

Melvin knew something had to be done or the widower
would lose patience and blame the lack of response on the
catalogue.

It was time for action.

Melvin picked up his pen. Tapping it on his chin, he thought-
fully studied the letter . . . a widower. Mathew McConnell was
obviously still grieving the loss of his wife these two years and
not in his right mind. Why else would he forgo the qualification

that any loving father would want for his children? No, this lonely, grieving widower needed love as much as his baby needed it . . . and from a woman with God on her side if she was to be of any help at all.

Intent on his task, Melvin tweaked a sentence, removed a few words—only a slight change but enough. Pushing his spectacles back onto the bridge of his nose, he read the new ad. "Yes, yes, this will do nicely." It had a certain ring to it. A certain romance that would speak softly to a woman of a tender heart and a godly belief . . .

There would be responses now. And Melvin trusted that the good Lord would show him exactly the right young woman whose letter he should forward on to Mathew McConnell— that baby needed a mother. She'd already been waiting far, far too long.

Anticipation filled Melvin, helping lonely couples was a calling. He had a way with words, and an inexplicable ability to read a letter and know what someone really needed.

Oh yes, he did indeed. It was a God-given ability, and Melvin Hitchcock had no qualms admitting as much or plans to let such a gift go to waste . . .

"Bible believers need not apply"—*ha!* Indeed they should and they would or his name wasn't Melvin Hitchcock of the very well-received *Hitching Post Mail-Order Bride Catalogue*!

CHAPTER ONE

Honey Springs, Texas
SUMMER 1870

A BORN KILLER. MELVINA ELDORA SMITH KILLED THREE
*people before the age of one—her mother at birth, her father of a
broken heart, and her poor, poor uncle Mutt outside a bar with
a runaway buggy . . .*

Ellie Smith fought off the chanting taunts of her past.
Taunts that had followed her from "the ill-fated day of her
birth"—as Aunt Millicent was fond of saying.

Three deaths before the age of one!

Aunt Millicent had assured Ellie and everyone else she
came in contact with for the last nineteen years that all three
deaths were most unquestionably Ellie's doing.

Oh, how Ellie wished she'd known them all. The loss of
her mother and father especially left a gnawing hole in her

heart. But according to Aunt Millicent it was nothing compared to the one in her heart, especially with the hardship of raising Ellie dropped straightaway into her lap. Over and over Ellie had heard this from as far back as she could remember.

The taunts of children on the playground and the whispers of adults carried the same message. "Murderin' Melvina." The hurtful nickname had clung to her all these nineteen years. Her penance for crimes committed . . .

But not any longer.

Today she'd left Murderin' Melvina behind, shortened Eldora to Ellie. Her new beginning as Ellie Smith was under way. Today her very own fairy tale began . . . She still could not believe it was possible.

Her chest felt like it would surely burst with anticipation as she stood on the weathered plank sidewalk beside the stagecoach she'd just ridden three hundred rough, dusty miles into Honey Springs. Even the oppressive summer heat couldn't stifle her exhilaration as she surveyed the bustling little Texas town that was now her home. She loved the assortment of clapboard buildings, some made of logs and some of bricks that were a backdrop for the busy people moving in all directions. The mercantile was across the street and the hotel was too. The livery sat at the end of the street. She took the rest in, but instead of focusing on the buildings, she studied the people. Fingers of excitement curled inside of her, tickling her so that she thought she might laugh with the thrill of it all.

Where is he?

At nineteen, Ellie was leaving her regrettable past—and Aunt Millicent—behind, daring to forge a new life. From the moment she'd stepped onto that stage she'd been in control of her destiny—well, she and God, but surely He had orchestrated this opportunity and was in on the plan.

Yes, God was finally smiling on Ellie. Good things were about to happe—

"Look out below!"

The shout from above had Ellie looking up just in time to see her heavy valise sail from atop the stage straight at her! Ellie jumped out of the way, barely in the nick of time, and the valise whizzed past her and thudded to the boardwalk in a plume of dust. Ellie's hat slid forward and she righted it with one hand as she clutched her Bible to her racing heart.

"Oops, sorry 'bout that, little lady," the grizzled driver shouted.

"That's quite all right, Mr. Muldoon," Ellie assured him. He and his shotgun had gotten her through some rough country without mishap and for that she was thankful. Sneezing when a loose feather from her hat tickled her nose, she swiped it out of the way and continued to scan the men milling about.

Where was he?

Two months ago Ellie had only dreamed of a different life. One with a husband and children to call her own—her unattainable happily-ever-after. But dreams were all she'd had. No man in Fort Worth with half a mind wanted to be stuck with a wife known as Murderin' Melvina. Then Aunt

Millicent had slapped a copy of the *Hitching Post Mail-Order Bride Catalogue* in front of her and given Ellie an hour to pick a husband or she would pick one for her.

Looking down in shock at that catalogue, Ellie had no idea that the book would change her life. Hesitantly, she'd opened it to a random page and, as if beckoning her gaze to fall upon it, there was Mathew McConnell's ad. The short, sweet words spoke to her heart.

Lonely, widowed rancher looking for love and a godly mother for his sweet, two-year-old baby girl who needs gentle arms to hold her.

Ellie had connected instantly—not even knowing what Mathew McConnell looked like. She'd looked her future in the face and decided right then and there to change the course of her life.

The very daring of the idea had energized her like nothing else ever had, like being freed from shackles!

And the most ironic thing of all: it had been Aunt Millicent's desire to be rid of her that had turned Ellie's life in this exciting new direction.

It just went to show a person that God, in His timing, could take a bad situation and turn it for good . . . just as the Good Book promised.

Mathew McConnell was the hope of her life.

The answer to her prayers. Her very own knight in shining armor.

Mathew offered her a way out of the life she'd been doomed to live and for that she would forever be grateful.

And baby Sophie . . . oh, the sweet angel, just like Ellie, had lost her mother at birth. Ellie had so much love just bursting to be showered on Sophie. The sweet, innocent child would never, ever carry the burden of her mother's death as Ellie had for her own.

Searching the passing people, Ellie's eyes jerked to a halt as they latched onto the dark, penetrating eyes of a tall, lean cowboy with a very unbecoming scowl on his ruggedly handsome face. "Goodness," she gasped, her fingers tightening on her Bible.

Dressed in dark britches, a gray, long-sleeved shirt tucked in at his narrow hips, a holster hung low on his right thigh. His thumb was looped beneath the leather belt just in front of the pearl handle of the holstered gun. Tall, lean, and dangerous.

And he was watching her.

Ellie wondered if he knew that he looked like he'd just eaten a very sour pickle. And how sad because it didn't become him in the least.

And why, she wanted to know, was he looking at *her* with that pickle-faced expression?

Hiking her chin, Ellie met the cowboy's insolent stare. How dare he! Of all the rude—He took a step in her direction! Ellie gasped and despite the road separating them, she took a step back on the platform. When he stomped from the plank sidewalk and strode toward her across that rutted road, Ellie's heart dropped straight to her toes. What was he doing?

Sidestepping horses and buggies, he crossed the busy street, taking purposeful strides toward her. Tightening her grip on the Bible she clutched to her chest, she denied the dreaded thought sliding over her—surely to goodness this man was *not* Mathew McConnell!

Why else would a perfect stranger be approaching me?

Her head was full of imaginations of the way she believed her betrothed would look. And while, at the moment, she couldn't disregard this man's dark good looks, the scowl that hadn't left his expression left much, *much* to be desired. Ellie was looking for a lonely widower looking for love . . . He should be looking happily at her.

This rugged cowboy looked like he was aching for a fight, or at the least had a belly full of green plums. Ellie glanced about her, maybe her eyes were deceived and his gaze was locked onto someone standing behind her.

"Miss Smith?"

Ellie's stomach curdled, her palms grew damp. "Yes." *Dear Lord, please don't let this be so.*

"Miss *Melvina Eldora* Smith?"

The name alone caused Ellie to cringe. Aunt Millicent always said a formal letter required a formal name, and Ellie had written the letter to the *Hitching Post* in the most formal way, wanting to make the best impression of her life—and with her aunt looking over her shoulder! Clearly a misconception on her part, since this dour, pickled-faced man obviously had no interest in making any kind of good impression on the likes of her.

Pulling her shoulders back, Ellie pushed her alarmed reaction down. "Mr. McConnell?" *Please, oh please let it not be so . . .* The quick nod of his dark head shot any glimmer of hope straight onto the dusty boards upon which she stood. Surely there was something amiss here. Some terrible, dreadful mistake.

❦

The dread that had been coiling in the pit of Mathew McConnell's gut from the moment the wide-eyed beauty stepped from the stagecoach tightened as she slowly nodded her feather-topped head.

"I'm afraid there's been a mistake," he nearly growled, eyeing the Bible in her hands before looking straight at her.

Eyes that were mingled shades of light and dark blues, like the colors of the bluebonnets that grew all over Texas, met his, just as a perfectly sculpted eyebrow snapped up. "Ex*cuse* me?" she said, none too happily.

Mathew should have tipped his hat to the lady, even if he was too angry to think of the manners his mother—may she rest in peace—had taught him. This was not the Melvina Eldora he'd pictured arriving to marry him—the woman who'd come to be a mother to Sophie.

"I specifically requested a *practical* woman." Snatching his Stetson from his head, he slapped it against his thigh. What kind of mail-order bride catalogue was this *Hitching Post* anyway? There could have been no mistaking his ad: *Widowed rancher looking for practical woman to keep house and be a mother to his baby girl. Bible believers need not apply.* And yet, here stood this, this *woman . . .* decked out in her feathers, ruffles, and lace from the top of her head to the tips of her dainty boots.

"Practical," she ground out. Her pert nose twitched just the slightest and her bluebonnet eyes flared with indignation. "You're saying I'm not *practical*?" Her voice rose on the last word as she glared at him and batted a feather out of her face.

"That's right." He'd started this so he might as well finish it. "And I *specifically* said Bible thumpers need not apply." His eyes fell to the Bible gripped in her white-knuckled hands.

"Bible thumber—I mean *thumper*?" Her eyes narrowed. "How *dare* you?"

"Well, don't get all riled up," he drawled. "You *are* holding that Bible like it's your last best friend in all the world."

Her mouth formed a perfect pink O and a tiny gasp escaped. "Yes. Well," she stammered. "Mister McConnell, I'm not certain what's going on here, but you are not the only one who's disturbed at the moment. You might be angry that a so-called Bible thumper has gotten off that stage. However, I can assure you that the sour face greeting me after my long and arduous stagecoach ride is quite a disappointment to me. A *very* large disappointment indeed." She huffed, pulled her shoulders back, and stood rigidly in place, staring up at him with the gumption of twenty frontier women.

Looking into those blazing eyes, Mathew was startled by the depth of emotion he saw dancing there—beautiful, unwavering eyes that held a mixture of ire—and *hurt*? A pang of regret hit Mathew and he found himself lost in that gaze and the emotions swirling just beneath the surface . . .

And he totally and completely lost his train of thought.

CHAPTER TWO

THE INSOLENT COWBOY'S WORDS STUNG, THOUGH HE surely had no idea how right he'd been. Her Bible had been Ellie's first and last best friend in all of the world. If she clutched it to her heart, it was because, unlike all the other words spoken to her throughout her life, God's words were the ones that had never hurt her.

God's words had taught her at a very early age to shield her heart, and doing so kept the cutting taunts of others from wounding her.

A part of her was glad to see Mathew struggle after hearing her reprimand. It gave her hope that he wasn't completely the ogre she'd feared he might be. But where could they go from here? This wouldn't do. She had to find good in this.

"I came here on good faith after reading your *lovely* worded ad," she said at last, extending him a chance to redeem himself.

His brows wrinkled. Eyes, deep and dark as a midnight

sky, flared. "Whoa," he said, as if halting a team of horses. "Did you say *lovely* words?"

She nodded. They had been lovely.

"I never said anything lovely. All I said was I was a widower looking for a practical woman to care for my baby. Bible believers need not apply."

The last words were enunciated as if Ellie were hard of hearing and might need to read his lips to understand them! She understood all right—clearly the man had problems. He was trying her patience no end . . . She crossed her arms tightly in front of her, fighting exasperation. She was about to do some enunciating of her own—and then his words sank in.

"Wait," she said, flinging her hand up. "That's what your ad said? That's *all* your ad said? And it said practical woman, not godly woman?"

He scowled. "Taking that ad out in that overrated catalogue was supposed to fix my problems." Raking his hand through his hair, he looked flustered, frustrated, and . . .

Cute.

Well, that was a positive. She could handle cute much more handily than tall, dark, and scowling. That fit more with what she envisioned when she'd packed her bags and stepped inside that stagecoach bound for her future.

Problem was, *she* wasn't what he'd envisioned either.

"This is that *Hitching Post* fella's fault," Mathew muttered, rubbing the back of his neck, very aware that Miss Smith watched him. "He did something to my ad or mixed it up with someone else's. Had to of. There was no misunderstanding my ad."

"If that's what you wrote it was definitely clear." Melvina bit her lip. "It was similar to what I read. Just different."

"Why did I let myself get talked into this?" he muttered. He had a good mind to put Melvina Eldora Smith right back on that stagecoach and send her on her frilly little way. And the skeptical way she was looking at him told him she was likely thinking the same exact thing.

But what about Sophie? What was he going to do with her?

A man didn't like admitting he was desperate, but Mathew was as desperate as he could get. He slapped his hat on his thigh. He had a ranch to keep up with. His ranch hand Lem did all he could, but he was getting up in years, and lately Mathew wondered if Lem was up to the job. Some of his cattle had gone missing and he needed to hire more help. On top of that, he had an active two-year-old running poor old Lem's wife, Maggie, ragged. Maggie had been a lifesaver after Beth died, but her arthritis had her so stove up she could barely get her joints to moving some days. She was struggling.

And with no other close neighbors, he'd let her talk him into this mail-order bride catalogue idea.

Trying to figure out his next move, he spun, staring hard at his wagon a few feet away. He didn't want some woman coming in here who would have any inclination to tell him how good God was. He'd once believed that it was true. Not anymore.

"Um, where is Sophie?" Melvina asked, cutting into his runaway thoughts.

He almost broke his neck turning back around. "Sophie?"

"Your child. Or did I misunderstand that too?"

Her eyes held his, her delicate chin lifted. Any hurt that he'd glimpsed before had disappeared behind a cool, controlled surface. Like a rock dropping deep in a pond, after the ripple has gone, leaving no trace that it had been there on the still waters. Almost as if she'd put on a shield.

"No, Sophie is real. She's with a neighbor."

The mask fell away and a smile danced upon her lips as the cool eyes warmed like sunshine.

Instant awareness shot straight through Mathew. His heart nearly hit him in the chin as it reacted to those sun-kissed eyes. *What is going on?*

She tilted her head slightly, feathers waving. "If you can find your tongue," she said with a lilt of humor in her voice, "maybe I should meet Sophie. Maybe *she* won't instantly take such a dislike to me."

Ellie hustled after the disgruntled cowboy who was making his way toward a buckboard a few yards down the street. Her oversized petticoats were heavy against her legs as she tried to hurry. Aunt Millicent had insisted she wear them. She despised the cumbersome clothes! Why did society demand such things? This was the frontier, for goodness' sake. She hoped she could soon be free from the proprieties that stifled her—that she could be free to be herself as she'd been the all too few times she'd escaped to old Mister Clute's farm. Thoughts of the rough-edged rancher who'd been the one true bright spot of her life snuck up on Ellie, fortifying her resolve as Mathew tossed her traveling trunk onto the buckboard, then grabbed her valise and tossed it on board without so much as a word. The man was as prickly as a cactus!

Ellie fastened her thoughts on seeing Sophie and determined that once she saw the sweet child then she'd decide what she was going to do. Aunt Millicent hadn't said anything about her coming home if things didn't work out. No, her aunt hadn't been able to get her out of the house fast enough. So where did that leave Ellie?

It leaves you with the option of having for once chosen your own destiny! Or your own doom. She was going to keep trusting God and she was not, not, *not* going to give up on Him with the first sign of trouble.

"So is the neighbor far?" she asked, hurrying close behind Mathew as he headed toward the front of the buckboard. He turned suddenly and she plowed right into him. Staggering back, her toe caught on her skirt and she pitched sideways. In an instant Mathew's hand wrapped around her arm, strong and steady. He held her upright.

"Are you all right?" he asked, sounding for the first time gentle. His voice was rich and smooth when not irritated. Her skin tingled at his touch.

"I'm . . ." Ellie lost her words, catching the flicker of warmth that flared in the depths of his deep molasses eyes.

Ellie's insides melted like butter and her breath locked in her throat. Mathew McConnell affected her in the most astonishing way. "I'm fine," she managed. "I'm clumsy sometimes."

Nodding, he released her as quickly as he'd grabbed her. "It's not far."

Fumbling with her skirt, Ellie reached for the seat rail. Mathew's hand once again cupped her elbow. He assisted her as she maneuvered the step and climbed up to the bench seat of the buckboard.

"Thank you," she said, but he was already striding around the front of the horses.

He climbed up beside her and took the reins. Her stomach fluttered at his nearness. "Is your ranch far?"

"About three miles."

"Oh, that's perfect. I lived in town in Fort Worth and always longed for the wide-open spaces," she said, fighting to settle her nerves.

Mathew just looked straight ahead.

The man wasn't high on talk. She fought the uneasy feeling that Mathew might send her packing. And much of that had to do with her Bible. How could a Bible make that much of a difference in the way the man looked at women? She'd never imagined the Good Book that gave her so much peace could be the cause of her losing her chance at a new life.

Surely God had not sent her here to be turned away.

Mathew had called her "frilly." He didn't even know her. He had no idea the life she'd lived or the grit that filled her bloodstream. She would not have survived without that unshakable determination. No, he had judged her without knowing her at all. As had everyone else in her life—other than Mister Clute. It was maddening.

"Does Sophie talk yet?" she asked, seeking to find common ground. He didn't speak for a long, heavy moment. Ellie held fast to her positive attitude and plastered a pleasant smile to her face.

"A few words," he said at last. "And she excels at walking, which is not always good since she tends to try and run like a deer."

Relieved, Ellie chuckled at the image. "I love it. We are going to have a wonderful time." She could hardly wait to see her . . . her baby girl.

Her own child. Closing her eyes, Ellie savored the dream. Opening them, she caught Mathew staring at her, though he instantly looked away, scowling once more.

Yes, as prickly as a cactus!

"It is a beautiful day for a new start." Ellie gave him a wide smile.

Despite things not being as she'd dreamed, God was good and she refused to think anything else. She would not worry, she would not worry.

She *would not* worry.

CHAPTER THREE

MATHEW TRIED TO CONCENTRATE ON DRIVING. Melvina had been nothing but helpful, which he found irritating, and she seemed totally unconcerned with the fact that she was nothing like the woman he'd hoped to marry, chattering and grinning like they were on a Sunday afternoon drive.

His gut twisted. Reminding him of happier times. Reminding him of Beth. Of the pain.

Mathew hardened his heart to the smiling, hopeful beauty beside him. What was he going to do?

He had to work. His daughter needed someone to care for her. Melvina had been the only response to his ad in months—and maybe that was only because of some mistake with his ad. The problem was he didn't have time to wait for a practical wife. Besides, the inept proprietor of the catalogue could mess up again! That would be about his luck.

"So when is the wedding?" Ellie asked, her big eyes as bright as the sunshine beating down on them.

"The *wedding*?" he wheezed. "But you haven't seen Sophie yet."

"I don't have to see her to know what I want. Despite getting off on the wrong foot with you, I want to be Sophie's mother," she said, her eyes imploring. "I've been sitting here thinking and I know I'm not what you were expecting."

She'd been chattering away—how could that be thinking? *He* couldn't even think with all her chattering.

Placing her hand on his forearm, she set his pulse immediately into a gallop. "I fell in love with your daughter the moment I read about her."

The truthfulness of her desire rang in the earnestness of her voice.

"I came to be the mother of your child. I've made a commitment to that. I promise that I can be what you are looking for. And I don't know what you have against frills and Bibles, but all of my clothes don't have ruffles, I promise. And I only brought this *one* hat."

What a relief—the thing was atrocious.

"That aside," she continued without pause, "I promise you, if you'll give me a chance I will do everything in my power to be a good and loving wife and to be a loving mother to Sophie."

Her hand on his arm tightened and her eyes grew soft with longing—Mathew thought his heart was gonna bust out of his chest and beat the horses to Maggie and Lem's place.

Sophie—this was about his motherless child, he reminded himself, tearing his gaze from Melvina's intriguing eyes.

He struggled to focus on what was best for Sophie, fighting to ignore how Melvina's touch was causing him all kinds of problems. He'd fought anything and everything that had come his way—the war, Indians, frontier conditions . . . bears, even outlaws. He'd survived it all. Surely he could survive a thumper.

Melvina hadn't backed down from the commitment she'd made to his child.

Despite not wanting to, he admired her for it.

Could he do no less for the commitment he'd made to her?

Truth was, so far she hadn't quoted scripture like he'd expected when he saw her clutching that worn Bible. She'd pulled her hand from his arm and now sat waiting for his answer.

"I planned on you meeting Sophie and then if all was agreeable with you, we could swing by Reverend Jacobs's after leaving Maggie's and make it official." Originally, he hadn't wanted to waste any time getting the hitching done. He hadn't wanted to give either of them time to change their minds. He needed this plan in action. He had cattle that needed tending, and a daughter who needed the same.

But looking into those huge eyes, his stomach felt queasy. This suddenly seemed rushed. ". . . *Or* you can have a few days if you need it," he added quickly when she didn't say anything. "Maggie would be fine with you staying with them for a little while."

"No," Melvina said, relief radiating in her voice. "I think your plan is *perfect. Just perfect.*"

He frowned. *Perfect.*

The woman was beautiful, no getting around that plain truth. So why had she answered an ad in a mail-order bride catalogue and traveled across the wilds of Texas to find a husband? If the Bible she was clutching was any indication, it could be that no man in the Fort Worth area wanted to be preached to any more than he did.

Dread lowered over him. "Fine," he grunted. "But let me make it clear once more before we set out: I specifically asked for no Bible thumpers." He paused, letting his words have time to soak in before adding, "But Sophie needs a mother, so I will make an exception. However, I insist that you keep your beliefs to yourself. Is that clear?"

She bit her full, delicate bottom lip as she studied him, her blue eyes darkening. His pulse picked up again as he looked at her lips. Meeting her gaze, he knew she'd caught him staring.

She smiled sweetly and a dimple appeared, creasing her left cheek. Her eyes twinkled mischievously, and Mathew nearly fell off the wagon seat.

"Are you always this grumpy and disagreeable, Mathew McConnell?" she asked in that lilting voice.

Feeling as cantankerous as old Prudence, the mule that claimed his ranch as her own, he grunted again, unable to form words to answer her. He was still trying to get past that dimple and that smile. And those lips.

Befuddled, Mathew looked straight ahead. "Yah!" He

cracked the reins, inclining the horses to travel at a faster pace. Melvina chuckled. Her laughter was a soft tinkling sound in the hot breeze.

She was determined, that was for sure. A good thing since determination was the one quality a woman needed to survive this frontier.

That and the ability to laugh even when things were tough. He glanced at Melvina. Her chin was lifted into the wind, her eyes bright as she took in her surroundings, and a smile lingered on her lips. He knew Melvina had that ability too, to laugh in hard times. He could sense it in her. So she might do all right here in Texas after all.

Right then and there he resolved he'd offer this woman his last name and his protection in exchange for care for his daughter. But not his love. Not his heart.

"Land's sakes, what a beauty!"

The plump older woman startled Ellie by bursting from the small whitewashed house. She limped slightly, skirts flapping, as she rushed to meet them.

"Maggie Sorenson," Mathew said, "this is Miss Melvina Eldora Smith."

"Well, I *certainly* hope so." The woman took Ellie's hand tenderly, smiling as if she hadn't seen another woman in months. "I didn't figure you found another woman between here and the stagecoach stop, Mathew! It's so good to meet you, Miss Smith."

Mathew began tending to the horses, giving Ellie a moment to relax. She might have teased him about being cantankerous, but it would have been to hide the shaky way she'd felt since his gaze had paused on her lips. Pushing the thoughts away, Ellie focused on Maggie. She liked the older woman instantly. "So good to meet you too, Mrs.—"

"Maggie. Just plain Maggie." Maggie harrumphed, waving her hand. "I ain't one fer such uppity nonsense."

Maggie's refreshing welcome touched Ellie's heart, so unlike Aunt Millicent and the way she clung to formality like a shield. A renewed sense of freedom washed over Ellie and she smiled. "Then I'm Ellie. Just plain Ellie."

Mathew almost broke his neck jerking around to stare at her. "*Ellie?* I thought it was Melvina."

"I like it," Maggie interrupted. "It suits ya. Ain't that right, Mathew?"

"I should have spoken up sooner," Ellie said. "Aunt Millicent insisted I use Melvina. But I prefer Ellie." Mathew turned back to his horses, fumbling with the leathers and then moving to the far side of the team. Maggie seemed to enjoy seeing him flustered. Smiling, Ellie realized she enjoyed it too.

Mister Clute had been the one who'd shortened Eldora to Ellie. He said the plucky name fit her better. And it did. He'd been the only one to call her Ellie, though she'd taken it up when thinking of herself. Now she was beginning a new life and she knew she wanted to completely leave Melvina Eldora behind. As Ellie she could enjoy having the freedom to be herself. And that was a wonderful thought.

CHAPTER FOUR

SITTING ON THE FLOOR BESIDE THE KITCHEN TABLE, holding a rag doll and sucking her thumb, was a rosy-faced little girl with big blue eyes and a curly blond cap of hair that looked as soft as her puffy pink cheeks.

"Oh!" Ellie froze in the doorway. Joy bloomed inside of her at the sight of the beautiful child.

Tears filled her eyes. "Is this Sophie?"

Maggie beamed. "You two were made for each other. Why, the child even looks like you."

Ellie scarcely heard Maggie, she was so intent on the child.

Sniffing, she blinked away tears of joy and thanked God for leading her here. She could endure whatever was to come for the chance to be a mother to this motherless child.

Sophie popped her thumb from her mouth and gave a toothless smile. "Doll." She held up her doll to Ellie.

Ellie knelt, tucked her skirts beneath her, and leaned close to Sophie. "She's a very pretty doll," she said, touching the rag doll's threaded hair, then touching Sophie's curls too. "You are beautiful, Sophie."

Sophie touched Ellie's cheek tenderly. Maggie clucked her tongue and looked at Ellie. "She's two years old and doesn't try to talk much. I'm a little worried about that. Sophie, this is your mama," she said, grunting as she stooped down. Ellie sucked in a sharp breath. She wasn't married to Mathew yet, so strictly speaking she wasn't her mama yet. However, from the moment she'd read his ad in the *Hitching Post*, Ellie's heart had been lassoed tight to this child. There was no letting go.

"*Ma*-ma," Sophie said, smiling up at Ellie. She stood and reached out with her damp hand to grab a fistful of Ellie's blond curls. "Mama."

"Wonderful." Maggie beamed at Sophie's words.

Ellie reached for the baby and cuddled her close. When Sophie giggled, Ellie knew this was as close to heaven as she would ever feel here on earth. Ellie's arms tightened on the child and she felt the hope of love. All of Ellie's life she'd longed for the love of another human being, longed to know what it felt like. If she lavished love on Sophie, there was hope that Sophie would return that love.

And if she did the same to Mathew, there was a chance . . . Surely love could blossom. She just had to play by his rules and be a *good* wife, and there was hope. Always hope.

"Maggie, thanks for watching Sophie." Mathew's strong voice broke into Ellie's thoughts.

Putting one hand on her knee, Maggie pushed up from her kneeling position. Her grimace of pain made it easy to tell the action was hard on her.

"You're welcome. I'm happy you've got this pretty little gal to soon call wife. Look at how your baby girl has taken to her new ma."

Hugging Sophie to her, Ellie smiled when the child's pudgy hand let go of her hair and flattened gently against her cheek. Her heart tightened at the touch and dug deep, the bond strong and swift. Mathew was unsmiling as he studied them. His dark eyes emotionless and his full, wide lips flattened in a grim line. Unease quivered in her belly.

"I think our Mathew isn't good at smiling," she quipped nervously, her gaze darting from him to Maggie who had punched her fist to her ample hips and was studying Mathew as well. At Ellie's words, Maggie threw back her head and hooted with laughter.

"Pegged him right off, ya did, Ellie. Our Mathew is scarce on smiles and even more scarce on talk." She grinned. "I think with that sparkle of mischief I see in your blue eyes you might just be the one to tug both from the depths of him."

Mathew's brows dipped. Once again Ellie thought the man cute with that scowl on his handsome face. But there was trouble in his eyes.

What pain was he fighting behind all of those scowls and gruff words?

"She's darling, Mathew. Just a sweet, sweet girl," she said. He'd removed his hat upon entering and now he tapped it against his thigh. "Then I guess we should be going over to the pastor's place."

"Mercy's sakes this is a great day," Maggie said. "A great day indeed. Well, what are you waiting for, Ellie? Jump up and get yourself hitched to that handsome lump of smiles standing over there."

Ellie stood and glanced again at Mathew. Nope, she hadn't missed it.

He was not smiling.

The man, when not scowling, was probably the most handsome man Ellie had ever seen. Something about him, that chiseled jaw, those dark, fathomless eyes that seemed to penetrate every dark corner of her being when he looked at her. That long, lean body . . . Yes, Mathew McConnell by far took the Most Handsome Man prize, and she was about to be his wife. It was amazing. But that being said, the man would obviously not have any trouble finding a wife. She hadn't missed the way the few ladies she'd seen walking along the streets of Honey Springs looked at him. So why had he resorted to sending that ad to the *Hitching Post*? She knew why she had. But why him?

She was suddenly struck by how alone he looked standing in that doorway.

Maybe he was heartbroken. Maybe he would always love his first wife. Maybe that was why God had led her here. *Maybe* she was here to help him smile again. Just like he and his baby were helping her have a new, bright future.

Ellie halted her runaway thoughts and stilled the nerves that were making her ramble on in her head.

Maybe she should just calm down. *"I will never leave you or forsake you . . ."* Her nerves eased as she repeated Joshua 1:5 once more. She'd been repeating that verse all across Texas, tossing and bumping inside that stagecoach bound for this. The good Lord had repeated Himself to Joshua four times to get it through to him. And Joshua being such a mighty man of God and all, she wasn't feeling too bad that she needed far more reminders than four.

"I'm ready—we're ready," she amended, hugging Sophie tightly, then she followed Mathew out the door.

Less than an hour after leaving Maggie's with Melvina and Sophie, Mathew was standing in the preacher's small study staring down into her disconcerting blue eyes. There was trust in those eyes and it unsettled him more than he wanted it to. She'd said to call her Ellie, but he'd continued to call her the more formal Melvina. She'd seemed startled when he'd said it, but she'd yet to mention it. He was glad. The last thing he wanted to explain was that calling her Ellie would be far more personal than he felt comfortable with.

"Take hands, please," Reverend Jacobs instructed.

Melvina lifted her hand, hesitated, and then, holding his gaze, she held it out to him. Swallowing a lump that suddenly lodged in his throat, Mathew took her slender fingers in his.

"Melvina Eldora Smith, do you take this man, Mathew McConnell, to be your lawfully wedded husband?" Reverend

Jacobs asked, his deep voice reverberating through the small room.

Mathew felt Melvina's hand tense in his. Her fingers trembled slightly and her gaze faltered momentarily before she nodded, and a small, gentle smile appeared. "I do," she said at last.

Mathew's heart weighed heavy in his chest.

"Mathew McConnell, do you take this woman, Melvina Eldora Smith, as your lawfully wedded wife, promising to love, honor, and protect her in sickness and in health, till death do you part?" Mathew tried not to think about the word "love" as he nodded his head, then spoke clearly, "I do."

In his heart of hearts he knew he could do everything the oath required except offer his love. Love had never been part of the deal. However, looking into Melvina's eyes and seeing the sweet smile she gave him, he felt an unreasonable tug of guilt.

This was a practical marriage, he reminded himself. He'd stated it clearly from the beginning. Why then, he wondered as the Reverend Jacobs pronounced them husband and wife, did he feel like he'd just done something terribly wrong?

※

"There's the house."

They'd just rounded a bend in the dusty track that wove through a stand of oaks. A hawk watched them from one of the tallest trees and a couple of red birds played tag against the blue sky. Ellie had been so lost in thought that she'd been missing the beauty surrounding them.

Tall, full oaks grew in clumps through expanses of scraggly mesquite trees. Ranch land stretched out from there, and they'd passed several streams where longhorn cattle grazed nearby and drank their fill. Mathew had told her these were his cattle and as far as she could see was his ranch land. She'd been startled by the size of it. Dusk was setting in. He'd said when he had hurried her from Maggie's that they'd have to be quick with the ceremony in order to make it to the house before nightfall.

He hadn't been joking. His ranch was about three miles from town, but that was just the boundary of it. If Ellie had wanted to live in the country, she was getting her wish.

"It's lovely." Built from stone and plank, the tidy-looking one-story house had a wide, welcoming porch. The front door was flanked by windows on either side and weathered gray. Both ends of the house had large stone chimneys.

"Did you build this?" she asked, amazed.

"I hope it will do," Mathew said, not looking at her. "Because there's too much work on the ranch needing my attention right now to take time to change anything."

"Change, why? It is absolutely the most charming place in the world. It's amazing." She and Aunt Millicent had lived in the home she'd been born in—the home her mother died in. Though it was nice, it had been far too stuffy for Ellie's taste. Over the years her aunt had been forced to take in sewing and had opened a dress store in the front parlor. She kept the rest of the house as a sort of shrine to the years she'd lost before Ellie had destroyed all their lives.

Ellie discovered the inside of the ranch house was just as impressive. It was easy to see that a woman had helped put the place in order in the cozy way the spacious living room and kitchen were situated. Three chairs and the wall bench were to one side, anchored in a warm, inviting way by a colorful rag rug and pillows that blended with it. The kitchen table was long and hand built from the gnarled trunks of the abundant mesquite trees, the top made of oak.

On the opposite side of the house, nearest the kitchen with its big stone fireplace, there was another room. Mathew carried her valise into that room. She followed him and stopped dead in her tracks, clutching the still-sleeping Sophie in her arms. The room was dominated by a fireplace that was smaller than the kitchen's and a large bed that sat next to a single window. There were no colorful rugs on the floor or pillows in the rocking chair that sat in the corner by the baby bed. Even so, the room drew her in. And shook her insides up like nothing she'd ever experienced as dawning suddenly began to set in . . . this was their bedroom.

Mathew set her valise down at the foot of the bed, then moved past her to the door. "I'll bring your chest in after I take care of the livestock." And then he was gone. And it was a good thing since Ellie felt certain he could hear her reckless heart making an outlandish racket inside her chest.

Where would Mathew sleep?

Oh goodness! She'd been so caught up in Sophie and the

wedding that her nerves about . . . her wedding night had somehow shrunk to the recesses of her mind.

Crossing the room, she kissed Sophie on the forehead and gently placed her in her bed. Then, chewing her bottom lip, she eyed that big stuffed bed.

CHAPTER FIVE

MATHEW WAS HOLDING A PITCHFORK FULL OF HAY when Melvina stormed into the barn. Despite the sun having dipped low and the dim light in the barn, he could see that her eyes flashed fire.

"I need to get something straight, something I somehow overlooked in my excitement of the day," she said, wringing her hands as she spoke, her cheeks flushed.

He tossed the hay over the stall to the milk cow, then jabbed the fork into the ground and leaned his elbow on the end of the handle. "Okay," he said, not sure at all what to make of this outburst.

"I . . . I need some time to . . . before . . ." She paused, her hand coming up to touch one of her burning cheeks.

Alarm hit him. "Are you feeling ill?"

"No. I need . . . Oh, fiddle." She stomped her foot and stuffed her hands onto her slim hips. "I'm not ready."

"Ready? For what?"

"I hadn't expected to share a room with you immediately," she blurted.

"Share a room?"

"Yes, I . . . I thought there would be two rooms. I . . . I've only known you for a few hours."

Her meaning dawned on him finally. "I moved my things into the tack room yesterday."

"Oh," she squeaked. "I see."

Her gaze swung to the door of the tack room. It was opened just enough that the cot could be seen. "It's not much of a room."

He hitched an eyebrow at her. "Until I have time to add on another room at the house, it will do."

Her head snapped. "Another room?"

"Another room, Melvina. I married you to be a mother to Sophie. That's all."

Her brows crinkled and her chest moved up and down rapidly as she took several quick breaths. Her hands came to her cheeks, then dropped to her sides. "I see," she said quietly. "Right. A *practical* wife." Then she turned and walked briskly back the way she'd come.

He knew he should go after her. Explain. Instead, he stood in the middle of the barn he'd built for the life he'd planned to have with Beth. He'd needed a mother for Sophie. He planned to keep her around. He'd married Melvina, given her his name and his protection. He wouldn't risk her life, or his heart—not this time. Not ever again.

No, he'd learned his lesson well. This was all he had to give.

❧

Standing outside exploring her surroundings with Sophie on her hip, Ellie still couldn't believe it had been a week since she'd married Mathew and become Sophie's mother. Looking up at the summer sun, its heat pelting down on them, she felt its warmth radiating through her. Though things weren't exactly as she'd expected them to be, it had been the best week of her life.

"There's my good girl." Ellie laughed, swinging a giggling baby Sophie into her arms. Sophie was a dream, and taking care of her filled Ellie's heart to bursting.

Then again, Sophie's daddy had her wanting to burst something over his head! She'd tried to help by taking care of the small chores around the yard like milking the cow and feeding the chickens. Mathew had told her a stern no. He'd said that taking care of Sophie and the household chores like washing and cooking should keep her plenty busy. He'd take care of the rest. She'd almost told him she'd spent time on Mister Clute's ranch, but she was trying so hard not to be argumentative, to be the wife Mathew wanted, that she'd held back and done as he'd asked.

Ellie had so looked forward to being a rancher's wife and getting involved with the ranching side of things. Even helping to round up cattle and such—but he'd cut her off before she could tell him that.

Not that she wasn't having a wonderful time with Sophie—she was. But . . . she'd hoped to fulfill that secret passion too.

Besides, without help, Mathew was hardly around and that wasn't good for Sophie either. Ellie wondered if he was avoiding them because of the way she'd confronted him about the household arrangements. The encounter had knocked her off solid ground and she was shaken. She hadn't wanted to give him the rights of a husband on the very first day that they had met and married. However . . . she hadn't counted on never knowing Mathew as a husband. On never carrying a child of her own. The discovery stung like a slap.

And he was barely around, leaving early in the mornings and showing up late each night to grab a bite before disappearing to his quarters.

Yet she thought about him almost every minute of the day. It was maddening.

"We're doing fine, Sophie. Just you and me," Ellie said.

"Pru-dy!" Sophie squealed just as the rumble of hooves sounded behind them.

Spinning around, Ellie was shocked to see a brown mule charging toward them. The hairy beast barreled down on them with the speed of a wild mustang, lips pressed back, huge teeth bared.

Ellie screamed, hugging Sophie to her chest. Ellie raced toward the closest building, the barn. She had to protect Sophie. She had to!

"Pru-dy!" Sophie squealed again, looking over Ellie's shoulder. *Is she trying to say pretty?* Ellie wondered as she ran.

Or tried to run. Her skirts tangled against her legs. Thick and cumbersome, the dratted clothing had her tripping and shuffling as she ran. Holding the armload of child to her, she didn't have extra hands to hold them up—petticoats were a curse!

Ellie had made it past the watering trough when she pitched forward. Trying to protect Sophie, Ellie twisted around and hit the ground on her back. The air whumphed out of her in a rush so strong she couldn't get it back. Gasping for new air, struggling, Ellie could only flounder helplessly on the ground, flat on her back, unable to breathe.

Laughing, unaware of the danger befalling them, Sophie sat on top of Ellie and clapped her pudgy hands together. Ellie heaved for air as the child giggled and the crazed mule plowed toward them. Just when Ellie thought they would be trampled for certain, the animal slid to a halt, plopped down on its haunches, and began to lick Sophie's cheek!

Mathew had lost more cattle. He'd found a spot where his fence had been deliberately cut. He was certain he had rustlers. He just had to find them. But right now he was headed home. He had to talk to Melvina.

He'd hurt her somehow. He could see the hurt in her eyes this morning.

And it ate at him all day.

But he didn't know how to fix it. He could only offer her what he had to give, and that wasn't his heart. He'd topped the last hill for home when he spotted Prudence thundering toward Melvina with baby Sophie in her arms. Mathew spurred his horse to a gallop, hoping to intercept the alarmed mule. But he'd been too far away to prevent the scene before him. He could only watch Ell—*Melvina* flying across the yard as if someone had lit a fire to her skirt.

Mathew arrived just after she flipped to the ground like a flapjack. He threw himself from the saddle, despite the almost full gallop, hitting the ground at a run. "Ellie, are you all right?" he asked.

Sliding to a stop, he pushed Prudy away. It was a hard thing to do since the mule thought Sophie was half hers.

Ellie's eyes were wide as she struggled to breathe, wheezing and gasping for air.

The fall must have knocked her breath out of her. He lifted Sophie from her chest in the hopes that removing the weight of the plump baby girl would enable her to breathe again. "Come on, Ellie, take a breath," he urged gently. With his guard down because of his concern, calling her Ellie slipped naturally into place. It was more personal than he'd wanted to allow them to get, but it felt right. Partly because the name did fit her personality.

Seconds later Ellie sucked in a deep breath and sat up with his help. She glared at the mule sitting calmly beside her on its fat haunches. "What—is that animal doing?" she asked in a shrill voice he'd never heard from her before.

"Protecting Sophie," he said sheepishly.

"Protecting her! She almost killed us."

Glaring at him, she clamped her lips together and stood up. He tried to help but she ignored his hand, gave the unconcerned little mule one last glare, then stomped stiffly toward the house.

Should he follow her? She was one mad lady—and she had a right to be.

Carrying Sophie who was chanting, "Pru-dy, Pru-dy," all the way, he stalked after her. He caught up to her at the porch.

"I should have warned you about old Prudence. That cantankerous donkey thinks she owns the place. And she watches out for Sophie. She's been out with a herd protecting the baby calves from coyotes, but we moved the herd closer this morning and she must have wanted to see Sophie." Now that the danger was over, his mind went straight back to Ellie running from the funny old gray bag of bones. He couldn't help himself—he chuckled.

Red as a ripe plum, Ellie gasped. "You are *laughing* at me!"

He tried not to laugh again. Fought hard not to, a hard thing to do when suddenly all he could think about was how cute the woman looked when she was furious. "Now, Ellie . . . calm down. You do have to admit that it was funny."

"I do not!" She crossed her arms.

He hiked a brow and grinned.

"Fun-ny," Sophie repeated and giggled.

His chest hurt with the laughter he was holding back. He was a little worried about her reaction at his finding this so blamed funny, but it just was. And she was cute as a baby porcupine when she was mad.

"Ellie. You know it was funny."

"Fun-ny, fun-ny," Sophie said proudly and clapped.

Ellie's lip twitched, causing his smile to widen.

"You know it's true. You would have laughed if it had been me in your shoes. You can't hold this against me too."

She bit her lips, both sides twitched, and suddenly she laughed, dipped her head, and hooted.

Hearing her full-bodied laugh pulled the first full-blown laugh from him that he'd had in two years. It hit him as he smiled at her. It felt good watching her laugh so hard tears rolled from the corners of her sparkling eyes. She rubbed them away with her fingers, then pressed them to her cheeks.

"You are mean, Mathew McConnell. And I think you have a really terrible sense of humor.

"And you've got Sophie laughing at me too."

"Me laughing too," Sophie quipped.

Ellie's smile as she scolded him reached inside of Mathew, warming the dark corners of his heart.

He stopped laughing and they stared at each other as if they couldn't look away.

Mathew's heart was doing crazy things in his chest. Like a crazy fool, he stepped closer to Ellie, tempted to reach his hand out and trace the line of her jaw. Instead, he clutched Sophie tightly.

"I have to go," he blurted and pushed Sophie into Ellie's arms. Snagging the leathers of his horse as he passed, he gave himself a good talking-to all the way to the barn and into the safety of the shadows inside. *What have I been doing?*

AN EVER AFTER SUMMER

Wondering what it would feel like to pull her into my arms and pretend that this was a real marriage.

"You are downright loco," he growled, his heart thumping and his blood rushing through his ears like the rapids of the Guadalupe River.

CHAPTER SIX

"I'm a fool. I'm a fool—yes, I am. Yes, I am." Ellie sang her frustrations in a sweet singsong voice as she held Sophie in the air and looked up at the grinning, drooling sweetheart. "How could I be such a fool, Sophie sweetie? How?"

"Foo-wel," Sophie repeated, drooling more as she stared down happily at Ellie. "I mam a foo-wel."

Despite her own angst, Ellie laughed and hugged her baby to her heart. No, she wasn't a fool for having come three hundred miles through dangerous territory to marry a man who *just* needed someone to watch his child. Not when that child was this angel.

Walking to the big wooden rocker sitting by the window, Ellie tucked a chattering Sophie in the crook of her arm and began to sing a lullaby. At least Sophie was everything she'd dreamed of, she thought as Sophie's bright blue eyes began to droop with the motion of the rocker. Soon her face went slack with sweet release into dream time. Ellie could watch Sophie sleep all day.

Sighing, Ellie brushed a blond curl from her forehead and then she stared out the window. The mule watched her from a few feet away. Ellie was not feeling very forgiving at the moment and did not look kindly on the hairy beast!

She had more interesting things on her mind. Mathew had begun calling her Ellie and he'd almost kissed her out there, before he stormed away. She was certain of it. Ellie's heart fluttered as she relived the moment when he leaned forward . . .

For a girl who'd never been close to having someone look at her that way, it was almost more than she could bear. More than she could hope.

And then he'd spun and strode away as if he couldn't get away fast enough.

"Please, Lord, help me. I am so confused," she whispered. Bowing her head, Ellie did what she'd learned to do growing up. She prayed. She thanked Him for His blessings, for Sophie and for Mathew and being here at all. She told God her fears about her situation and her desires and at last she asked God to give her patience that she would let Him show her the way.

Lifting her gaze, she stared out the window once more.

Patience was not easy for her, in this situation especially. She wanted things to move faster than they were. But she had no idea how to do that. She'd tried everything she could think of—making small talk, not talking at all, trying to simply show him what a wonderful wife she could be if he let her. Her nerves were shot.

She wanted that kiss from her husband.

She'd wanted it with all of her heart.

There, she had admitted it. Admitted that she longed to feel his arms around her and his lips on hers.

Aunt Millicent would be appalled.

But he was her husband. And Aunt Millicent's opinion of her no longer mattered, she reminded herself.

Mathew strode from the barn, drawing Ellie's attention.

Carrying a saddle, he looked as though he could fight the world itself.

He tramped across the yard toward the corral that sat a little ways away from the house. Several horses were kept there and he'd told her early on that they were horses he was going to break and for her to keep Sophie away from them.

He dropped the saddle in the dirt. Entered the pen and within seconds had a particularly irritated black horse roped. Looking wildly angry, the colt snorted and pawed the earth. Mathew gave it some slack as it yanked its head violently. Ellie's breath caught when it reared up, standing on two legs, its front hooves clawing dangerously at Mathew!

"Today is your day," Mathew said to the two-year-old colt who had a very bad attitude. Mathew was brewing to release some frustration. From the looks of it, Ruthless was too.

He'd worked with the colt for a few days and he was still skittish and untrusting. Straining against the rope, Ruthless pawed the earth and reared as Mathew leaned back, his arms straining, dirt flying as they fought each other. Mathew wound the rope around the breaking pole and snugged the angry horse so close to it that the animal couldn't so much as lift his head. Still the stubborn horse kicked up dirt and dug at the ground with his hooves. Breathing hard from the fight, Mathew got the bit and bridle on him—no easy task. Then he headed out of the corral for the saddle. He was already damp from exertion, and the frustration he felt from his situation with Ellie hadn't diminished at all . . .

Mathew welcomed the challenge.

Ruthless offered an avenue for him to vent—

"What are you *doing*?"

Mathew whirled around to find Ellie, looking wild-eyed herself.

"What are you doing out here?" he snapped. He needed to get rid of his frustration, not pile on more.

She pointed at the colt. "Are you about to ride him?"

"That's the plan," he said, not happy to see her *or* her attitude. "If Ruthless is willing."

"Willing to kill someone," Ellie scoffed.

Her lack of confidence stung. "No one's dying today, Ellie."

"That is not funny. It looks like he needs more time. More work before you haul off and climb on his back."

"Ellie, what do you know about ranching? Nothing, that's what. You tend to woman's work and leave man's work to me."

"But—"

"No, Ellie, get on back to the house and leave me be," he snapped. At this point he was so frustrated he was past caring.

Her eyes shadowed. Beautiful eyes that had him losing his train of thought all over again even in his anger.

"That isn't fair. Mathew, I can help. I haven't been given the chance to show you what I can do."

This land was not easy on a woman. His mother and then Beth were proof, and also Maggie and the way she was breaking down with her joints and ailments. "No." The word wrenched from him. "I hired you—I mean I married you to look after Sophie."

Ellie went very still and the color drained from her face.

Mathew knew he'd made a big mistake the moment he'd said "hired." If he'd been too dumb to realize his blunder, the grim look spreading across Ellie's face would have pointed it out to him straightaway.

"Hired me! Hired me. Of all the . . ." She faltered on the last, huffing so hard he was sure he saw smoke come out of her ears. She spun and stalked back the way she'd come.

They sure did do some stalking away from each other, he thought as her skirts flounced and her hips swayed. She muttered halfway across the yard. He couldn't understand what she was saying, but it was obvious that it wasn't good. She was pert near to the porch when she swung back around and stalked straight back to him.

She didn't stop until she was toe-to-toe with him, so close she had to tilt her head back to glare up at him.

"You might look at me as just a hired hand but, Mathew McConnell, I have news for you—you married me! That's right. We are lawfully wedded in the sight of man and God, and I'm tired of tiptoeing around here not knowing where I fit in. I've done that all my life. I came west to get rid of that feeling. I am your wife. An-and I'm here to tell you that I want children. I want brothers and sisters for Sophie. You may not want me like a husband should want a wife—or want this marriage to be real. But . . ." Her voice trailed off. She looked at the ground and then back up at him. "I do. A real home and family is all I've ever dreamed of. Fair warning to you," she said, her hand on her hip. "I did not come here to be your hired help. Nor to be told what I can and cannot do."

And then she spun away and stormed back the way she'd come.

Mathew watched her go. The woman was beauty and fire and sass all in one. He'd had to fight the urge to pull her into his arms and kiss her to silence. Instead, grabbing the saddle at his feet, he headed into the corral.

It was time to ride—he just hoped Ruthless was still ready for a fight, because he sure was.

CHAPTER SEVEN

ELLIE STALKED TO THE HOUSE. *"HIRED ME?"* EVIDENTLY taking a mail-order bride was Mathew's way of ensuring he kept the hired help on forever. Wasn't this just the way? Here she'd just told the Lord she'd wait on His lead. That she'd be patient. And just look at this fine mess.

Well, she'd gone and done it now. She'd hauled off and blasted Mathew with both barrels.

But she couldn't take back her words. They were true. In her heart of hearts she desired more children. Loving on Sophie had only made her want them more. *Mathew*—the man could irritate her so. And hurt her too.

Why was it that his words could hurt her like no one else's could?

Ellie stepped onto the porch and went through the door, heading toward her room where Sophie slept. Mathew McConnell thought he knew her—had judged from day one by the dress she'd worn and the Bible she'd held close to her heart. "Ha," she muttered softly, entering the bedroom. Sophie was sound asleep. "Your daddy doesn't know me at all," Ellie whispered, then headed to her trunk at the foot of the bed.

She was tired of hiding behind the stifling airs and proprietary manners that Aunt Millicent had always insisted on, being told all her life what she could and could not do!

It was time to be true to herself.

Lifting the lid of her traveling trunk, Ellie dug to the bottom through all the fluffy dresses Aunt Millicent loved. They went flying in all directions as Ellie reached the bottom of the trunk.

Back home, Ellie had found herself following the creek to old Mister Clute's small ranch, which hadn't been too far from town, when she couldn't take Aunt Millicent's never-ending rants any longer. It was there she'd discovered that she'd loved the country. There she'd begun to dream of life on a ranch.

Knowing she was going to be a part of a ranch had been an added bonus to accepting Mathew's proposal and fulfilling her dream.

All her life she'd been put down, told what to do . . . and rejected. The one person who'd accepted her had been old Mister Clute. She'd thought things would be different here, more like they'd been with her old neighbor. But nothing was different. Mathew was treating her just as her aunt had.

Ellie lifted her clothes from the trunk, the feel of them giving her fortitude.

It was a new day for Melvina Eldora Smith *McConnell.*

Mathew, the stubborn man, might think he was going to deny her all the dreams bulging inside her heart—but he had another think coming!

※

"Whoa, there," Mathew snapped. Having gotten the saddle onto Ruthless's back without getting killed, the next step was getting on his back still alive. And that was the tricky part.

Easing his boot into the stirrup, he saw the colt's ears twitch, a sure sign the fight would be on. Ready to rid himself of the clashing emotions raging inside him, Mathew shoved his boot into the stirrup, threw his leg over, and held on! The battle was on.

The horse was greener than green, as rank a ride as any Mathew had ever ridden. Ruthless, infuriated and fearful, reacted violently. Mathew knew deep in his heart that there was some fear in him too, that he and the horse had that in common. They were both fighting that as much as each other.

The angry animal bucked and twisted and tried its best to unseat him. Lying back in the saddle, Mathew held on. Sweat poured from Mathew's brow. His muscles burned from using all of them—his thighs, forearms, his gut—to stay in the saddle. Ruthless was not tiring, instead, he kicked repeatedly, traveling about the corral like a Texas twister. Mathew had the skill to hang on and not eat dirt where the horse was concerned.

But with Ellie he was buried neck deep in dirt.

Ruthless had him riding a wicked buck midair when movement out of the corner of Mathew's eye snagged his attention. A small person in baggy pants and a big shirt came flouncing out of his house, hat in hand, blond hair shining in the sunlight.

Her expression grim as she stalked his way.

Mathew was so startled he almost lost his seat. His hands went slack for a moment.

Ruthless took advantage of his distraction—immediately twisting into the fence, scraping Mathew's legs against the corral rungs. An instant of lost concentration was all it took for the horse to send Mathew flying from the saddle and straight over the top of the fence. Something struck him hard. Stars burst inside his head, bright and hot, and then he bit the dust.

The alarmed blue eyes of his wife staring down at him through a white rain of cascading stars was the last thing he saw before the world went dark.

❦

I killed him!

"Mathew," Ellie cried, dropping to the dirt as she stared at his pale face. Blood spit at her from the gash on his head—it was a gusher!

Jerking her shirttail out of her britches, she grabbed it between her teeth and yanked—and almost broke her teeth! The shirt was no thin petticoat, and it refused to rip.

Wishing for the first time in her life that she was wearing the ridiculous piece of clothing, Ellie panicked—she was just about to yank off the shirt and hold it to his forehead when she spied his knife in its holder tied to his belt. Fumbling for it with trembling hands, Ellie freed it from its home and stabbed the blade into her shirt tail, slicing off a large section of the fabric.

She wadded it up and held it firmly over the wound.

She'd seen head wounds before, and she prayed it would stop after a few minutes. This was her fault. She'd gone and let her temper, her pent-up rebellion, get the best of her.

She'd thrown her prayers and promises of patience out the window and let herself take control.

Poor Mathew. He'd been so startled at seeing her dressed in her britches that he'd lost concentration. He was beautiful in the saddle, a born rider, and she'd done him in with a pair of britches.

Not even considering that her timing for a confrontation could wait until he was off the dangerous animal, oh no, she'd stormed outside determined to have her way right then and there.

And just look what it had gotten her . . . very likely a soon-to-be-dead husband!

"I've mourned the day you were born, Melvina. Good riddance and woe to the man who takes you in." Her aunt's parting words as she'd climbed aboard the stage echoed in the recesses of her heart. So thrilled to be on her way, and so hardened to the bitter words of her aunt, Ellie never considered that she might well and truly bring catastrophe to her new family. Tears of fear clogged in her throat. *Murderin' Melvina.*

"Please don't die," she whispered, watching the blue cloth turn a dark red. "Dear Lord, please, *please* stop this bleeding."

Her prayer rang out loud and pleading as her fingers turned sticky with Mathew's blood. "I'm no good to anyone. I've been here a week and already added my husband to my list of . . . of . . . dead." She eked the last word weakly.

Looking at the pale, oh so handsome face of her near dead husband, she knew the truth. She *was* born a killer.

Tears slipped from her eyes. Lifting the soaked rag, she peeked at the gash. There was a knot forming there and the blood flow had eased. She willed him to open his eyes. Sweat made trails in the drying blood. She needed to cool him down.

Running to the water trough, she filled a bucket and hurried back. No time to boil the water. Taking his knife she sliced off the other side of her big shirttail. She dipped it into the cool water and gently pressed the cloth to his forehead, careful to wipe around the wound and not over it. He moaned but didn't move. His dark lashes didn't even flicker.

She had to get him out of the scorching sun. Standing, she grabbed him under the arms. Grunting, she put her full weight into the effort. The man was six feet something and weighed far more than she did. He didn't budge. She planted her feet, took hold of him, and tried harder—throwing her whole body into pulling him. Straining, her hands slipped and she fell backward flat on her bottom in the dust.

Huffing, she wiped sweat from her brow and searched for help. Spotting Prudy watching her from the corner of the barn, Ellie's heart sparked with hope.

"Ah! Come here, pretty Prudy," she called, striding toward the mule. Prudence looked up but didn't look too trustful. Ellie grabbed a rope hanging on a post by the barn and, quickly making a loop, threaded the rope through. Yes, thanks to Mister Clute, she wasn't as helpless as Mathew had thought her to be.

Whipping the rope to twirling above her head, she walked to the edge of the barn and let the rope fly. At the same instant, Prudy broke for clear pastures. Ellie had anticipated this and the rope landed perfectly around her neck—a fact Prudy did not like. Not in the least!

A horrible noise erupted from the animal as she continued running full blast for high country. But Ellie held tight to the rope. When it went taut, Ellie was jerked off her feet, flying through the air briefly before landing in the dirt for the second time that day. Ellie held tight, though. Mathew's life depended on her. She was dragged behind the wildly circling mule, bouncing and bumping like a rag doll, dragged through dirt and rocks.

When she hit a large bump, Ellie screamed, flopped over, and stared at the sky as it raced by. Ellie's hand slipped, the rope jerked from her hand, and only then did she realize her hand was wrapped in the rope. She was in a pickle now.

"Prudence, whoa, mule!" Mathew's deep, commanding voice rang out.

He was alive. Ellie had never heard such a wonderful sound as his voice. Wanting to cry with joy, she cranked her head and saw him staggering to stand as she flew past him in a cloud of dirt.

"Hellllp me," she chattered, skidding over several rough

patches. "Ow! Oh!" She'd be mortified if she wasn't in so much pain!

"Prudence, halt this minute, you stubborn mule," Mathew bellowed.

To Ellie's relief, Prudy arched her path toward the barely standing cowboy, slowed, and trotted his way.

CHAPTER EIGHT

ELLIE WOULD HAVE FLUNG HER ARMS AROUND MATHEW'S neck if she could move.

And if the sky would stop spinning.

"Are you all right?" he asked, blood covered but glorious looking to Ellie. "What in the world are you doing?" He looked a little unstable as he reached down, grimacing and tugging the rope from around her aching hand. When she was free, he held his hand out to her. "Can you stand?"

She reached for his offered hand. "Thank you," she managed as they both staggered while she gained her feet. "You were out cold and bleeding like a waterfall," she said, staring into his dazed eyes. "I was trying to get Prudy to help me get you out of the sunlight."

"You were doing a fine job of it too." A grin tipped his lips as he swayed. She feared he wasn't going to stay upright long.

"Funny," Ellie said, woozy herself, wrapping an arm around his waist. Pulling his arm across her shoulders, she forgot the pain of her bumps and bruises the instant she realized she was snuggled up against him.

"Walk, cowboy. We need to get you into the house before you pass out again."

"Why, thank you, little lady," he said, sounding odd, his speech slurred and his feet fumbling beneath him.

If she hadn't known better, she'd say the man was drunk. He was trying to help, trying to support some of his weight as they swayed and weaved their way to the house with Prudy trailing them.

Something wasn't right.

They managed to make it up the step onto the porch and then through the doorway. From the back room she could hear Sophie crying. The wails so distraught that Ellie knew she'd been crying for a while.

From the yard, Prudy joined in the melee, hee-hawing her unhappiness at being left outside.

Ellie concentrated on getting Mathew to the bedroom, praying he wouldn't collapse before they made it to the bed.

Poor Sophie was standing up in her crib when they entered, her face stained with tears. Thankfully she calmed down when she saw them. "Mama," she hiccupped as she watched them stagger past her toward the big bed. Ellie's heart melted even as she struggled to get the baby's pa settled.

"Here we go, ease on down here," Ellie commanded gently, her hand splayed out across his flat stomach as she eased him to sit on the side of the bed. He swayed as he sat. Their faces were so close she could feel his breath on her skin. His eyes, dazed and a little crazy looking, held hers. Grinning lazily, he touched her cheek.

"You sure do look pretty," he murmured, and before she knew what was happening he pressed his lips to hers.

Ellie's breath caught at the tenderness of his touch. Wonder and bliss, her first kiss! The longing for love filled her as she joined in, timidly at first and then with gusto. Suddenly Mathew's lips stilled and to Ellie's disbelief he pitched backward—passing straight out, he hit the mattress like a rock!

His eyes closed, his breathing even . . . and a broad smile on his face.

☙

Someone was banging cast-iron skillets inside his skull.

Easing his eyes open, Mathew squinted at the ceiling and tried to get his bearings. He remembered Ellie coming out of the house in man's clothes and Ruthless taking him to task at the corral fence.

Things were fuzzy after that. Just like his head. He lifted a hand off the bed—bed? He was on his bed. How had that happened?

He moved to sit up when a wave of dizziness slammed into him.

Ellie padded into the room, the sound a loud echo in his skull. "You're awake. I was so worried. How do you feel?"

He tried to focus. There were *two* Ellies. Which he thought was nice since she was so pretty; it didn't hurt to have two of her to look at.

"If the room would stop spinning I'd be happier." He closed one eye—nope, still two. Both Ellies planted their hands on their hips. He could see a faint flush on her cheeks. Both sets, Ellie One and Ellie Two. His head ached and he reached to rub his temple—

"No!" they cried, rushing forward. Ellie One grabbed his hand and tugged it away from his head. "I feel weird," he mumbled. Looking down, he saw blood on his shirt.

"You hit your head, Mathew. You can't rub it or the bleeding will start again."

Bleeding. He had a flash of Ellie's arms wrapped around him.

"What happened?" He fought a wave of nausea.

"You were thrown from that horse and hit your head on the rail over the gate. You bled something fierce and then you were baking in the sun . . ." The words rushed from Ellie, and suddenly it all came back to Mathew in a wave.

Ellie in britches! Then, coming to, he'd struggled to focus, seeing her throw a lasso on Prudy as if she were a seasoned cowpoke!

"You can rope," he said. "And you got dragged by Prudy."

He looked her up and down. She still wore the britches and there was splattered blood all over her.

"Yes, well, I can explain that. First, though, I'm sorry. I didn't mean to startle you so with the change of clothes.

I know your getting hurt was my fault. You saw me and it almost got you killed."

"Yup, it threw me." He gave a shrug and saw worry in all four of her beautiful eyes. He concentrated and finally the two Ellies merged into one. The pain began to recede just a bit. "Don't blame yourself. Ruthless is a tough colt with a mind of his own. I should have never let him sense I wasn't paying attention."

"No, it was my fault." She looked away. "You ride well . . . You really do."

Her eyes darted to meet his, instantly dropped to his lips, and Mathew's insides filled with longing and an overwhelming need to kiss her.

Kiss her. Their gazes locked and she turned pinker than a cherry blossom. The color crept from beneath the cotton shirt and spread up her slender neck to her jaw and then to those trembling lips—and suddenly Mathew was hit with a full-blown flashback of kissing Ellie!

"Ellie." He sprang to his feet, wobbled, and slammed back down onto the bed. "I *kissed* you." No wonder she looked so embarrassed. He'd sat right here on this bed and kissed her. She'd been helping him and he'd kissed her.

And then he'd passed out.

He was such a knucklehead.

Ellie stiffened, her jaw lifted. Her eyes flashed above flaming cheeks. "I *am* your *wife*." Her eyes overly bright, she stomped loudly from the room.

Mathew wobbled. He'd really made a mess of things now and that was pure fact.

Ellie fought tears—she would not cry. Yes, she'd almost killed him, and she was truly sorry for that. But he'd kissed her and passed out smiling, and left her with the most amazing feelings of hope and longing.

And then he hadn't even remembered it.

Reaching the stove, Ellie grabbed some rags and lifted the lid on the heavy pot of stew. Stewing herself, with the need to throttle her husband.

How dare the man look so insulted by the fact that he'd kissed her!

Married couples kissed. But he didn't want to have a baby with her and he didn't want to kiss her. Ellie fought hard not to let this stab to her heart penetrate. But her heart had been weakened by his kiss—his wonderful, amazing kiss.

Tears slipped over the edges of her eyes. Drat them—she swatted at them with the cuff of her shirt. She focused on Sophie playing and singing in the corner with her doll and a tin cup. She was here for Sophie; she was here for Sophie.

She sniffed. She would not cry.

"Ellie."

The air left her lungs—*Oh, dear Lord, how long has he been standing there?*

"Ellie, look at me. Please."

She swiped at her eyes, hoping it would look as if she were pushing stray hair from her temples. Turning, she found Mathew just two steps away from her.

Gripping the back of the cane chair, he was as pale as moonlight.

"You shouldn't be up," she admonished. "I—I was just about to bring you some stew." Ignoring the awkwardness coursing through her, she slipped her arm around his waist. Instantly a wave of longing flooded her.

"You need to sit," she said gruffly, her eyes downturned.

"No. I don't want to sit. Ellie, we need to talk."

"True," she agreed breathlessly. "We do. However, you falling out on the floor because you're too stubborn to sit down isn't going to help us get much talking done," she fussed. When she looked at him at last, his lips lifted into a darling crooked smile.

"Are you always so bossy?"

"Maybe," she hedged, looking away, her stomach dipping at his nearness . . . She was a lost cause. Her lips still burned from his kiss hours ago, and of their own accord her eyes sought his lips once more. He smiled. Her gaze flew upward to find him watching her.

Her heart kicked about so hard that it put Ruthless's ruckus to shame.

"Ellie. I haven't meant to hurt your feelings," he said gently, his fingers pushing a wayward strand of hair from her temple. "You have to understand there are some things I can't give a wife. I've tried to explain that, but I've done a poor job of it. One of those things is my heart, and because I can't give you all you deserve, I won't take advantage of you."

Reality wrapped around her like a cold, dark night. She was unlovable; it was true after all.

"Please sit down before you fall down," she urged, trying to resign herself to what she'd never before been able to accept.

And she *really* couldn't handle it if he fell and the bleeding started up again.

He swayed and grabbed hold of Ellie, pulling her close. Ellie flung her arms around his waist and staggered, barely keeping him from toppling. Breathing hard, he held on to her, and when Ellie looked up his eyes were as wide as a full moon. Ellie felt faint—it was like an ailment or something when he was around!

Her head swam. He smelled of leather and pine, and Ellie realized she could happily breathe his scent for the rest of her life. The feel of his corded arms holding on to her was magical. Though he might not want her, he knew how to hold her so that she felt safe and wanted . . . Confusion tangled in her heart.

His arms tightened around her. She felt his heartbeat quicken against her own heart, and she thought he was going to kiss her again.

How could it be that he didn't want her and yet his kiss had been pure bliss?

Ellie's head spun with the delight of it. She closed her eyes and waited . . . Another moment ticked by, then he took hold of her arms and firmly set her away from him.

"We have to talk, Ellie."

CHAPTER NINE

MATHEW YANKED THE OTHER CHAIR OUT FROM THE table and sank into the one she'd pulled out for him earlier. "We have to talk—no getting mad and walking out. There are some things I've got to know."

Numb, Ellie sank into the seat. She felt as if she were the one who had struck her head. She was thankful for the gingham table cover she'd placed on the table that kept her shaking hands from his view.

"You're a beautiful woman, Ellie. I need to know what happened in your life to bring you here as a mail-order bride. And *where* did you learn to rope like that?"

With all they had to talk about—the kiss, the fact that he didn't want her. And he wanted to talk about roping?

Unbelievably, relief washed over her, glad to have the moment to back away from the problems at hand. To find solid ground.

They were actually going to sit at the table and talk to each other. This was good.

The *Hitching Post* had set them up so quickly and there had only been a couple of letters between them. Both of their situations hadn't given them a lot of time to spend on a long correspondence. As things had turned out, she was certain Mathew hadn't seen her actual letters anyway. They'd been filled with her love of the Lord, and if he'd read them, he would have known she was a believer before she'd stepped off that stage.

"Well, it's a little embarrassing actually," she admitted.

"If we are going to become friends and make this work, then we should get comfortable with things. Even the embarrassing things."

Friends. Ellie couldn't speak for a moment as the very thought sank in . . . she'd so longed for a friend. She had told God she would be patient and then immediately she'd plowed forward and caused all this trouble. He was steadfast even in her fickleness.

Sophie crossed the room and grabbed her arm, smiling up at Ellie. Picking her up, Ellie breathed in her baby scent and cherished the way Sophie snuggled contently into the crook of her arm. Ellie met Mathew's eyes with courage.

"All my life I've been a little of a black sheep. You see, my mother died giving birth to me, so I have that in common with Sophie. Also, before the year was out, my father died . . . Aunt Millicent said it was of a broken heart. He just couldn't take the loss of his beloved wife. My aunt said he couldn't stand to look at me, so he left raising me to her. A job she didn't want since she too grieved the loss of my mother, her younger sister. And then her husband, Mutt, died not long after that. Uncle Mutt had started drinking because of the stress of having me to raise. And so when he was coming out of the saloon one night, he staggered in front of a runaway buggy and was killed." She'd gotten the story out without much emotion. "My aunt never let a day go by without reminding me of the misfortune I'd caused. And her friends' children picked up on what their parents were whispering about, so they teased me relentlessly."

Ellie had been looking down as she finished that part of her story.

"You were a child, Ellie," Mathew said softly. "None of that was your fault."

The fact that Mathew would reassure her sent a gladness coursing through her.

"I know I'm not supposed to speak of it, but I can't talk about my past without telling what the Lord has done for me, Mathew. I found solace in His Word. I've had to live with the consequences of those deaths, but the guilt for it doesn't belong to me." To her happiness, Mathew simply nodded when she'd said she needed to speak about her faith.

"You weren't responsible," he said, looking from her to Sophie.

"I've longed all my life to feel the closeness of a family that I've never known. When I came here I became pushy and headstrong because I wanted it all so much. I was aggressive when I should have been patient. I'm sorry. I love—your child so much. And I'm so grateful to be here."

Mathew looked thoughtful.

Finally, with pain in his eyes, he said, "I'll admit that it's been hard for me to give my whole heart to Sophie. She reminds me so much of Beth. And it hurts looking at her sometimes and knowing what I lost. It shames me now, thinking about it. But I would never treat her as you've been treated."

His words were quiet as he studied his child. Ellie's throat constricted with emotion as he touched Sophie's soft hair. "I needed someone to love her like I couldn't. That was why I let Maggie talk me into finding a mama for her." He lifted his gaze to her and gave a quick shrug.

"Thank you for being honest," Ellie said. Sophie had taken hold of his finger and was chattering away to it as if she had lots to tell her pa's finger. It dug into Ellie's heart and caused an ache so strong that Ellie knew right then that she was here to help mend this relationship. *Thank You, Lord*. The prayer filled her and she smiled.

"You do love Sophie, Mathew. You just have to make peace with the past and open your heart to her."

He didn't say anything, though his eyes held a light she hadn't seen before.

"Tell me more of your life," he said, his eyes searching hers, digging deep. "And don't forget to tell me about this roping you've been hiding behind those frilly clothes."

No one had ever asked her to talk of her life. Feeling suddenly lighthearted, she chuckled. "You are really worried about my britches. You see, my aunt was forced to find work after my uncle died. She opened a seamstress shop in the front parlor of our home, and I was trained to help her at an early age. I started working in the shop almost before I could walk, picking up scraps of material and tidying up. And later I was taught to sew. Aunt Millicent and the ladies were overly fond of frills and ruffles and an overabundance of petticoats. I hated every minute of it, I'm sorry to say. Cooped up in that house, forever reminded that I was the reason my aunt had to work to live. Every spare minute I could find I would escape to this small ranch not too far from town. Old Mister Clute owned it and he was getting up in age. He caught me trying to learn to ride one of his horses one day and took a shine to me. He wasn't much for words, but he taught me to rope and to ride. I'd even help him with his roundups because he was getting too old to get around."

"Well, I'll be," Mathew said, sitting back in shock.

"It's true. See, he'd lost his son in the war. After that he closed himself off from the world. These here are his son's clothes. He'd saved them in a trunk and he gave them to me. Those bothersome skirts were constantly in my way and he knew it. They'd get dirty too, and Aunt Millicent was getting furious about me disappearing and coming back filthy. It just made sense and helped keep our secret from her. She would have put a stop to my shenanigans if she'd known exactly what I was doing. Which she did when the truth came out three months ago."

Mathew leaned forward, looking much steadier than he had. "What happened when she found out? And how?"

"Mister Clute died." Sadness hit her. He'd been as close to a friend as she'd ever had. "His brother came and took over the ranch. When I asked him if I could help him out, he laughed at me and went straightaway and told Aunt Millicent. As you can imagine, she was horrified that I'd been going behind her back, and especially that I would wear pants. She informed me that it was time for me to find my own way in life and stop embarrassing her. That said, she laid the *Hitching Post* on the table in front of me and told me to find a husband, preferably one that didn't live in Fort Worth."

"So it was your aunt's wish," Mathew said, clearly taken aback. "You didn't want this?"

Ellie shook her head. "Well, I was in shock at first. After a few minutes, I opened up the catalogue and immediately saw your ad. My heart latched onto your words as if you had written them directly to me. When I read how Sophie had lost her mama at birth, I felt drawn to her. I felt compelled by God to come so she would grow up feeling loved and wanted."

"Something you never felt," he said gently.

The compassion in his voice caused her throat to knot up with emotion. She could only nod.

"I'm sorry you went through all of that." Mathew covered her hand with his, then stared at their hands while tracing his thumb slowly over her wrist. He swallowed hard, as if he too had a knot in his throat. After a moment he lifted sincere eyes to hers. "Thank you for opening my eyes to the injustice I was doing to my daughter. Beth wouldn't have wanted me to give her baby any less than the love she would have lavished on her had she been alive." He smiled. "She would have liked you."

Joy flooded Ellie's heart. "I'm so glad. And I hope you will want to tell Sophie of her mother when she is old enough. It will do her a world of good to know that her mother loved her."

They stared at each other for the longest moment, and though there was so much between them that was confusing and unfinished, this was ground to build on. Sophie deserved it.

"Mathew," she said, drawn to go on. "I need to tell you that I'm glad to be here. But I'm giving you fair warning that I just know God has a plan for my life. The Bible says He will give me the delights of my heart. And I've been holding on to that promise ever since I read your ad. It sustained me all the way here during that long stagecoach ride. And I'm not giving up on it now."

Mathew patted her hand like a brother and drew it away. Feeling him withdrawing emotionally, she stood, hoping she hadn't gone too far again. She wanted everything. Love, children, forever . . . and she knew he could see it in her eyes.

"How about some stew?" she said, breaking the connection. "It will help you feel better." She placed his daughter in his arms to anchor him to the chair since he seemed steady enough to stay upright now. "Love on your daughter for a few minutes while I get the meal ready. It will do you both a world of good."

CHAPTER TEN

"I AIN'T NEVER SEEN NOTHIN' LIKE IT," LEM SAID, A week after Mathew's accident.

"What's that, Lem?" Mathew asked. They were searching for a couple of missing calves that Mathew hoped had just wandered off from their mothers. He was now certain he had rustlers systematically picking off his herd and he was going to have to put his attention to catching them soon.

"Maggie's got the notion to have a party. Says Ellie needs to be introduced around. And that's all fine and dandy to me, but you ain't never seen the likes of the work that thar woman's got me doin'. Do this, Lem, do that. No, you ain't done it right—do it this a-way. I'm right fond of you and your new wife, but if this keeps up, I ain't gonna be fond of my own much longer."

Mathew chuckled despite his wandering thoughts. Which kept going to Ellie as they had all week. His heart had cracked a little while Ellie told him about her past that night sitting at the kitchen table. How could her aunt be so cruel? So heartless? And how had Ellie survived it?

"Maggie comin' over the other day was a good thing," Mathew said. "Ellie really enjoyed it."

Lem grinned. "Maggie tried to put some of my britches on soon as we got home." He laughed. "You shoulda seen her. She looked like she'd been squeezed into a sausage skin."

Mathew chuckled, pretty sure Lem would be in a heap of trouble if Maggie knew he'd just told him that. "You better watch out," he warned.

Lem hiked a bushy brow. "I told her I'd buy her a bigger pair if she wanted them, long as she'd start mucking out the stalls."

That got a hoot out of Mathew. "You said that and you're still walking around?"

"I can run faster than her with them bad knees of hers. And that there is the only reason—" He spat a stream of tobacco. "I'll tell ya that for sure. I hear Ellie's done taken over up at the house."

"She's taken over the chickens and milking the cow. And feeding the calves too. Her and Prudence have become fast friends. I'm telling you there was no holding her back once she'd yanked on those britches."

"Maggie said she was riding some too."

"Yup. She's riding some of the gentler stock I've broke, helping soften them up some more so they don't go wild on me again. I worry, but she's a good rider, I have to admit. Tell you the truth, she was born to be a rancher's wife. If it wasn't for Sophie, she'd be out here helping us right now."

"You told her 'bout the rustlers, though, right?"

"That's the only thing keeping her and Sophie from being out here. For Sophie's sake she's staying close to the house. She wants me to teach her to shoot a gun."

"Look out, ever'body," Lem said, grinning widely.

"Yeah, that's what I said."

Lem sobered and he shook his head. "Mathew, I ain't never heard of such as that aunt of Ellie's."

So Ellie had confided her past to Maggie when she'd come for a visit, Mathew realized. He suspected Ellie had needed a woman to talk to and Maggie was the best.

"There are small-minded people in this world," he said, shaking his head. "Ellie tries to make something good out of the injustice that was done her." Her attitude made him ashamed of the hard time he'd given her when she got off the stage holding her Bible.

He wiped the sweat from his brow. They were heading down a ravine, their horses carefully picking their steps. "I've got to confess, Lem. This is eating at me . . . I've known the love of my parents, and of Beth. Ellie hasn't known the love of anyone. She was barely tolerated by her aunt and then kicked out first chance the old bat got."

Lem looked over his shoulder, having moved in front on the narrow trail. "The two of you aren't—"

"I can't, Lem. It's just not in me." He had to admit sleeping on the lumpy mattress in the barn was getting old, especially when he thought about Ellie with her hair hanging loose and the feel of her soft lips against his—he stopped his thoughts in their tracks. No sense going down that road. Ellie had made it extremely clear she'd like more from their marriage, that she wanted children. But when he'd married her he'd vowed to protect her, and he aimed to do just that. Even if that meant protecting her from himself. They both knew from experience what could happen in childbirth and it wasn't going to happen to Ellie because of him.

Lem's eyes narrowed. "Boy, you got more room in that stubborn heart of your'n. All you got to do is open up."

There was more involved than that now, and Mathew knew it. He didn't want anything to happen to Ellie. He couldn't stand to think of it.

"Look-a-there," Lem hooted, spotting a calf caught in a bramble.

Mathew was relieved to have something to distract Lem from the subject at hand. Dismounting, they went to untangle the little fella.

It hit Mathew hard, knowing even his cows had him looking out for them. Caring for them. Ellie hadn't even had that.

The calf bawled as Mathew tore the brambles off of it.

Looking into the young calf's big brown eyes, Mathew's stomach felt ill thinking of Ellie as a child. "Everyone should have someone looking out for them," he said more to himself than to Lem. He lifted his gaze to his friend, who held the animal still. "This calf has us. Ellie deserved someone looking out for her—"

"She's got you," Lem said, puzzlement in his eyes.

"Yeah, and she'd look me square in the face and tell me God was looking out for her. But God wasn't looking out for Beth."

Lem looked sorrowful. "Son, you got to let that go. God's got mysterious ways. Everyone is appointed a time to die when they are still in the womb. That ain't got nothin' to do with you."

Mathew tore away the stickered vines. "God forsook Beth, sweet Beth. And left her baby motherless." Left him with a gaping hole in his heart out here in the middle of the wilderness where they'd planned to build a life together.

Ellie's face, so brave in the face of everything he'd seen thrown her way, blurred his vision. He pulled the calf free and pulled it into his arms.

"Let it go, I'm tellin' you. Quit thinking about what you ain't got and think about what you have."

"Lem, it's not that easy. Look, I'm gonna head on home. We'll see y'all at the party. Ellie is so excited about it."

"Maybe you should do some prayin' on the ride home."

Instead of responding, Mathew hoisted the calf in front of the saddle, then climbed up behind it. "Tell Maggie thanks, we'll see you there in a few hours," he said as he tugged on the reins, turning his horse around and urging him to a quick pace. It was time to get home.

❀

The sun was hanging low on the horizon as they headed toward Lem and Maggie's late that afternoon. "Do you think there will be a lot of people there?" Ellie asked, barely able to contain her excitement.

"Probably all of Madison, Brazos, and Leon County."

"Really?" Ellie gasped, bouncing Sophie on her lap as the buckboard rolled along the bumpy road. Mathew chuckled, sliding his warm gaze her way, teasing her. That look sent her heart fluttering. She'd learned to control her temper somewhat and take her time where Mathew was concerned.

In her rush to have it all and not be patient with the Lord's plan, Ellie had nearly messed up everything.

No, she was relying on God to help her not overwhelm Mathew.

She'd first wondered why a man like him would need to send off for a mail-order bride. Well, no maybes about it, he absolutely had a broken heart.

He'd loved Beth as Ellie could only dream of being loved. He'd said he couldn't give his heart to Ellie, and now she understood. When you loved someone like that and lost as he had . . . how could you ever risk opening up like that again? Or even have any love left to give after having felt so deeply?

No, Ellie could only pray that she could show Mathew the depth of her own love for him and that at some point he might be able to share enough affection toward her that their marriage could become one of contentment. Maybe she could love him enough for both of them.

"I can't believe they are having a party for *us*," she said. Imagining the evening ahead, she smiled happily at Mathew.

He chuckled. The husky sound of it and the sparkle in his eyes had her breathless and thinking of nothing but the moment.

"You deserve it," he said, touching her hand and sending her heart into a gallop.

"Paudy fo us," Sophie said, looking expectantly from Ellie to Mathew. She'd begun forming short sentences within the last few days and sometimes they were understandable. Ellie laughed in delight.

"Yes indeed, baby girl. A paudy for us."

There were buggies and wagons all over the place as they drove into the yard. Maggie had set up the party in the barn and the doors were flung open wide to let the breeze in. Mathew took Sophie and then helped Ellie from the wagon. She smoothed the skirt of the yellow calico dress with the simple lace collar. Her excitement overshadowed any and all nerves.

"You look lovely this evening, Ellie," Mathew said.

Ellie's gaze swung to him—she wasn't quite sure how to respond to his compliment. *A thank-you would be a nice start.* His eyes were warm with appreciation. Ellie heaved in a very unladylike breath. "Thank you. I . . . I removed some of the ruffles and that awful thick petticoat—" She clamped her mouth shut, not comfortable discussing undergarments with him. Even if he was her husband.

His rich chuckle rumbled deep in his chest. "It suits you much better this way." He held out his arm. "May I have the pleasure, ma'am?"

Ellie took his arm and they walked together toward the festivities.

"Look who is here," Maggie exclaimed as they stepped inside the large barn.

Ellie was so happy to see her new friend and hugged her hard. "This is wonderful. You've gone to so much trouble, though. You shouldn't have."

"I ain't done nothin' I wasn't happy to do. Now come on in here and meet your neighbors. And tell me how this handsome cowboy of yours is treating you." She winked at Mathew as she took Sophie from him. Mathew shook his head and grinned.

"Well, land's sakes! That's a smile if I ever saw one, and I didn't have to draw it out of you like thick molasses." She looked at Ellie and beamed. "You done good, girl. Real good. Now come on, you two. We got folks to meet and mingle with, and then there's gonna be hours of dancing. Lem—Lem!" she yelled, motioning to Lem, who was deep in conversation with several other men. "Get yourself over here and greet Ellie."

Ellie spent a delightful hour meeting people who were happy to meet her. There were several younger women, new brides themselves, who lived out on surrounding ranches like she did. Though there was distance between them, it was nice knowing she had females she could hopefully one day call friends rather than simply neighbors.

Soon the music began to play. Cute little man that Lem was, with his barrel chest and short legs, he played a fierce fiddle. Ellie found herself standing beside the punch bowl tapping her toes to the music. Mathew had been hovering close to her side for most of the first hour, even putting his hand on the small of her back as she was being introduced around. Ellie couldn't help but feel proud that this handsome man was hers and that he seemed more than pleased to call her his.

When she and a group of younger ladies began comparing the progression of their babies, Mathew excused himself and headed over to talk with the men.

She watched as he approached and the others slapped him on the back in what appeared to be congratulations, so many times that she was certain he would have bruises by morning.

When the music started, Mary, Elizabeth, and Rebecca had all hurried to pull their husbands onto the dance floor. Ellie eased to the side of the refreshment table, out of the way as she sipped her punch and watched, memorizing the steps as couples twirled around the center of the barn. Dancing had always looked so fun.

Mathew was deep in conversation with two men outside beside the front doors. Ellie wondered what they were talking about. Sophie played over in the corner with several of the other babies as a group of older women and young girls watched over them. Maggie had insisted that Ellie have a good time and not worry about Sophie. She was in good hands.

"You should be dancing," Mathew said, coming up behind her, leaning close to her ear.

Ellie's heart jumped inside her chest. "No." She was so happy he was here to stand beside her. "I don't dance. But it's lovely to watch and I love the music. Lem and the band play wonderfully."

She turned her head, looking over her shoulder at Mathew. He remained behind her, bent slightly, staring into her eyes. His warm breath on her skin sent a shiver through her.

"You don't dance? You didn't tell me that. I'm not much of a dancer myself, but I'd take you for a spin if you'd like."

She looked at the floor, then met his eyes. "No, that's all right. Watching is fine."

Questions and skepticism in his eyes, Mathew moved beside her as he glanced at the dance floor, then back at her. "Every young girl I know loves to dance, Ellie."

She couldn't meet his gaze but gave a quick smile, willing him to just let this go so they could enjoy the rest of the evening.

Unexpectedly, Mathew took her chin between his fingers and lifted her face so she was forced to look him in the eyes. "What's going on, Ellie?"

How could the man read her so well?

"Oh, fiddle, Mathew. I don't know how to dance, if you must know." There, she'd admitted it. His mouth fell open ever so slightly before he clamped it shut.

"Everyone knows how to dance," he said after a heartbeat.

She shook her head as the music slid straight into a second song.

"Why don't you know how to dance? Don't tell me, dear old Aunt Millicent never took you to a dance." Mathew's face was incredulous.

It almost made Ellie smile. "I went to only a few dances. But honestly, Mathew, this isn't important."

"No, Ellie," he said gently, holding down his anger. "It is important. Why don't you know how to dance?"

Ellie huffed. "Well, if you must know, I was never *asked* to dance." There, she'd admitted that too.

CHAPTER ELEVEN

MATHEW COULD NOT BELIEVE HIS EARS. ELLIE A *WALL-flower*. Frustration at the injustice of it all engulfed him like a Texas grass fire. "Your part of Fort Worth was full of fools." He stepped in front of Ellie, hating the sting of humiliation in her eyes. He'd come to know Ellie as the most vibrant and alive person he'd ever met. She played with Sophie with the abandon of a child herself and she looked at the work on the ranch as an adventure.

Tamping down his anger, he pulled Ellie into his arms. "May I have this dance, Mrs. McConnell?"

Her eyes flew wide in shock. "No." She shook her head and pushed against his arms.

"What?" Baffled, Mathew held on. "Ellie. Dance with me."

"Mathew, no. I . . . I can't," she hissed softly. "I've never danced before. I don't know what to *do*."

He smiled, glad that he was about to be the one to dance

with her first. "Take my hand, Ellie. Trust me." He held her worried eyes with his, willing her to trust him. She breathed in deeply, her lips grim as she looked from his offered hand to his eyes. He smiled. "You're not scared, are you?"

Her blue eyes fired up and her jaw jutted out. *There's some spirit*, he thought, knowing the barb would bring back that fire that he'd come to love. She jammed her fingers into his hand, hiked her chin, and held his gaze. He pulled her closer and his heart kicked like a bull.

Despite trying not to, had he fallen in love with Ellie? Somehow that thought wasn't as troubling as it had been in the not-too-distant past.

"You lead," she ground out. "I'll follow."

He grinned, touched his forehead to hers, processing his emotions. "I like the sound of that, Ellie." Fighting the urge to kiss her, he warned instead, "Hang on, honey, and go with me." And then he spun her out onto the dance floor, practically lifting her up as he went.

Tonight his wife was going to dance like nobody had ever danced before.

***

The stars were shining as they waved their good-byes. Ellie glanced into the bed of the wagon where Sophie was snuggled, fast asleep on the soft blankets Mathew had laid out for her. "Sophie had a wonderful evening," Ellie said as Mathew turned the horses onto the road and headed toward home.

"How about you, Ellie? Did you have a good time?"

Mathew's gentle question wrapped around her like a warm blanket, and Ellie could not help but long for his arms once more. "I had a *glorious* time." Her gaze locked with his and a shiver raced through her.

"Good," he said, grinning. "You are a fast learner."

"I had a great teacher. I'm thinking you must have never missed a dance growing up." The man had danced with her until she thought her feet would fall off and then they'd danced some more. She hadn't wanted to stop. Stopping meant his arms wouldn't be around her any longer. Oh, how she loved this man. How could she not?

"I had my fair share of dances, it's true," he said. Clucking, he urged the team to pick up their pace a bit, then he looked back at her. "But no one has ever been more fun to dance with than you."

Ellie's breath caught and her heart stilled. *Oh, Mathew, if you could only love me.*

Not knowing what to say, Ellie simply smiled and then looked up at the stars. There were thousands of them tonight.

They traveled in silence. Her heart was overflowing with the beauty of what she and Mathew had shared tonight. She didn't want to spoil any of it by asking . . . by pushing for more.

She wouldn't be greedy. She must be content.

They'd turned off the road and were crossing their land now, the lane illuminated by the soft moonlight and the canopy of brilliant stars.

"Did Beth love to dance?" Ellie asked at long last. The

question burst from her in the silence and it was between them before she could stop it. She was hopeless!

Mathew sat up straighter and she wasn't sure he was going to answer. "Yes, she did," he said at last. Then, meeting her gaze, he added, "Almost as much as you."

Pressing her lips together, she held back the smile that yearned to bloom at his words. "Do you miss her terrible?" she asked softly, feeling for him.

He nodded. "I think I always will."

He sounded so wistful, it was just as she'd thought. Heart clutching, she closed her eyes and let his words sink in. They had come to this companionable relationship, but that was all it would ever be.

Mathew slowed the buckboard until it came to a halt. "Ellie, look at me."

Ellie thought her heart would burst. She couldn't look at him. How, oh how could she be jealous of a dead woman?

Forcing herself to have some dignity, she looked at him and smiled. "She was a very lucky woman."

He'd stopped the buckboard just before a bend in the road beside a stand of trees. "Ellie, listen to me." He took her in his arms. "I am a lucky man. A blessed man," he said. He was lowering his lips to hers when suddenly three cows rounded the bend in the road, flanked by two riders.

Mathew let go of Ellie, pushed her behind him protectively as he reached for his gun.

"I wouldn't do that if I were you," said the man who approached on their right, the click of his rifle's hammer sounding as he aimed it straight at Ellie. It gleamed ominously in the moonlight.

Mathew went stone still beside her. "Don't move, Ellie. Don't speak. Just go easy."

To them he said, "Don't do anything you'll regret in the morning." One man had a beard, its outline visible in the light, though his hat shadowed the rest of his face. The taller one with the gun wore a duster and she couldn't see his facial features beneath his hat either.

"I'm thinkin' we ain't got much choice in the matter. Seein' as how you know these are your cattle."

Ellie couldn't move. Stealing cattle was a hanging offense. So what would they have to lose if they hurt them in the process? Or worse?

"Why don't you toss that six-shooter you're holding this direction. Or I use the little lady for target practice."

Ellie gasped. "Mathew—"

"Hush, Ellie. Just hold tight." Mathew tossed his weapon to the ground.

They were now at the mercy of these varmints. Ellie glanced over her shoulder at Sophie. Sweet Sophie. She would do what she needed to save her baby.

The bearded rider walked his horse over and looked down at them. "Boss, they've got a baby over here."

"That so."

"Yeah, I don't know about no baby."

"Get out of the wagon, you two," the boss guy demanded, ignoring his partner. "And bring that baby with you."

Ellie could hardly breathe. She prayed that God would help them. Prayed that Mathew wouldn't do anything careless. Maybe if they just did as they were told, they'd be spared.

She reached for Sophie. Mathew started to help her but the man with the beard leveled his rifle on him. "You stay still."

Ellie pulled Sophie into her arms as gently as she could, but the child woke up and immediately began to wail.

"Get that cryin' baby to shut up," the boss ordered. "And get down off that wagon."

Mathew nodded and Ellie eased out of the wagon, clutching Sophie to her. Once they were on the ground, she tried to soothe Sophie, but she could not be consoled. Maybe it was waking up in the dark in a strange place that had her disturbed. Or seeing these strange faces. Ellie clung to her and prayed for God to intervene.

"Now you get out of the wagon," the bearded man commanded. Mathew took his time, never taking his eyes off the man. A dangerous look in Mathew's eyes set alarms off inside Ellie. What was he thinking about doing?

"You know they have descriptions of you," he said, moving to stand at the head of the wagon. "I talked with the sheriff this evening and he said he got the Wanted posters today. Your days in this area are numbered."

"What we gonna do with these three? Leave 'em, they can't do nothin' to us," the bearded outlaw said. "We need to get out of Texas. Fast."

"Take them into the woods and get rid of them. Now git," the boss man spat out. "And quit your bellyaching."

Mathew had placed himself between the two riders, and Ellie was pretty certain he'd done it for a reason. Part of that reason was to distance them from her and Sophie, who were standing on the other side of the wagon. Sophie was still carrying on. Ellie was so distraught she was sure the baby could sense it.

An owl hooted from the woods and Ellie shivered. Would this be the end of them?

"Why don't you two think this through," Mathew said calmly. "If you start now, you'll be well on your way out of this county by morning. We'll keep our mouths shut and give you time to make it out. Just let my wife and baby go. Killing a woman and child is going to bring a rain of fire down on you. You'll be hunted down—"

The boss galloped his horse over to Mathew and poked his pistol at Mathew's chest. "Keep your mouth shut," he snapped.

"But, boss, he's got a point. If'n we kill 'em, we'll never have any peace."

To Ellie's dismay, the boss leveled his gun on his partner. "Climb down off that horse and do as I've told you or I'll shoot you myself. Do you hear?"

Muttering, the man did as he was told. Grumbling, he poked Mathew in the back and shoved him with his gun. "You heard the man. Git!"

Mathew's jaw tightened but he said nothing as he met Ellie's gaze over the wagon. Ellie was rocking Sophie, trying desperately to quiet her cries, and she realized Mathew was not going to go down without a fight. He was not going to just let these men walk them into the woods and shoot them. He would die trying to save them.

Oh, Lord. "Please listen to him," Ellie blurted over Sophie's wails. "You've just stolen some cattle. You don't want to do this."

"Ellie, quiet now," Mathew demanded. "Stay right where you are."

"Hey," the boss growled. "I'm giving the orders here, and I'm telling the little lady to make nice and get over here with you."

Mathew had a rifle jammed in his back. He was only about three steps from the rustler on the horse, that man's gun now pointed straight at Ellie. Tension was so high, electricity vibrated in the air. Ellie didn't move, couldn't move—it was as if God had put a hand on her shoulder and was holding her in place just as a low, thunderous rumble sounded through the trees.

Thunder? Sophie's tears had soaked her shirt, and Ellie clutched the dear child closer to her heart and bent her lips to her sweaty hair. "Please, please calm down, little darlin'," she whispered, but Sophie wailed louder and the thunder drew closer—Ellie recognized the sound just as Prudence burst from the trees, charging straight forward.

Chaos erupted!

The two horses hitched to the wagon bolted and broke for home, startling the outlaws. Mathew grabbed the rifle from the man on the ground and wrenched it from his hands just as Prudence hit the man full force and plowed right over him.

The boss man was trying to control his horse as Mathew dove for him, grabbed him, and yanked him from the rearing horse. The outlaw hit the ground with a thud. A gun went off, and Ellie realized she was standing in the open with Sophie in her arms!

"Dear Lord, keep Mathew safe," she yelled and ran for the trees. Shots rang out behind her. She planted her back to the first oak she came to. Sophie had stopped crying and in the shadowed darkness Ellie could see the whites of her eyes; they were as round as saucers. Feeling the little girl's limbs and torso, Ellie satisfied herself that none of the gunshots had hit her. Breathing heavily, Ellie prayed hard, then turned, keeping Sophie as close to the trunk as she dared to peek around the edge.

To her relief, Mathew had the gun and it was aimed at the outlaw whose arms were in the air. The second outlaw wasn't doing as well; he was flat on his stomach with Prudence sitting on top of him.

It was over.

"Ellie," Mathew yelled. "Are you and Sophie all right?"

Ellie almost cried at the fear and concern she heard in his voice. "Yes," she called, feeling weaker than she ever had. He was safe.

They were safe.

God had seen them through.

And Prudy did own this ranch now and could sleep inside by the fire this winter if she wanted to. Anything. Anything at all that mule wanted that mule could have!

CHAPTER TWELVE

At dawn's light, Ellie had strong coffee brewing. She stood by the window, waiting. Mathew had tied the two outlaws together and lashed them to a tree. Then he pulled a saddle from one of the outlaw's horses and placed it on Prudence. Once that was done, he held Sophie while Ellie climbed into the saddle. He put Sophie in front of Ellie and let Prudence take them home.

He went for the sheriff.

Ellie had rocked her sleeping Sophie for the next four hours and waited. Finally she'd placed her baby into her bed, closed the door, and made coffee. Then she'd made biscuits. And she waited some more. Before long she'd make something else just to keep her hands busy.

Where is he?

So much had happened since the first time she'd scanned Honey Springs and asked that same question.

Her life was so much richer than it had been then. Things weren't as she'd dreamed, but she could live with that. If only he'd come home and she could see his face.

He'd said he missed Beth. She'd heard the love and regret in his voice. Closing her eyes, she accepted the blessings that she had gained and she tried not to long for what lay behind the doors God had closed.

Hoofbeats. She looked out the front door and saw him coming.

So strong and powerful in the saddle. Hurrying outside, still in her dress from the party, she didn't care if she fell down. She raced across the yard, skirts flapping and tangling as she ran. At the edge of the corral she stopped, put her hand to her forehead, and watched him gallop her way. The man was born to ride.

Jumping from the saddle, he didn't stop until he had her in his arms.

Ellie buried her face in his chest, her hands gripping his shirt. She breathed in the very essence of him. *Thank You, Lord, for bringing him home.* "You're safe," she sobbed.

"It's all right, Ellie. It's over." He ran his hands down her back and over her arms and then he hugged her tight and his lips brushed the skin of her neck. Ellie went still in his arms, letting herself savor the moment.

"I thought I was going to lose you, Ellie," he said, his voice breaking.

Had he said what she thought he'd said?

He lifted his head and took her face in his hands. "Ellie, I love you. I've been trying to deny it. But I was a fool."

Warmth and light exploded inside Ellie at his words. Her heart was bursting and she couldn't contain the smile that took over her face. But did she dare believe— "Oh, Mathew. I thought when you told me you would always miss Beth that there was never any hope for me."

He sobered. "I will always miss Beth. She is part of me, and always will be. But you are too, Ellie. You are my blessing from God. I have been too blind to realize it. I feel so humbled that God would send me you—" He stopped speaking and his brows dipped into that scowl that she'd come to love. "Wait, you haven't said—"

"I *love* you, Mathew," Ellie said with emotion, then she pressed her lips to his. "I've loved you from the first moment I read the ad—"

Before she could say anything more, Mathew covered her mouth with his, kissing her with all the love and longing she'd dreamed of. Skin-tingling, toe-curling, heart-pounding love poured into her and left her breathless. There was the promise of a future and a family in that kiss, and Ellie's knees would have given out beneath her if Mathew hadn't been crushing her so tightly in his arms.

Suddenly he pulled back to look at her. "Wait, I didn't write the lovely words you fell for."

She laughed as joy filled her soul. "The promise of you and Sophie was in those words. They gave me courage to change my life and a hope that I could have a future with you. And I loved the idea of you. And knowing you, being with you each day, has only made my love stronger."

"I love you, Ellie McConnell. And I want to spend the rest of my days showing you just how much."

"Now that is what I love about you, Mathew. You are a man of your word." Ellie smiled and took his hand. "I think it's time you moved into the house."

Mathew threw back his head and laughed, a deep, rumbling laugh that filled Ellie with happiness. What a life they would have. "Lead on, Ellie. Let's get started."

Ellie winked at him. "I couldn't agree more," she said, and together they walked toward their home, their baby, and a future that promised to be richer and fuller than any fairy tale or happy ending Ellie ever could have dreamed of. God was so good.

They walked to the house and Ellie hugged Prudence once more—she had been standing at the front porch like a sentinel since bringing them safely home.

"Thank you, Prudy. You saved us." Ellie kissed the old mule's forehead. Prudy had heard Sophie's wails and come searching for her baby, and she rescued them.

"Hey," Mathew said, "*I* rescued you and Sophie."

"Now, Mathew, don't be jealous. You know perfectly well that Prudy galloped in and saved the day."

"She might have started it, but I finished it."

"Why, Mathew, surely you aren't jealous of a little ole mule," Ellie teased, unable to help herself.

"Well, of course not." Mathew opened the door and scowled.

"That's good. Because I have a special place in my heart—" Ellie's teasing was cut short when he swept her into his arms and covered her lips with his.

And then he carried her over the threshold and kicked the door closed behind them.

Ellie met his kiss with her heart. They were home . . .

And Prudy was on guard.

Autumn's Angel

Robin Lee Hatcher

This means that anyone who belongs to
Christ has become a new person.
The old life is gone; a new life has begun!

2 CORINTHIANS 5:17 NLT

September 10, 1870

Beyond the window of the passenger car, the plains of western Nebraska lay flat, lifeless, empty. Dawn had begun to lighten the sky from black to pewter. The night was nearly over, but Luvena hadn't slept a wink, even though exhaustion permeated every fiber of her body. And after seemingly endless days of travel, she was certain she looked as terrible as she felt—wrinkled, gritty, and bedraggled.

Elsie, her eight-year-old niece, shifted from left side to right, her head resting in Luvena's lap. Luvena smiled as she brushed unruly hair back from the child's face. She envied the girl. Luvena had been like that as a child, able to sleep anytime, anywhere. But no more. Not with so many responsibilities weighing on her shoulders.

Her gaze shifted to the seat opposite her where Elsie's older brother and sister also slumbered. Lying lengthwise, Ethan, age ten, took up most of the seat, his feet hanging off the edge into the aisle. Merry, the eldest of the siblings at fourteen, was squeezed up against the wall of the coach, her head and shoulder pressed against the sooty window in the little space left for her by her brother.

Looking at the children, her heart broke once again over all they'd lost, over the end of their dreams—and over the end of her own too. Once upon a time, she'd dreamed of becoming an opera singer. A girlish, unrealistic dream most likely, but one she'd relished. Her vocal teacher had declared Luvena possessed the voice of an angel and promised that she would be a sensation if ever she performed on the stage in New York City or the capitals of Europe. Luvena had chosen to believe her—for a time. That was before her family was plunged into disgrace. These days, she rarely sang where anyone might hear and compliment her. Not even in church. It hurt too much.

Drawing a deep breath, she pushed such thoughts away. She had no time for them. In another twenty-four hours, she and her little brood of orphans would disembark in Promontory, Utah. From there they had three or four grueling days of travel by stagecoach to Boise City, the capital of Idaho Territory. And there, at last, she would meet the man she was to marry. The man who would provide a home and security for the children of her sister.

Please, God, let it be a good home. A happy home.

She glanced down at the letter in her hand. How often had she read it since leaving Massachusetts? Ten times. Twenty. Perhaps more. She could almost recite it from memory. As for the photograph he'd sent—she looked at it again—it was small and grainy, but Mr. Birch appeared clean and respectable. No beard or mustache. He wasn't too old either. Thirty-one to her twenty-three years. And although he didn't smile in the photograph, neither did he look disagreeable.

As long as he is good to me and kind to the children, as long as he is a Christian and has integrity, it doesn't matter who he is or where he lives or what he looks like. I'm not marrying for love. I'm marrying because it's the practical thing to do. The same reason hundreds of other women choose to travel west and marry complete strangers. People have been arranging marriages since almost the beginning of time. It will be all right. It will.

She closed her eyes, leaned her head against the back of the seat, and began to hum a favorite hymn, hoping the inspiring lyrics would help drive away her doubts.

Please let it be all right.

CHAPTER ONE

CLAY BIRCH TOOK THE LAST BITE OF HIS LUNCH AND pushed the empty plate away from the edge of the table. A quick glance at his pocket watch confirmed the stage was running late.

He shouldn't have come down to Boise to meet Miss Abbott. There was so much work to be done back in Grand Coeur. He should have sent her more money and let her come all the way to him by coach. But this had seemed a little more courteous to his future bride. More civilized. He needed to make a good first impression *before* she saw her new home. Grand Coeur would be somewhat of a shock to a woman from Boston. The town wasn't yet a decade old, and it still bore all the markings of its gold camp beginnings.

He looked at the photograph he'd received from his intended and wondered again why a young woman as beautiful as Luvena Abbott needed to find a husband through the

Hitching Post Mail-Order Bride Catalogue. It seemed to him that men in the East should have been lining up to propose to her. Even if the photograph had been kind to her, she would still be comely enough for any man he knew.

But her appearance wasn't her most important asset. He'd wanted a wife who was young and strong, someone willing to work hard, someone with a keen mind and good business sense. He'd made it clear in his application that he had no interest in widows with children. Since the end of the war, the country was crawling with widows and their fatherless children, and he didn't want or need another man's offspring complicating his life. He wasn't cut out to be a stepfather. Besides, Grand Coeur wasn't an ideal place for kids. Not yet. There wasn't even a schoolhouse. No, what he needed was a woman who would be as focused as Clay himself on making the Grand Coeur Opera House the best venue of culture and entertainment west of the Rocky Mountains. And since Miss Luvena Abbott had experience in the management of an opera house, she had been the logical choice among the few responses he'd received to his advertisement.

Of course—he grinned at the thought—he didn't *object* that she was easy on the eyes. He supposed it didn't hurt for a man to enjoy looking at his wife.

Clay heard the thunder of horses' hooves and the creak and rattle of the coach moments before the stage rolled past the restaurant's window. He rose, left payment for his lunch on the table, and hurried outside. With long strides, he crossed the street, thankful it had been warm and dry for weeks. Better the excessive dust than ankle-deep mud. He reached the boardwalk outside the Wells, Fargo office before the driver hopped down from his perch and opened the door for the passengers.

He drew a deep breath, feeling his gut churn with nervous anticipation. This was it. For better or worse, he was about to meet his bride.

First out the door of the coach was a boy with sandy-colored hair and a scowl for anyone who met his gaze. He looked like he wanted to punch somebody. Anybody. Next came a girl with the same color hair; she was perhaps fourteen or fifteen years of age. Wrong coloring and wrong age for Miss Abbott. The girl turned and helped an even younger girl to the ground. They were without a doubt sisters to the boy. The younger girl, who clutched a doll to her chest, had a face streaked with tears.

"Ethan," the older girl said, "get out of the street. Hurry up." She held her little sister's hand and stepped onto the boardwalk a short distance away from Clay.

He felt sorry for her. He understood what it was like to be the oldest sibling in charge of younger ones. Seven years had separated him from Jacob, the first of his four half brothers. When his brothers were little, Clay had often been called upon by his mother to help feed or bathe or tuck one boy or another into bed. He'd loved them, but that didn't mean he'd loved acting as their nursemaid. Sometimes they'd made him so mad he'd—

Movement in the coach doorway drew his attention.

A woman leaned forward so that all he saw at first was the crown of a gray bonnet adorned with a long white feather. But when she straightened, he knew this was Luvena Abbott. The photograph hadn't lied.

Her hair was blue-black, like the wings of a raven, her complexion pale and flawless. Her eyes were deep pools of brown. She was more petite than he'd expected. From where he stood, he guessed the top of her head would barely be as high as his shoulders, even with shoes on. His hands could encircle her waist, he was sure.

Before moving away from the coach, she looked at the three children now standing on the boardwalk. Her expression revealed exasperation, and seeing it made him grin. After traveling for hours or days with those kids in the close confines of the coach, she might just be thankful for a quiet wagon ride with just the two of them. He was looking forward to that himself.

Her gaze shifted, and he saw that she recognized him from his photograph as well.

Pulling off his hat, he stepped forward. "Miss Abbott?" He made it a question, even though he knew the answer.

"Yes. And you are Mr. Birch, I see."

"I am indeed. Welcome to Idaho Territory. I hope the journey wasn't too difficult."

"Difficult enough. I'm grateful to be here at last." She stepped onto the boardwalk, her gloved fingers brushing at her skirt. As if that would help rid it of the accumulated dust.

He'd been right about her height. The top of her head, not

counting the hat, didn't quite reach his shoulders. He wondered if she would tip the scales at a hundred pounds. Possibly, but only just. "I take it you arranged for your larger trunks and furniture to be shipped to Grand Coeur, as we discussed."

She nodded. "Yes."

"Then let's get whatever you brought with you and put it in my wagon." He indicated the borrowed farm vehicle across the street. "We want to get to Grand Coeur before it's too late in the day. I'd like you to see the town at its best." That was a careful way of saying he wanted to get there before the saloons got too full and their customers got too rowdy.

Luvena turned toward the stagecoach and pointed toward the luggage that the Wells Fargo driver and station agent were unloading. "Those two smaller trunks there and those two carpetbags are ours."

Ours. He liked that she said it that way, even if she hadn't traveled light. Good thing he'd borrowed a wagon instead of a buggy. Still, she'd said *ours* instead of *mine*, and he knew they were going to get along. It was a good start for their union.

He stepped off the boardwalk, ready to claim the identified luggage.

Then he heard Luvena Abbott say, "Children, we're going in that wagon over there. Ethan, take Elsie's other hand and you all get settled in the back of it. Mr. Birch wants to be on our way without delay. We'll be to our new home soon. This is the final part of the trip."

Despite the warmth of the day, Clay went cold all over.

Luvena waited until she was certain the children were headed to the right vehicle before she returned her attention to Clay Birch. She found him looking at her with what she could only call a stupefied expression. "Is something amiss, Mr. Birch?"

His gaze flicked to the opposite side of the street and back to her. "Are those children with *you*?"

Oh, for goodness' sake. She was so exhausted she'd completely forgotten her manners. "I'm sorry. That was rude of me, Mr. Birch. I should have introduced them." She glanced across the street again. "Of course, you can tell which one is Ethan since he's the only boy. Esmeralda is the oldest girl. We call her Merry. Elspeth is the youngest and she is called Elsie. But I'm sure I told you that already."

"Told me what?"

"What everyone calls the girls."

He shook his head slowly.

Was he, perhaps, not very bright?

"*Miss* Abbott?"

"Yes."

"Not Mrs.? You've never been married. Right?"

"Of course not." She rubbed the crease between her eyebrows, wishing he would simply get their luggage so they could be on their way. She was tired and her exhaustion worsened by the moment.

He frowned at her, looking more like the unsmiling photograph he'd sent her than he had moments before. "Then who do those children belong to?"

"Mr. Birch, I don't understand you. These are the children of Oliver and Loretta Browne, my sister and her husband. And they belong with me, of course. Where else would they go?"

"To their parents might be a good idea."

She sucked in a breath. Was he beyond dense? Was he cruel too? Oh, she hadn't expected this. "You know very well they have no parents or grandparents still living. I am their family now. Their only family." She became aware that others had stopped what they were doing to stare at them. Heat rose in her cheeks. "Please, sir. May we go?"

Anger flashed in his blue eyes as he managed to stuff a carpetbag under each arm and grab a trunk handle with each hand. Then he marched across the street and delivered them into the back of the wagon where the children were now seated. She hurried after him, thinking he would assist her up to the wagon seat. Instead, he turned on her, his temper checked but obvious.

"What sort of game are you playing, Miss Abbott?"

She motioned with her head, then led him away from the children, stopping near the team of horses. "I don't know what you mean, sir."

"Yes, you do. I made it clear in my first letter that I was not interested in marrying a widow with children. Surely you must have understood that I meant any woman with children, even those who aren't her own. Why else would you fail to mention that you were the guardian of three orphans?"

She drew back from him. "That is untrue."

"Untrue?" He whipped off his hat and raked his fingers

through his hair, a gesture of frustration if ever she'd seen one. "Are you calling me a liar?"

"No. I'm sorry. I'm simply confused. If you didn't know about the children, why did you send the money for their passage on the train and stagecoach in addition to mine?"

"I can assure you, I did not pay for them to come with you."

"But you did! I couldn't have managed the expense without the funds you sent." She opened her handbag and withdrew the letter that had been folded and unfolded countless times. "Here is your last letter. Here is where you told me when and how to travel." She pointed at the paragraph. "Right there. As plain as day."

He set his hat on his head again before taking the stationery from her and perusing the words on the page. When he looked up, the anger was still in his eyes, but it didn't feel as personal. She saw him draw a long, deep breath. "Miss Abbott, it seems you and I have been the object of some sort of hoax. This letter isn't in my hand."

"What do you mean?"

"I didn't write it."

"But . . . we exchanged photographs. You asked me to marry you."

"Yes." He shook his head. "I wrote several letters to you. I sent you my photograph. I did offer marriage, and I did send money for your fare. But I didn't say I wanted you to bring children with you. That wasn't part of my offer."

Luvena felt her knees go weak and her head go light, and before she could will either sensation to go away, she crumpled forward.

CHAPTER TWO

CLAY CAUGHT LUVENA BEFORE SHE COULD FALL AGAINST the nearest horse and spook the team. Limp as an empty gunny sack, she was. He'd experienced many things in his life, but he'd never seen a woman faint like that before. What could he do but sweep her feet off the ground and carry her to the back of the wagon?

"What'd you do to her?" the boy demanded when Clay put her down.

"I didn't do anything. She fainted."

The older girl—Merry, was it?—moved over to cradle her aunt's head in her lap. "Aunt Vena? Wake up." She lifted her eyes to Clay. "Do you have any smelling salts?"

"Sorry. I don't make it a practice to carry salts with me." He was certain the girl missed the sarcasm in his voice.

Luvena moaned softly. After another moment, her eyes fluttered open. "Oh dear," she whispered.

Merry helped her aunt sit up.

"I do apologize, Mr. Birch," Luvena said. "I am overtired. That's all. I'm not given to fainting spells, I promise you. I'm quite healthy and strong."

He nodded, although he didn't really care if she was given to fainting spells or not. What he wanted now was to be rid of her and those children. He needed to return to his own town and his own work and forget he'd ever heard of Luvena Abbott or the *Hitching Post*. "Maybe we'd better figure out what we're gonna do next."

Her eyes widened. "Aren't we going to Grand Coeur?"

"Miss Abbott, don't you think—"

"Mr. Birch, I have only a few dollars left to my name. We have no place to go even if I had money for the fare. What few belongings were left to us—that aren't in those bags you carried across the street—are being shipped to Grand Coeur. We came to this territory because I was promised a husband and a home for my nieces and nephew. I don't know why anyone would change your letters to me and presumably my letters to you, but whatever the reason, it wasn't my fault. I did not lie to you. I give you my word. And it seems we"—she motioned toward the children—"are all at your mercy."

Clay was trapped. By her words. By the fear in her eyes—not to mention by his own limited funds. He didn't have the money to send her back east, let alone all four of them. And she had come to him in good faith. There was that too.

Faith . . .

He'd been so convinced this idea—finding and taking a wife—had come to him as a result of prayer. He'd imagined it clearly, a marriage between two people who wanted to be a force for good in a raw land. But children? No. Children weren't part of his future. He wasn't cut out to be some kid's father or stepfather or even an uncle by marriage. He wouldn't wish that on anybody.

But if he got his hands on whoever at the *Hitching Post* was responsible for this fiasco, he would wring their neck. He would make them regret the day they were born. He would—

Reining in his anger a second time, he took a step back from the tail of the wagon and cleared his throat. "I guess we'd best be on our way. We'll figure something out later on. Nothing we can do about it now."

"Thank you, Mr. Birch."

"Do you feel well enough to sit on the wagon seat with me? You'll be more comfortable there than in the back. The road to Grand Coeur is kind of rough."

"Yes, thank you."

He helped her sit up. Then he placed his hands on her waist—he was right; he could span it with his hands—and lifted her to the ground. The blush he'd seen earlier returned.

When he'd sent for Luvena Abbot, he'd thought he knew all he needed to know about her—young, healthy, strong, never married, and some experience with the operation of an opera house. Now it seemed neither one knew what had been truth and what had been fiction in the letters each received. Not that discovering truth from fiction would make him willing to marry her. She still had those three kids, and kids still weren't part of his carefully made plans for the future.

❦

What am I to do? What will become of us? However shall I take care of these children if I don't have a husband?

The wagon left Boise behind them, and only after the capital city was out of sight did Luvena realize she hadn't noticed anything about it. Except for the sign that had read Wells, Fargo. She remembered it because she had seen it above Clay Birch's head.

The silence—and her uncertainty—began to press in on her. "There *is* an opera house, isn't there, Mr. Birch?"

"Yeah, there's an opera house. Guess whoever tampered with our letters didn't leave out that bit of information."

"Would you tell me about it?"

"Not much to tell. Yet." He glanced at her, then added, "It's still undergoing renovations." Clay looked straight ahead and slapped the reins against the horses' rumps, asking more speed from the team as they began the ascent up a winding mountain road. "Maybe we should just start at the beginning, like there never were any letters."

"That would be helpful."

"I was born and raised in Illinois. The only child of Tom and Clarissa Birch. My father . . . died when I was six and my mother married John Thompson not long after. I've got four younger half brothers. I fought for the Union during the war. I was in one of the first battles and one of the last. The brother closest to me in age, Jacob, joined up before he turned eighteen. He was killed in 'sixty-four."

Luvena knew what that felt like, losing a beloved sibling, although her sister had died in a much different way. "I'm sorry."

"I wasn't interested in going back to work for my stepfather. He owns a couple of stores in the town where I grew up. So I struck out on my own. Went to California first, then slowly moved north. Worked in a number of mining camps along the way. Finally wound up in Grand Coeur, still thinking I might strike it rich someday. But eventually I learned, as most do, that that's a fool's dream for all but a very few. Who knows where I would have gone next if I hadn't won the old theater in a lucky hand of poker."

"Do you gamble frequently, Mr. Birch?"

He laughed, no doubt at the shock revealed in her question. "Not hardly, Miss Abbott. Not at all anymore."

Could she believe him? Could she believe anything he said?

"The truth is I won that place by blind luck or divine providence. Not by any skill on my part. And when it came into my hands, all I wanted to do was sell it, take the money, and move on. But then an upright man of God helped me see a truth that changed my life." His voice softened, as did his expression. "I got religion, as some folks call it. The truth of the Bible became real to me. Jesus too. Time was, getting rich was the most important thing to me, but now I'm hoping to do something good for others."

Luvena's breathing eased a bit. Only a good man would want to do good for others.

"I got the idea to turn the old theater into an opera house where fine actors and singers could come to perform." He clucked to the horses. "I don't pretend that it will change the world, but it might change Grand Coeur a little at a time. Sometimes just giving folks a glimpse of something beautiful can make all the difference in their lives." He was silent for several moments before he added, "I realized soon enough that I needed someone who was willing to work beside me to make the opera house a success."

"A partner?"

"A wife." He looked at her again. "It made sense to me at the time."

"There was no woman in Grand Coeur who interested you?"

"I didn't want to marry just any woman, Miss Abbott. Unmarried women of quality and virtue are in short supply in towns like Grand Coeur, and I didn't have the time to try to find and court someone in Boise City. So I decided to advertise for a wife. I've known a few men who found wives from the East through advertisements, and they seemed happy with how things turned out."

"And out of the responses you received to your advertisement, you chose me."

"Yes."

Perhaps he would change his mind if given enough time.

Perhaps he would remember the reasons why he'd chosen her and—

"Miss Abbott, Grand Coeur's no place to raise children."

❀

Luvena Abbott seemed to be everything Clay had asked for in a bride—and many things he hadn't dared hope for. Without question she was beautiful. But she also was genteel, educated, well mannered, well spoken. He suspected she was stronger than she looked, her fainting spell notwithstanding, and she believed in taking responsibility for her family. An admirable quality, he begrudgingly admitted.

He jerked his head toward the bed of the wagon and lowered his voice. "What happened to their parents?"

Sadness flitted across her face. "It was an accident at sea. My sister and brother-in-law were sailing with friends when a violent storm caught them by surprise. The boat capsized. Their friends managed to hang on until they could be rescued, but Loretta and Oliver drowned."

"Leaving you the only one to raise their children."

"Yes."

"But without the means to do so."

Softly, "Yes."

There was something about Luvena that spoke of refinement and money. Perhaps it was the way she carried herself or the proud tilt of her chin or a certain tone in her voice. Whatever it was, something didn't add up. Why didn't she have the means to care for them?

As if she'd read his mind, she said, "I was raised in Boston and my family spent summers in Newport. Both of our homes were built by my paternal grandfather when he was not much older than I am now. I suppose the Abbotts were quite rich, although it certainly wasn't something young ladies of good society were supposed to discuss or even think about. Then my father"—she looked into the distance—"lost his business and all of our money. He lost all of my brother-in-law's money as well. Father did not deal well with the shame of it all. He used a pistol to take his life." She paused again, clearly trying to control her emotions.

Clay held his breath.

"Mother and Loretta and I became outcasts among most of our friends after that, though there were a few who were kind to us." She drew in a deep breath and let it out. "When Mother learned we were to lose both of our homes, she took to her bed. She died of the shame, I think. In some ways, it was almost like what my father did . . . only slower. After the funeral, I went to live with my sister and brother-in-law."

Clay wasn't sure what to say—and so he said nothing.

Luvena looked at him again. "I couldn't support my nieces and nephew, Mr. Birch. I received an education but not for anything so practical as a means to make a living. Marrying was my only real option. I was raised for it. But no man of good society was going to ask for my hand in marriage. It seemed that everyone up and down the Eastern Seaboard knew of my family's disgrace. Then I saw a copy of the *Hitching Post*." A tremulous smile curved her mouth. "I decided to answer an advertisement. As it turned out, *your* advertisement. I needed to take the children away from the gossip as well as provide them with a place to live. They'd lost too much already to remain where they were as outcasts. Your letters . . . your photograph . . . your opera house . . . you were the answer to my prayers." Tears welled in her eyes, and this time she couldn't keep them from falling.

The answer to her prayers. The words hit him like a fist to his gut. Not to mention the way her crying made him feel. Like a snake.

What did I get myself into?

One thing for certain. He was going to write to the publisher of that catalogue and demand his money back. And while he was at it, he was going to give whoever interfered with their letters a piece of his mind.

CHAPTER THREE

GRAND COEUR WAS NOT THE SORT OF PLACE LUVENA had imagined. She hadn't expected a smaller Boston, but this was so . . . so much less. It was a frontier town, rough-hewn and dirty. She'd expected small. She hadn't anticipated . . . *this*. Why would anyone want an opera house here?

She lost count of the number of saloons they passed on their way from one end of town to the other. And in all that way, she didn't see a single female on the boardwalks. Worse yet, most of the men she saw were unwashed and unshaven, many undoubtedly crawling with vermin.

"Whoa, there." Clay drew in on the reins, stopping the team. Then he looked over at her. "Well, we're here."

Weary, hungry, despondent, Luvena turned to see his home. The place she'd expected to be her home as well. But what she saw was a three-storied building made of red brick. The only brick building she'd seen on Main Street.

"Is this the opera house?" she asked, already knowing it must be.

"Yes. Want to see the inside?"

She was too tired to care, but she nodded.

Clay hopped to the ground and turned to help her descend more gracefully.

"Children." She looked at them. "Come with us."

"I'm hungry, Aunt Vena," Ethan said.

"I know. We'll get something to eat soon." She hoped she spoke the truth. They were dependent upon Clay Birch's charity at this point.

Clay frowned. "Maybe we'd better have supper and get the kids settled for the night. I can show you the opera house tomorrow."

"Thank you." Relief flooded through her. "That might be for the best."

Clay tied the team to a hitching post, and the five of them walked two blocks to Polly's Restaurant. They discovered only a couple of tables were empty when they went inside. They moved to the larger one farthest from the entrance.

Clay held out a chair for Luvena. "The food here's plain but good. Restaurant's been around almost from the start, although this is their second building. First one burned down in a fire years ago." He sat in the chair next to her. "That's why the owner of the Grand Theater built it from brick. Costly, but less likely to be destroyed in a fire."

The Grand Theater? More than a little pretentious. But

perhaps no more so than Clay's intentions to start an opera house in this little backwater town.

A waitress arrived. At least Luvena knew that there was one other female in Grand Coeur besides her and her nieces.

Clay ordered the first choice on the menu for all of them—boiled ham, cheese, carrots, corn bread, and mince pie. They waited in silence for the food to arrive.

Luvena was almost too weary to look at her surroundings and, when she did, became uncomfortable from the stares of men at other tables. "Why are they all looking at me like that?" she whispered to Clay.

"I reckon because they haven't seen a woman as beautiful as you in a month of Sundays." He winked, then smiled. "If ever."

It was strange, the way his comment made her feel. Although some had called her "pretty enough" in years past, she'd come to believe her eyes were too far apart, her brows too arched, her mouth too wide, her lips too full, and her teeth too large for anyone to consider her beautiful. Those flaws in her features might have been overlooked if there wasn't a scandal attached to the Abbott name or if the family still had their wealth. But with the scandal and without the Abbott fortune, being "pretty enough" wasn't enough. She'd become completely unattractive to the men of her acquaintance, and she'd grown used to thinking of herself as unattractive too.

But Clay Birch thought her beautiful, and something warm blossomed inside her heart because of his words.

Clay wasn't sure what just happened. It was as if the earth shifted beneath his chair. His pulse quickened. His mouth went dry. Voices in the restaurant receded to a dull hum in his ears. And he felt an almost irresistible urge to kiss Luvena Abbott, if only to discover if she tasted as sweet as she looked.

Heaven help him!

Apparently God was listening, for their supper arrived at that moment. As plates were set before them, Clay's world righted itself again. Conversations throughout the room returned to their normal level.

Luvena and her wards looked at him expectantly, but it took a moment to realize they were waiting for him to bless the food. Living alone, he was used to saying a quick, silent prayer before eating. It seemed that was a habit that must change if he was to marry her.

If he was to marry. Where had that "if" come from? Everything had changed when she'd arrived with children. He didn't intend to marry her now. He couldn't. It wouldn't be prudent. It wouldn't be fair to them or good for him. Only, how was he to be rid of them? That was the most pressing question in his mind.

He closed his eyes and gave thanks for the food. Then he focused his attention on his plate, making certain not to invite any further conversation around the table. Even the youngest girl—Elsie?—seemed to understand. Few words were exchanged throughout the meal. Perhaps they were all too tired or perhaps his mood warned them to be silent. He didn't much care the reason as long as they kept quiet.

When everyone was finished eating, Clay paid for the meal and escorted the little group back toward the opera house. The sun had fallen behind the mountaintops in the west. Long shadows darkened the town. Prospectors were already filling up the saloons. This was what he hadn't wanted his bride to see. Not yet. He'd hoped to bring her to town, get her settled in for the night, give them time to get better acquainted, and help her understand what he wanted to accomplish in Grand Coeur.

But what did any of that matter now? Luvena needn't know or understand. They wouldn't be married. She wouldn't be staying. Not any longer than it took him to figure out what to do with her and those children.

CHAPTER FOUR

WHEN LUVENA AWAKENED THE NEXT MORNING, SUN-light spilled through the window of the small bedroom. Next to her in the bed, Merry and Elsie slept soundly, the older girl cuddled up to the younger. But sounds from the front of the house told her she was not the first one to rise. She sat up and looked at the floor. Buried beneath a couple of blankets, Ethan slumbered on. Which meant it must be Clay Birch who was rattling pots and pans beyond the bedroom door.

Nerves fluttered in her stomach.

Clay had slept in his office at the theater. Or at least that was where he'd said he was going when he left her and the children in the house the previous night. But now he'd returned, and if her nose was correct, he was preparing breakfast.

She rose from the bed and slipped her arms into a dressing gown before smoothing the wild appearance of her hair with a brush. One more glance at the children told her even hunger wasn't likely to wake them for another hour or so. She would let them sleep.

When Luvena stepped into the kitchen doorway, Clay had his back to her as he turned sausage in a hot skillet. The meat sizzled and hissed.

"Can I help, Mr. Birch?"

He looked over his shoulder. "No need. I'm used to fending for myself." He motioned with his head toward the table. "Sit yourself down. This won't take much longer."

She moved to comply.

"Want coffee?"

"Yes, please." She covered her mouth as she yawned.

"This will help." He set a large mug of coffee on the table, along with a sugar bowl. "No milk or cream. Sorry."

"That's all right." Cream and sugar were luxuries she'd learned to do without.

Clay turned back to the stove, and a short while later he set a plate of eggs and sausage before her. Then he sat opposite her with a plate of his own. After a quick blessing, he picked up his fork and began to eat.

How did you sleep? What are you thinking about us? How much longer before our belongings arrive? The questions tumbled in her mind. *Where do you mean to send us if we can't stay? Whatever shall we do to survive? No family. No friends. No money. No skills.* She played with the food on her plate, worry stealing her appetite.

Clay's voice intruded on her thoughts. "Would you like to see the opera house?"

"Yes," she answered, surprised by her quick agreement.

"We'll go as soon as you're dressed."

His words made her feel strangely exposed, even though she knew she wasn't. She fingered the top button of her dressing gown at the base of her throat.

"But you better eat some of that breakfast first, Miss Abbott. Can't afford to waste it. And besides, I'm pretty sure a good wind could blow you away."

She obeyed. After all, her future and the future of her nieces and nephew lay in this man's hands.

Before Clay could take Luvena to the old theater, the children woke up and were hungry. The eldest girl, Merry, offered to help him with the second round of breakfast preparations, but as he'd done with her aunt, he told her it was easier to do it himself.

When the children were all seated at the table and eating the food that Clay had prepared, Luvena told Merry to keep an eye on her younger siblings. "Mr. Birch and I won't be long. We shall be right next door at the theater if you need me."

Despite his first negative impression of the Browne children when they'd exited the stagecoach yesterday, Clay had to admit they were well behaved most of the time.

He and Luvena went out the back door of the small house and made their way to the rear entrance of the brick building next door. The sounds of saws and hammers met their ears.

"Come this way," he said.

They climbed the back staircase to the third floor of the theater. The hallway was dark, but it was only a short distance to the door that opened into the balcony of the theater; there was plenty of light there. Below them lay the stage apron and, off to the far side, an area for a small orchestra. Before them were the rows of wooden balcony seats.

Clay stopped and grasped the handrail as he looked down. "The Grand Theater was a hurdy-gurdy house."

"What kind of house?"

"Hurdy-gurdy. A dance hall."

"Oh."

"The place made money, but the owner wasn't the best of businessmen. Or so I was told. He wasn't choosy about what sort of acts appeared on the stage. A two-headed calf or a great thespian were all the same to him. He invested nothing back into the theater. Eventually he let it fall into disrepair. Then I won it in a game of poker, like I told you." He looked down at the workers below who were laying new boards on the stage. "I don't suppose anyone would consider me a refined or cultured man, Miss Abbott, but I've seen how people can be transformed by performances of great artists. The audience may think they're just being entertained for a few hours, but it can be so much more than that. It can make them long for something better. It can make a man long to *be* something better. When I was in Washington, D.C., during the war, I saw a performance of *The Barber of Seville*." He shook his head slowly. "I didn't understand a word they sang, of course, but that didn't matter. The music moved me, and I laughed in the comic parts along with the rest of the audience. I felt happy for that one evening, even in the midst of civil war."

"You surprise me, Mr. Birch."

"Yeah. I imagine I do." He looked at her. "I bet you've attended many operas in your life."

She nodded.

"And plays by Shakespeare?"

She nodded again, this time with a small smile bowing her lips. Her invitingly kissable lips.

He cleared his throat as he looked away once more. "I suppose what I want to do here seems silly to someone like you."

"No, it doesn't. It doesn't seem silly at all." Her smile broadened. "I admire you for what you want to accomplish, Mr. Birch. Music stirs my heart too."

At least that part of their letter exchange had been true.

⁂

Luvena had no trouble envisioning what Clay wanted to do in this town and in this building. She found his enthusiasm contagious. Yes, the theater was small and modest in comparison with some of the great concert halls and opulent theaters she'd visited before her father's death. Still, she believed he could accomplish something amazing in this place, even with limited funds.

An hour after they first entered through the back door of the theater, they exited through the front door into the golden sunlight of midmorning. Main Street appeared busy today. People—including more women—were out shopping and conducting business. A couple of men on horseback rode toward them in the middle of the street. Both of them grinned and tipped their hats in her direction before they turned the corner. At which point, both riders looked over their shoulders, straight at her.

Mercy. She wished the men in this place wouldn't stare like that.

"They haven't seen a woman as beautiful as you in a month of Sundays," Clay's voice echoed in her memory. *"If ever."*

She felt the warmth of a blush rise in her cheeks. Oh, how she hoped Clay Birch couldn't tell what she thought.

"Maybe we should—" He broke off suddenly, then said, "Here comes Reverend Adair. Guess he wants to be one of the first in town to welcome you."

Luvena hoped against hope that she looked composed as she turned to face the reverend. She'd known Clay less than twenty-four hours, but he'd said enough for her to know he held this minister in high regard.

Delaney Adair was a distinguished-looking gentleman. Perhaps in his mid- to late fifties, his hair was pure white, including his close-trimmed beard. He smiled broadly, and she had the distinct impression that he did so often.

"Clay, I was on my way to your house." Reverend Adair stopped on the boardwalk before them. "And this must be your Miss Abbott. Welcome, my dear, to Grand Coeur. I'm Reverend Adair."

"Thank you, Reverend. It's a pleasure to meet you."

He took her hand in his, smiling all the while. "Your photograph did not do you justice."

Clay said, "I just finished giving Miss Abbott a tour of the theater."

"Exciting, isn't it?" Reverend Adair looked back and forth between the two of them. "I'm sure you'll help Clay find the best performers for the opera house's grand opening."

"Of course, if I can be of help to Mr. Birch, I'd be delighted."

The reverend continued, "Now to the purpose of my call. I don't like to perform a wedding ceremony without having a talk with the couple first. Would you come to my office tomorrow? The two of you. Shall we say nine o'clock?"

Luvena expected Clay to tell the minister there wouldn't be a wedding, that he didn't want to marry her. But that wasn't what he said.

"All right, Reverend. We'll be at your office at nine in the morning."

She managed not to gape as she looked at Clay, but she felt certain her surprise still showed on her face.

"Good. Good." Reverend Adair squeezed Luvena's fingers again, then gave Clay a hearty handshake before turning and walking away.

Meeting her questioning gaze, Clay shrugged. "Tomorrow will be soon enough to tell him what's happened."

Luvena supposed he was right. And she had other, more important things to worry about. Like how would she feed, clothe, and shelter her nieces and nephew in this town on the edge of the civilized world?

CHAPTER FIVE

LATER THAT MORNING CLAY RETURNED TO THE theater. Alone this time. He talked with the men remodeling the stage before going into his office on the main floor in the back. For the next few hours, he read through mail and answered correspondence and studied his accounts. The latter made his eyes begin to blur after staring at them too long. He leaned back in his chair and rubbed his eyes with the pads of his fingers.

Maybe I was crazy to think I could do this.

He'd borrowed money to pay for the improvements he was making to the theater, using the building and the house next door for collateral. If he didn't make a success of things, he could lose it all in a heartbeat. If the workmen didn't finish on time. If materials cost more than he'd estimated. If he didn't manage to bring in the right performers. If the audiences stayed away.

So many ifs. Too many ifs.

And then there was Luvena Abbott. What was he going to do about her? And about those kids who were with her?

He groaned in frustration. If he'd never decided he wanted a wife—a proper wife—to help turn him into a successful businessman, he wouldn't be in this predicament now. Why had he thought he needed to marry? He'd managed well enough up to now. Alone. What made him think—

You were tired of being alone. That's why you wanted a wife.

There it was. That was the truth he'd tried not to admit to himself. But there it was. He'd finally let it in. Yes, he was tired of being alone. In the years since the war ended, he'd bounced around the West from camp to camp, from town to town. Just him and his horse. If this theater hadn't fallen into his hands because of that card game, he wouldn't still be in Grand Coeur. He would have moved on. Looking for something. Looking for peace and contentment and a bit of happiness. Alone. Always alone.

But because of the good reverend, Clay had discovered he was never truly alone—the Lord was always with him—and yet the longing for someone to share his life's journey was still there. The Bible said it hadn't been good for Adam to be alone and so God had made a helpmeet for him. Clay figured that meant the Lord cared enough to make a helpmeet for him too. But nothing in the Bible told him when he might meet her or how he might find her.

"Maybe this wasn't the right time for it, and even if it was, Luvena sure isn't the right woman."

A floorboard squeaked and then a young voice said, "Who're you talking to?"

Clay glanced up. Peeking around the edge of the doorway was Ethan Browne. Clay ignored the boy's question, asking his own instead. "What are you doing in the theater?"

"Just looking."

"You shouldn't be in here. Go back to the house."

"Aunt Vena said I was in her way." Ethan stepped into the small office.

Suspicion loomed. "Did she send you over to find me?"

"No." The boy shrugged. "I just wanted to see the theater. Aunt Vena said it was nice."

"Well, you've seen enough. Now go back to the house. Your aunt will wonder where you are."

"Aunt Vena's cleaning. She won't miss me. Like I said, I was in her way."

"Cleaning?" He hadn't asked her to do that. Of course, if they'd married, it would have been her place to do so, but as things stood between them, it felt wrong.

Ethan sniffed the air. "I like the way it smells in here. What makes it smell so good?"

"Fresh lumber. The carpenters are replacing the boards on the stage."

"Can I go see what they're doing?"

"No." Clay stood. "I'm taking you back to the house."

Ethan mumbled a complaint, but he turned and led the way out of Clay's office.

They entered the house through the back door. While

Ethan hurried on through to the parlor, Clay came to a sudden stop when he saw Luvena on her knees, scrubbing the brick floor of the kitchen—the same type of brick used on the exterior of the theater. Her hair was hidden beneath a large kerchief wrapped around her head, and the hem of her dress was tucked into the waistband of an apron, leaving most of her white petticoats in view.

"Miss Abbott," Clay said—and waited for her to blush.

She obliged as she scrambled to her feet, pulling her skirt free to cover her petticoats once again.

He liked what that added color did to her appearance, and it took great effort to keep from smiling. "You've had an exhausting journey from Massachusetts. Shouldn't you rest for at least one day?"

"I needed something to do, and the house needed a good cleaning."

Luvena Abbott was a lady, through and through. She hadn't been taught how to scrub floors as a girl. He'd bet his life on it.

"You don't mind, do you?" she asked, brows raised.

"No. I don't mind." He let his gaze roam. She'd done more than scrub the kitchen floor while he was over at the theater. "You've been busy this afternoon."

Amusement curved the corners of her mouth. "Idle hands are the devil's playground." As quickly as it had come, the smile disappeared. "Mr. Birch, we must talk about . . . about what we are going to do. The children and I cannot continue to stay in your home since there is to be no wedding. And I must find some way to provide for them. I do not want and cannot accept your charity any longer than necessary."

He believed her. There was pride in her eyes. Not the kind of pride that said a person thought they were better than others. No, hers was the pride of someone who believed what the Bible said—if any would not work, neither should he eat. She didn't want life handed to her on a platter. She didn't want her hands to be idle.

His admiration for her increased with that understanding, but admiration didn't change the fact that he couldn't be a parent to those children. For their sake, if not his own.

So what's the answer?

❀

Luvena waited for Clay Birch to respond. She'd learned that he wasn't quick to speak. At least not most of the time. She liked that about him. He was thoughtful. He weighed and considered his words. Even in his anger yesterday, when he believed she'd lied to him in her letters, he hadn't been cruel with his words. Or in any other way. He could have left them in Boise City to fend for themselves. He could have been indifferent to her financial circumstances. But instead, he'd shown compassion. She believed him to be good and honest and upright. All attributes she'd hoped for in a husband.

If things were different, if we'd met under other circumstances, perhaps— She cut off the thought. It served no purpose to wish for things that might have been.

"Maybe we should take a walk, Miss Abbott, so we won't be interrupted."

She knew what he meant: *So the children won't hear what I'm going to say.*

He continued, "I can show you more of the town, and we can stop at the mercantile to get supplies for our supper."

Hearing the kindness in his voice caused tears to well in Luvena's eyes. She quickly looked away, hoping he hadn't seen them. "I'll tidy up first. It won't take me long." She hurried into the bedroom and closed the door.

There was no dressing table, this being a bachelor's room. The only mirror was a small oval above the washbasin on a corner table. Not large enough to see her full head and hair, let alone her entire body. She would have to make herself presentable without the aid of a mirror. At least she could be thankful she was no longer freshening up in the tiny lavatory of a train's passenger car that rocked from side to side.

With her face washed, her hair smoothed and controlled with hairpins, and her apron removed, Luvena said a quick prayer for wisdom, then opened the bedroom door. Clay sat on a straight-backed chair in the corner of the parlor . . . with Elsie on his knee. They were looking at an open book in the young girl's hands.

The sight of the two of them caused the breath to catch in Luvena's chest. Yesterday she'd assumed Clay Birch didn't *want* children because he didn't *like* them. Or at least didn't like other men's children. But that couldn't be true. *Look at him.* No, this was not a man who disliked children.

Somehow Luvena found her voice. "I'm ready, Mr. Birch."

He looked up. "So am I." He leaned forward so he could meet Elsie's gaze. "Thanks for sharing your book with me."

"You're welcome, Mr. Birch."

Luvena hadn't seen Elsie look this happy in many weeks. She decided right then, whatever else she had to face, she would be grateful to Clay Birch for that.

He moved the girl off his knee and stood. "Okay, let's go."

Luvena looked at Merry.

The girl grimaced, sighed, and nodded in quick succession. "I know. I know. Look after them while you're gone." Apparently Mr. Birch's charm had failed to affect the older sister as easily as it had the younger.

The thought made Luvena smile.

Clay grabbed a burlap sack from the floor near the door, and the two of them left the house. They followed Adams Street past the opera house and turned right onto Main Street. As they walked, Clay shared more about Grand Coeur than he had the previous evening. Luvena learned not only the street names but the names of the sheriff, the town doctor, the publisher of the tri-weekly newspaper, and the banker. She learned that the Presbyterian church—she could see it up on the hillside—had been the first and only church in Grand Coeur for several years, but now there were also a Catholic church and a Lutheran church.

Three churches, but more than ten saloons.

Several blocks later, when they turned right again—this

time on Jefferson Street—Clay pointed out a dressmaker's shop. "Reverend Adair's daughter, Shannon, told me once that Mrs. Treehorn is the finest dressmaker in the territory." He laughed. "Although what she thought a bachelor would do with the information, I have no idea."

Luvena liked his laugh. "Perhaps she meant it for your future wife." *Perhaps she meant it for me.*

"I would believe that, only she told me before I'd given any thought to marriage." His grin broadened, as if he'd remembered something more. "You'll like Shannon when you meet her. She's quite the lady."

Luvena's lighthearted feeling fled, replaced by something not as sweet. Jealousy? But that made no sense. She had no right to feel jealous of anyone, especially not when it came to Mr. Birch.

They walked on, and Clay pointed out the area south of Grand Coeur known as Chinatown. "There's been trouble here in the past, although not as much lately. Some miners don't think the Chinamen have a right to be here or to mine their own claims. The truth is, many of the Chinese are more successful because they aren't afraid of hard work and long days. And most don't waste what gold they find on liquor or women in the saloons."

Another turn to the right, now onto Lewis Street, brought their destination into view. After what Clay had just told her, she was surprised when she saw the name of the store—Wu Lok's Mercantile.

As if Luvena had expressed her surprise aloud, Clay said,

"Wu Lok's got the best prices and the best selection in Grand Coeur. Everybody knows he's fair and honest. Even folks who think the Chinese should be sent packing shop in this store to save money." He pulled open the door. "Come on. I'll introduce you."

Inside the mercantile, Clay introduced Luvena to Wu Lok and to several customers as well. With each introduction, there was a moment of awkwardness. He could tell people expected him to say that she was his intended or to announce their wedding date. Luvena must have felt the awkwardness too, for as soon as their shopping was done and they stepped outside, she broached the subject they'd avoided throughout their walk.

"There won't be much opportunity for a woman like me to find employment here in Grand Coeur. Will there?"

"No."

"I'm not an accomplished seamstress like Mrs. Treehorn, and I'm not trained as a teacher. Whatever else is there for me to do?" Fear laced her words. Fear, but also determination.

But of course. Wasn't it obvious? He should have thought of it before. "For now, you can work for me."

"For you?"

"Yes, you can help me manage the opera house. With your experience, it'll be the perfect fit."

She shook her head slowly. "To what experience do you refer?"

That was when he knew. The mysterious letter writer at the *Hitching Post* had struck again. "You never worked in an opera house, did you?"

"No. Whatever made you think—" She broke off as understanding dawned on her too.

"What do you know about opera, Miss Abbott?"

"I received vocal training as a young woman. Before the death of my parents."

"Did you ever perform on the stage?"

One of those small smiles that he was learning to anticipate played across her mouth. "Not really. I sang in church on occasion, and I was in a local production when I was fourteen. My vocal instructor said I had perfect pitch, and that if I'd been born to another family, I might have had a career singing. I don't know if that is true or not, but I believed it for a while. I hoped for it for a time. But, of course, such a thing would not have met with my parents' approval, even if . . . things had turned out differently."

She'd wanted to be an opera singer but her family wouldn't have approved. Why did that bit of information tug at his chest?

Luvena forged on. "Mr. Birch, my family were patrons of the arts before our money was lost. I have seen numerous operas and plays performed in Boston and Newport and New York. Even in London. I believe I may still be of help to you." She paused to draw a breath. "If you'll allow me."

What choice did he have? What choice did either of them have? She had no money at all and what funds he had were tied up in the Grand Coeur Opera House. It seemed, even without marriage, that their futures—at least their immediate ones—were tied together.

He would have to get used to sleeping in his office.

CHAPTER SIX

WHEN LUVENA PUT THE TWO YOUNGER CHILDREN TO bed, life didn't seem as hopeless as it had seemed that morning. She would work for Clay Birch, helping him with the opening and running of the opera house, and in addition to the modest salary she would receive, she and the children would have a place to live and food to eat. Plus, he'd promised her a bonus if the theater made a profit at the end of three months.

It wasn't a great deal of money, but it should be enough so she and the children could leave Grand Coeur and settle someplace where there were more employment opportunities. Or perhaps more marriage opportunities. After all, the scandal that had stained her name in the East was rather meaningless here in the West. Or so she hoped.

After kissing Ethan and Elsie good night, she left the bedroom. She found Merry still seated in the rocking chair, mending a tear in the skirt of her favorite gown.

At fourteen, Luvena had been—and still was—rather hopeless with a needle and thread. But then, she'd had a lady's maid seeing to her every need until her father's misfortunes. Merry had been much younger when financial loss and scandal struck, robbing her of such luxuries.

"Do you have enough light?" Luvena asked as she moved closer to the rocking chair.

Merry glanced toward the nearby lamp. "Yes, Aunt Vena. I can see."

"What a fine job you're doing. No one will ever know the fabric was torn."

"I'm not sure how much longer I'll be able to wear it. There's no more fabric to be let out." Pink tinged her cheeks.

Luvena understood why. Although Merry most likely had her full height, she was still developing a woman's figure. The bodices of her clothes had grown snug in recent months.

Luvena settled onto the sofa. "Mr. Birch pointed out a dress shop when we went to the mercantile this afternoon. Perhaps Mrs. Treehorn, the proprietress, could help us remake a few of your dresses."

"It would cost too much."

"Perhaps not. It wouldn't hurt to ask."

Merry's eyes widened as she sat straighter in the chair. "Maybe I could do some piecework for the dressmaker. Surely I could make a little money that way."

"I can't ask you—"

"Yes, you can, Aunt Vena. I'm old enough to help provide something. I know sometimes I don't act like it, but I am."

"What about school?"

"Is there one?"

Luvena had no answer to that. Clay hadn't pointed out a schoolhouse during their walk, and she hadn't thought to ask him. She'd simply assumed there was one for the children to attend. Oh dear. How would she manage if not? She was even less suited for teaching than she was for sewing.

"Aunt Vena?"

"Yes, Merry."

"We're going to be all right. God's watching out for us, like you always tell us. He wasn't surprised about those letters the way you and Mr. Birch were. He knew about it all the time and brought us here anyway. It must be part of His plan."

Tension drained from Luvena's shoulders. "How very wise you've become, Esmeralda Browne."

Merry smiled.

"I believe I'll go sit on the back stoop and enjoy the cool night air." Luvena stood. "Would you like to join me?"

As if in answer, Merry yawned. Then she chuckled. "No, thank you. I think I'll go to bed and finish mending this dress tomorrow."

Luvena stepped over to the rocking chair and placed a kiss on the crown of her niece's head. "Sleep well, Merry."

"You too, Aunt Vena." The girl yawned again.

Luvena left the parlor, passing through the kitchen on her way to the back door. She took pleasure in the tidiness of the room. Much had been accomplished today, despite the upheaval of emotions and weariness from many days of travel.

Tomorrow would bring new challenges, no doubt, but for now, she felt an unexpected peace.

❦

Clay was standing in the dark behind the theater—wrestling with the present, fighting with the future, trying to find a way past the dilemma he found himself in—when he saw the back door of the house open and Luvena Abbott step onto the small back porch, light spilling around her from the kitchen. Then the door closed and night enveloped her again. Without the glow of the moon, he couldn't see any other movement, but he guessed she remained on the stoop.

"Father"—her words drifted to him on a soft breeze—"I thank You for all You are doing, for all You have done. In my life. In the lives of Merry and Ethan and Elsie. Help me know what we are to do next."

He supposed his thoughts—the wrestling, fighting, and answer-seeking—had been a kind of prayer, but her simple words were far better. They were a more faith-filled prayer, revealing an uncomplicated trust. Something he hadn't mastered. It drew him across the short stretch of ground. As he came closer, a twig snapped beneath his boot, and he heard a gasp of surprise.

"It's me, Luvena."

"Mr. Birch?"

Only when she called him by his surname did he realize he'd used her given name. Had she noticed? It felt natural. Would she mind?

"May I join you?" he asked.

"Of course."

He turned and sat on the top step next to her. She moved slightly away—he assumed to give him more room—though he was sorry for it.

"It's a beautiful evening," she said.

"Autumn's in the air. It'll be too cool to sit outside soon."

"What is winter like in these mountains?"

"It can be harsh. Most years there's deep snow for several months."

"I like the snow."

Clay wished he could see her face and not just a shadowy form. He was certain she smiled. "I like it too. Except when it's piled up to the roofline and I can't get out for days at a time. Then I start to feel boxed in." He shuddered at the thought. Close spaces had troubled him since he'd been locked in a closet as a boy. He shook his head to free himself of the bad memory.

"Do you know what Merry said to me before I came outside?"

"What?"

"That God knew about the changes to the letters and brought us here anyway, so it must be what He wanted."

Now *that* was a different way to look at their current situation. He'd been so busy being angry with the turn of events in the past twenty-four hours, he hadn't considered there might be a divine hand guiding them.

Was it true?

He rubbed the back of his neck, unsure what to say. Unsure what he felt or believed.

"Mr. Birch?"

"Yes."

"I'm very grateful for the compromise you have made. Offering employment, I mean, when you weren't obligated to help us in any way. I will do everything in my power not to disappoint you."

"I believe you . . ." *Luvena.*

The desire to take her in his arms, to draw her close, to kiss those generous lips, enveloped him like a fire. If not for those kids—

He stood before he could give in to temptation. "I'm going to turn in. Good night, Miss Abbott."

"Good night."

He was almost to the back door of the theater before he thought he heard something more. Before he thought he heard her say, "Clay."

CHAPTER SEVEN

CLAY WENT ALONE ON SATURDAY MORNING TO MEET with Reverend Adair. Why subject Luvena to any embarrassment that might result from discussing their situation with the pastor? Besides, if they weren't to marry, they had no need to speak to the minister as a couple.

"Well," the reverend said when Clay had explained about the altered letters and Luvena's nieces and nephew, "this *is* an odd turn of events, is it not?"

"It is."

"And you're certain the children make the union between you and Miss Abbott impossible?"

"I am."

"I ask because my son-in-law's nephew, Todd, was nine when he came to live in Grand Coeur, and he's turned into rather a fine young man, despite his surroundings these past six years. Wouldn't you agree?"

"That's quite a different situation."

"Is it?" The reverend steepled his fingertips and touched them to his lips.

"Yes. For one thing, Matthew's job with Wells, Fargo was settled and secure from the start. He wasn't embarking on a new venture that could well end in financial ruin. He could support his wife and nephew, and he had the time to dedicate himself to raising the boy well."

"Yes, that is all true."

Clay leaned forward in his chair. "Reverend Adair, this isn't Miss Abbott's fault, but neither is it mine. I was up front about not wanting a woman with children for a wife. My new opera house is no place for young kids and, like it or not, neither is this town. And I'm sure not the right man to become a father to them. I wouldn't be good at it. I'm too much like—" He broke off abruptly.

Reverend Adair's gaze was penetrating, and Clay began to fear the minister would see the things he wasn't willing to talk about.

The older man broke the lengthening silence. "But because you're willing to employ Miss Abbott, even for the short term, you will still have the children around the theater sometimes. Won't you?"

"I suppose. But not for long. Not permanently. This is a temporary solution. As soon as other arrangements can be made, Miss Abbott and the children will leave Grand Coeur."

Reverend Adair leaned forward. "I believe there is

something you aren't telling me, Clay. Something that has nothing to do with Miss Abbott. Something that weighs heavily on you and has for a long while."

Clay tensed. "There's nothing more to tell." It was an outright lie, and he figured the reverend knew it.

"It might help to talk it through."

"No."

"Mmm. Well, it seems your mind is made up, then."

"Yes." It surprised Clay, the regret he felt.

"Would you mind if I paid Miss Abbott a call? Perhaps our church can be of some assistance to her. I might know of someone down in Boise City who could give her employment and find a suitable place for her and the children to live."

"Sure." He shrugged. "Sounds good to me."

"Then I shall do so." Reverend Adair rose. "And I shall continue to pray for you both."

Clay stood too. "Thanks. I reckon we'll need it."

"Mmm."

The two men shook hands, and Clay left the reverend's office.

He'd expected to feel relief after talking to his good friend and trusted mentor. But he didn't. Instead, he felt more unsettled than before, though he couldn't put his finger on the reason why.

"Would you mind if I paid Miss Abbott a call?"

Strange question. Why would Clay mind if the reverend called on Luvena? Especially if he could be of some help to her.

"I might know of someone down in Boise City who could

give her employment and find a suitable place for her and the
children to live."

Clay hoped—if the person the reverend had mentioned
came through with a job and house—that it wouldn't be too
soon. After all, he'd asked Luvena to help him with the opening of the opera house. He was depending on her now.

Since Clay hadn't wanted Luvena along when he met with
the minister—and she hadn't wanted to go—she decided
the morning was a good time to go exploring. She and the
children had been inactive too long. They'd been shut up in
railroad cars and stagecoaches and even this small house for
what seemed an eternity.

But it wasn't the town that Luvena wanted to see. It was
the forested hillsides that beckoned to her. And so, as soon
as the breakfast dishes were washed, dried, and put back on
the shelf, she and her young charges set off. It took a few tries
before they found the right road to follow, but soon enough
they left Grand Coeur behind them. The cool nights of
September had begun to turn the leaves on the aspens to gold.
The colors weren't dramatic yet, but they made a nice contrast
amid the green of the tall pines.

Grand Coeur, she'd learned, was close to five thousand
feet above sea level. Luvena could tell the difference between
here and where she'd lived her entire life. The air was thinner
and drier. Not better or worse. Just different.

After walking a long while, they caught sight of a stream

running through a draw far below them. Two men stood in the water. They were bent over, and each held something between his hands.

Ethan said, "I think they're panning for gold."

"I believe you're right," Luvena answered.

Their voices must have carried through the forest because both men straightened and looked up. Something about the miners' posture gave Luvena the feeling they weren't happy to be watched as they worked their claim.

"Let's go, children."

Pine needles crunched beneath their feet as they followed the trail higher and higher into the mountains. If there were more men anywhere about, Luvena didn't see them. Now it was small forest creatures who peeked at them from branches overhead and from beneath bushes down below. A chipmunk gave them a noisy scolding for intruding upon his woods. With the sun nearing its zenith, golden light battled with the shadows for dominance.

Ethan and Elsie raced each other to the crest of the trail. Luvena smiled as she watched them. They were well-behaved children. Considering all the upheaval they'd endured in their young lives, their happy natures were nothing short of miraculous.

"It's pretty, isn't it, Aunt Vena?" Merry asked, motioning to the view of the valley below.

She nodded. "Yes."

"I like it, though it's different from back home."

Back home.

For just an instant, Luvena imagined she caught the whiff of a sea breeze, tasted salt upon her tongue, saw white sails as boats skittered along the surface of the water, and heard the sound of laughter as her family played along the shore. Her family. Her beloved family. Her sister. Her father. Her mother. Missing them—and the sadness that came with it—hit her so hard she almost couldn't draw breath.

"Aunt Vena! Merry!" Ethan called. "Hurry up!"

She lifted her gaze to the top of the rise. Her nephew waved at them, and she and Merry waved back. The action caused the intense sadness to ease. She still had family. She had Merry, Ethan, and Elsie. None of them was alone. They had one another. They would be all right. They would make a new life for themselves. They would make a new home and new memories. She wouldn't allow fear to take root in her heart. She would embrace the future, whatever came.

Tossing a challenging grin at her niece, she said, "Come along, Merry. I'll race you to them."

Luvena held her skirts and ran as fast as she was able, but Merry caught up with her. They arrived at the top of the hill in a dead heat. Luvena sank to the ground at Elsie's feet, mindless of the dirt, laughing between gasps for air. The children joined in, and the sound of their laughter mingled with hers was the balm she needed to chase away the last dregs of sadness.

When Clay learned from one of his workmen that Luvena and the children had been seen walking north on Canyon Road, his first response was irritation. Hadn't he made it clear that he preferred they all stay close to the house unless he was with them? After an hour passed, irritation became anger. But when they still hadn't returned another hour beyond that, he grew worried. So he saddled his horse and rode into the mountains. Higher into the mountains. Deeper into the forest.

He heard their laughter a minute before he saw them. The happy sound spilled through the forest, bouncing off trees, making it impossible to tell which way it came from. But then his horse rounded a bend in the trail and Clay followed the path with his gaze to the top of a rise. There they were, all four of them, on the ground, the younger two rolling about.

He forgot why he'd been irritated, angry, and worried. Now all he wanted was to join them. To feel as carefree as they sounded. Clay nudged the gelding with the heels of his boots and rode toward them.

Merry was the first to see Clay. She poked her aunt's arm. Luvena's smile vanished along with her laughter as she got to her feet, followed moments later by all the children.

Drawing close, Clay reined in. "I didn't think I'd have to ride this far up to find you." He leaned a forearm on the pommel of the saddle. "You shouldn't be out here without an escort, Miss Abbott. None of you should."

"Surely we are safe in the middle of the day. There are four of us, after all."

There were stories he could have told her about mining camps throughout the West and the wicked things dangerous men were wont to do. Stories that would make the hair on the back of her neck stand on end. Maybe give her nightmares. But he didn't want to frighten her. Her or the children. Oddly enough, he wanted them to like Grand Coeur. To believe in it, the way he did, that it would one day be a good and decent place for families to put down roots.

"You're all going to be starved before we get back to town." He stepped down from the saddle. "We'd better start back."

"I'm already starved," Ethan said.

Clay grinned at the boy. "Figures."

"Come on, Elsie." Ethan headed down the hillside with an exuberance common to boys.

"Ethan," Luvena called, "don't get out of sight. You stop and wait for us." Looking at Clay, she said, "I hope he heard me."

Elsie didn't chase after her brother. Instead, she took Merry's hand and the sisters set off at a more sedate speed. The two adults followed in the rear, Clay leading his horse.

"How was your meeting with Reverend Adair?" Luvena asked after several minutes of silence.

"He was disappointed there wouldn't be a wedding. But he understood the reasons for our change of plans."

Why, he wondered, did those words feel false as they left his mouth?

Perhaps because the change of plans had been his decision and his alone. Not theirs. His. Luvena would have married him if he'd been willing. That was why she'd come to Grand Coeur.

But he wasn't willing. Nothing would change his mind. Nothing.

CHAPTER EIGHT

A FEW DAYS LATER LUVENA SAT AT THE DESK IN CLAY'S office, reading through the various letters, playbills, and advertisements he'd collected. Clay had set a date toward the end of October for the opening production of the Grand Coeur Opera House. Luvena's task was to bring in a professional opera company or a soloist who would impress the audience and make them want to continue to patronize the theater from then on.

Perhaps it was an impossible undertaking. It surely felt impossible as she looked at the papers spread before her. What did she know about hiring a troupe of seasoned performers? What had made her think she could handle this job? She was no expert. She'd attended theater and opera with her parents, and she'd taken lessons and appeared in one small production years ago. That was all. She didn't know enough. She was certain to fail.

But she had to try. She had to do her very best. Her nieces and nephew were depending on her.

Clay's depending on me too.

A pleasant shudder moved through her as she pictured him in her mind. Since Saturday, when he'd come looking for her and the children in the mountains above Grand Coeur, Clay hadn't spent a great deal of time with any of them. So she'd found herself listening for his footsteps, looking up at the slightest noise.

Waiting for . . . something.

Hoping for . . . something.

In the night, when she lay awake in bed, hearing the children's steady breathing, she could admit her disappointment. She was disappointed because Clay wouldn't marry her. Disappointed because she wasn't enough, because she couldn't make him want her *despite* the children. Maybe she would feel better if she disliked him. If he was cruel to her or mean-tempered with Ethan and Elsie or dismissive of Merry. If he had horrible table manners. If he was weak of mind or body. But he wasn't any of those things. He was good and kind and handsome. He was a man of true faith. He believed in what he was doing and was willing to work hard to make it succeed.

Releasing a sigh, Luvena forced her eyes to focus on the papers before her once again, silently ticking off what had to be accomplished—find the right singer or troupe; put together a stunning opening production; help the opera house turn a profit; earn a bonus; leave Grand Coeur; find a man who would marry her and care for the children.

Help me, Lord!

As if in answer to that pitiful but heartfelt prayer, her gaze fell upon a familiar name. Ada May Innsbruck. Her pulse quickened as she took up the handbill and moved it closer to the light. Ada May Innsbruck, a star of the stage, first in New York and now in San Francisco, was currently scheduling a tour of western theaters. At one time, Ada May had been a dear friend of Luvena's sister. As far as she knew, that hadn't changed when scandal struck the Abbott family. Perhaps Ada May didn't even know about their tragedy. Was it possible Ada May might consider coming to Grand Coeur as one of the stops on her tour?

Her heart continuing to race with excitement, she rose from the chair, the slip of paper still in her hand, and went looking for Clay. She found him in the lobby, overseeing the hanging of a large mirror.

"Mr. Birch?"

He turned.

"I think I've found someone for the opening."

"Who?"

"Her name is Ada May Innsbruck. She sings beautifully and is a gifted actress. Best of all, she is presently booking appearances in towns between San Francisco and Denver." Luvena held out the handbill for him to take. "I know Ada May. I feel certain she would come if she hasn't already filled her tour dates."

He read the advertisement. "Is she as good as this says?"

"Better." Luvena grinned. "We should telegraph her

husband in San Francisco immediately. Mr. Innsbruck is Ada May's manager."

"How well do you know her?"

"Well enough. She was a good friend of my sister."

"Can I afford her?"

"You won't know unless you ask."

At last, Clay returned her smile. "Then let's go send that telegram."

As Clay and Luvena walked toward the Wells, Fargo office, a weight seemed to fall from Clay's shoulders. Remodeling the old Grand Theater into the new Grand Coeur Opera House had been the easy part of this endeavor. In his mind, finding the right artist to perform for the reopening was the hard part. If this Ada May Innsbruck was as good as Luvena said . . .

He glanced to his left. And, as if sensing his look, Luvena turned her head. A smile instantly curved the corners of her mouth.

It was going to work out. They were going to pull this off. He felt it deep in his bones. He might have told her such if they hadn't arrived at the Wells, Fargo office just then. He opened the door, motioning for her to step inside ahead of him.

Matthew Dubois greeted them from the other side of the counter.

"I didn't know you were back, Matthew," Clay said.

"We returned yesterday."

"How was the trip to Virginia?"

"Good. Shannon enjoyed showing me where she grew up and introducing me to old friends. She loved showing off the children too. But sometimes it was difficult for her. Reminders of the war are everywhere, and many people she knew are now gone." Matthew's gaze shifted over Clay's shoulder.

"Sorry." He turned to look at Luvena. "Miss Abbott, this is Matthew Dubois. He's Reverend Adair's son-in-law. Shannon's husband. Matthew, this is Luvena Abbott."

"A pleasure to meet you, Miss Abbott."

"And you, Mr. Dubois."

"Delaney tells us you won't be staying in Grand Coeur as expected. Shannon is disappointed. She remembers all too well how difficult it was for her when she came to Idaho Territory. She didn't like Grand Coeur much at first, but she's grown to love it. You would too."

"Matthew," Clay interrupted before Luvena could respond, "we need to send a telegram."

"Of course." Matthew placed paper and pencil on the counter in front of Clay.

He, in turn, slid the items to Luvena. She hesitated a moment before taking up the pencil. Then, looking between the handbill and the telegram form, she crafted the request to Ada May Innsbruck. When finished she handed the message to Matthew. He looked it over, nodded, and moved to the desk that held the telegraph equipment.

Clay sent up a silent prayer for a positive response from Mrs. Innsbruck. Not simply her availability and willingness to come to Grand Coeur but also that she would charge a reasonable fee.

Matthew returned to the counter. "It's sent. I'll let you know when we get a reply."

"Thanks." Clay paid for the telegram.

"I hope it turns out." Matthew's gaze shifted to Luvena. "It was a pleasure meeting you, Miss Abbott."

She nodded to him.

"My wife will want you and Clay and your family to join us for dinner sometime soon. You can expect an invitation before long."

"That's very kind, Mr. Dubois. I'll look forward to it."

"*. . . you and Clay and your family . . .*" Matthew's words echoed in Clay's thoughts as he and Luvena walked back to the opera house. "*. . . you and Clay and your family . . .*" There was something right about the sound of it.

But how could it sound right when he knew just how wrong it would be?

CHAPTER NINE

24 September 1870

Mr. Melvin Hitchcock
Proprietor, Hitching Post Mail-Order
Bride Catalogue

Dear Mr. Hitchcock,

I am writing to advise you that someone
employed by your catalogue company revised
the letters I exchanged with Mr. Clay Birch
of Grand-Coeur, Idaho Territory. I now find
that he and I are not to be married as expected
because he had expressed his unwillingness to
become a stepfather to any children. A crucial
fact that was removed from his correspondence
to me. Now, because of this, my sister's children
and I find ourselves without the home and

means of support we thought were secured when we left Massachusetts.

While Mr. Birch has not cast us out, we cannot continue to accept his charity. Therefore, I must ask that an advertisement of my own be included in your catalogue, free of charge given the circumstances. Please be certain it includes the information that I am the guardian of three children (ages eight to fourteen). I do not wish for there to be any further misunderstandings. I am writing a few other particulars regarding myself on the back of this letter and trust you will use them for an appropriate listing.

I also trust that whoever was responsible for this interference with our letters will be summarily dismissed from your employment. That is the very least that should happen to the individual.

Sincerely,
Miss Luvena
Abbott
Grand Coeur,
Idaho Territory

The letter finished, Luvena blotted the ink, folded the paper, and slipped it into an envelope.

There. Done. She should have written to the *Hitching Post* the very day she arrived in Grand Coeur. She should have expressed her shock and dismay over the cruel joke perpetrated upon her and Clay. Whoever was responsible, she hoped they received their just desserts.

And now the search for a husband would begin again. It shouldn't feel any worse than it had before, the idea of moving to a new place and marrying a stranger for the support a husband could provide. But it did feel worse.

When she'd first considered the listings in that catalogue, she hadn't known any unmarried men who would overlook the tragedy in her family. Nor had she known any men who made her feel the way Clay Birch made her—

No, she wouldn't think that. Clay had made up his mind the moment she'd stepped out of the stagecoach and identified Merry, Ethan, and Elsie as belonging with her. He hadn't changed his opinion in the past nine days, nor was he likely to.

As if summoned by her thoughts, Clay appeared in the doorway of the office, grinning broadly. "You've done it, Luvena!" He waved a slip of paper in the air.

Luvena. Her name thrummed in her ears as she rose and moved to the side of the desk. "Done what?"

"Mrs. Innsbruck has agreed to come to Grand Coeur."

"I'm delighted for you, Mr. Birch." She couldn't help but return his smile.

"We might even draw folks up from Boise." He closed the distance between them. "It wouldn't have happened without your help."

"You would have found someone, I'm sure."

"Perhaps. But not someone as well known. Besides, she's coming because of you." He spoke the words softly, his gaze holding hers.

Luvena's heart leapt, and it took great resolve not to reach up and caress his cheek. Something she had no right to do. She was not his fiancée. She would never be his bride.

The smile faded from her lips as she took a step backward and reached for the envelope on the desk. "Please excuse me. I have a letter I must post, and I'm hoping it will make today's stage. Then I must see to the children's lunch."

"Of course." He also took a step backward. He also lost his smile.

Good. He'd understood her subtle reminder of why he should not stand so close and why he should not call her by her Christian name. At most he was her landlord and employer. By his choice. A choice they both must live with.

"I suggest you send it by Wells, Fargo," he added. "They're generally more reliable than the postal service."

With a nod of acknowledgement in Clay's direction, Luvena left the theater and hurried along Main Street toward the express company's office. Feeling close to tears—and hating herself for it—she kept her gaze fastened on the boardwalk a few steps in front of her.

Mr. Birch isn't anything to me. He isn't. I shall find another man to marry.

Luvena was so deep in thought she almost walked into

another woman outside the Wells, Fargo office. The woman gasped, and it was that sound that brought Luvena to a sudden halt.

The heat of embarrassment rose in her cheeks. "I beg your pardon. I wasn't watching where I was going."

"It's all right." The woman—striking looking, with fiery-red hair and cat-green eyes—laughed softly. "Neither of us was harmed." She looked as if she would turn and continue on her way, but then she stilled again. "You must be Miss Abbott."

"Yes, I am."

"I'm Shannon Dubois. My husband and I were traveling with our children when you arrived in Grand Coeur. I would so have liked to have been here to welcome you, but here we are now. So, welcome!"

"That's very kind, Mrs. Dubois."

"Please, won't you call me Shannon?"

"If you wish."

Shannon reached out and squeezed Luvena's upper arm, the gesture warm and genuine. "I have a feeling we shall become great friends."

Luvena felt a catch in her chest, as if she'd lost something dear to her. If she could stay in Grand Coeur, they might have been friends. But now—

"Matthew and I would like you to come to dinner after church tomorrow. And your nieces and nephew, of course. Do I have that right? Two girls and a boy? Or is it the other way around?"

There was something about Shannon Dubois's smile that refused to let Luvena feel sorry for herself. She returned it. "You have it right."

"Good. I thought so. Just the opposite of us. We have two boys and a girl in our home. But I mustn't detain you from your errand any longer. You will meet the children tomorrow." She started away, then tossed back over her shoulder, "Oh, tell Clay he is invited to dinner too."

⁂

Well after Luvena left the office, the soft scent of her cologne lingered. Clay found it an oddly disturbing fragrance. Earthy. Sensual. Unforgettable. At last it drove him out the back door of the theater where he stopped and filled his lungs with fresh autumn air.

"Ethan, keep your eye on the ball."

Clay turned in the direction of Merry Browne's voice. On the vacant land south of the house, Merry prepared to throw a ball toward her brother who held a bat high and behind his head. Some distance in back of Ethan, Elsie waited to chase the ball if he missed it.

Baseball. A sport that had grown in popularity from coast to coast. During the war, he'd participated in many friendly games with other Union soldiers. Those games had helped keep boredom at bay and his mind off of blood and death and the acrid smell of smoke that could linger in a man's nostrils long after battles were over.

He walked toward the Browne children.

Merry threw the ball. Ethan swung at it and missed. Elsie chased after it.

"You need to widen your stance," Clay called to the boy.

Ethan straightened and looked Clay's way, suspicion in his eyes. "You ever played baseball?"

"As a matter of fact, yes. I have."

"When?"

Clay took Ethan by the upper arms and angled the boy's shoulder toward Merry. "Back when you were still in diapers." He couldn't see Ethan's frown, but he knew it was there all the same. "I've even seen the Chicago White Stockings play."

Ethan looked up and behind, skepticism giving over to excitement. "You have?"

"Yep." Clay turned the boy's head forward. "Your feet need to be a few inches wider than your shoulders. There. That's good. Keep a bit more weight on your right foot. Bend your knees a little. A little more. Now hold the bat about here. That's right. Keep your head steady." He backed away from Ethan and stepped off to the side. "Okay, Merry. Throw him a good one. Ethan, be ready for it. Don't try to hit it too hard. That'll come later."

The boy missed Merry's first pitch, but he connected with the ball the next time, surprising his older sister as well as himself.

"That's it!" Clay shouted. "You did it!"

Looking as proud as if he'd hit the ball over the roof of the theater, Ethan held the bat toward Clay. "You do it, Mr. Birch."

"Maybe later. Right now I'm hungry. I thought I'd fix something for lunch." He turned on his heel and started toward the house. To his surprise, the three Browne children left their game and followed him inside.

Merry said, "Aunt Vena was going to make lunch after she finished writing to the *Hitching Post* catalogue."

Clay stopped in the middle of the kitchen. "The *Hitching Post*? Why was she writing to them?"

"Same reason as before." Merry shrugged. "To find herself a husband."

"To find herself a husband."

The words reverberated through Clay.

"To find herself a husband."

So what had he thought she would do? He'd offered her and the children this house to live in temporarily. He was paying her a modest salary, one he could ill afford to pay. And he'd promised her a bonus if the opera house turned a good enough profit after its opening—which would take a miracle. Short-term fixes, all of them.

"To find herself a husband."

When he'd burst into the office a short while ago, proclaiming the good news about Ada May Innsbruck, he'd wanted nothing more than to pick Luvena up and spin her around in celebration. Well, maybe he'd wanted one thing more than to spin her around. He'd wanted to kiss her. Truth was, whenever he was with Luvena, he wanted to kiss her. Sometimes when he wasn't with her, he still thought about kissing her.

"To find herself a husband."

It wouldn't be hard for Luvena to find a man willing to marry her. She was beautiful and intelligent. Despite her being only twenty-three, she was a capable and caring mother to her wards. She wasn't afraid of hard work. A man would be a fool not to—

"My goodness." Luvena's voice rescued him from his thoughts. "I didn't expect to find all of you in the kitchen."

Clay turned toward the parlor. Luvena stood framed in the doorway, looking even lovelier than she had in the theater office. How was that possible? She wore the same dress and her hair was unchanged. Perhaps it was the way the light fell through the parlor window. Or perhaps—

"We're helpin' Mr. Birch make lunch," Elsie said.

A quick glance told him the kids had, indeed, started while he'd stood there lost in thought.

"Sandwiches," Ethan added, slapping a slice of cold roast beef onto bread.

Luvena took a step into the kitchen. "I hope they weren't in your way, Mr. Birch."

"No. Not at all." He cleared his throat. "I guess you got your letter posted in time."

"Yes."

For some reason he didn't understand, he wished she would tell him what she'd written to the catalogue. He didn't want secrets between them.

"And I met Shannon Dubois," she continued. "She invited all of us to dinner after church service tomorrow."

"Guess what, Aunt Vena?"

"What, Ethan?" She looked toward her nephew.

"Mr. Birch taught me how to swing my bat better. And I hit the ball Merry threw!"

Luvena's eyes widened as they shifted back to Clay.

He shrugged. "I learned a little about the game during the war. Just shared it with the kid."

There was a warmth permeating the kitchen. Not one caused by the sun overhead or the stove against the opposite wall. No, it was a warmth created by the people in the room. All of them. The Browne children too. It came from their hearts and their laughter and their smiles. It made the small house feel like . . . like a home. It made all of them feel like a family. Clay hadn't felt that way in many, many years. Maybe never.

A gentle smile played around the corners of Luvena's mouth. "You continue to surprise me, Mr. Birch."

She couldn't be any more surprised than he was himself.

CHAPTER TEN

LUVENA HAD ENJOYED THE PREVIOUS SUNDAY SERVICE at the Presbyterian church. Reverend Adair was an excellent preacher with a fine, clear voice. But today melancholy wrapped itself around her heart as she sat in the same pew as Clay Birch, her nieces and nephew between them—Ethan next to Clay, Elsie next to Luvena, Merry in the middle.

Like a family.

Would she have preferred that Clay sit elsewhere? No. She wouldn't. In truth, she wished she was beside him. It would feel so right, even if it made her sad. Soon enough she and the children would leave Grand Coeur, and it wasn't likely she'd see him again. She would miss him. She would miss him more than she should. The letters they'd exchanged hadn't been many. Her time in Grand Coeur hadn't been long. But she would miss him. Terribly so.

Reverend Adair began the closing prayer. Luvena closed

her eyes, but rather than attending to the minister's words, she pictured the five of them as they'd been in the kitchen yesterday. They'd all been happy in that moment. Even Clay. She was sure of it.

Why isn't that enough for him, Lord? What could I do to change what's happening?

Clay liked her. Perhaps his feelings for her weren't as strong as her feelings were for him, but he did like her. But that wasn't enough to change his mind.

Don't go.

The words stirred inside her heart. Her own thoughts? Or God's voice?

Don't leave.

The reverend said, "Amen," and the congregation repeated the word. Clay rose and stepped into the aisle, waiting for the children and Luvena to exit the pew.

What choice do I have but to leave? I must marry. I've no other option.

Outside, the air was golden on this late September day. While they waited for the Dubois family to come out of the church, Clay introduced Luvena to a few people she hadn't met the previous Sunday. He should have been introducing everyone to her as his wife instead of as Miss Abbott.

The thought stung, and her melancholy increased with each forced smile, each nod of the head, each shake of the hand.

Ask him. Talk to him.

Ask him what? Talk to him about what?

Shannon Dubois—holding a toddler of about one year,

the little girl wearing a frilly dress and bonnet—stepped into the sunshine. Matthew followed right behind his wife, bent at the waist as he held the hand of a small boy, perhaps three years of age. Shannon said something to her father, then came down the steps to the street. "Sorry to keep you waiting."

"You didn't," Luvena replied, glad for the interruption from her thoughts.

"Come along then. We'll make the rest of the introductions once we reach the house. That's it on the hillside there." Shannon pointed toward their destination.

They set off walking, the two women leading the way.

"I'm so glad you agreed to come." Shannon shifted the little girl in her arms, now bracing her on a hip.

"What's her name?" Luvena asked.

"Adelyn, after my mother. We call her Addie."

"She's adorable." Luvena touched the little girl's soft cheek with her fingertips.

Shannon laughed softly. "You won't hear any argument from me." She cast a quick glance behind her. "You have a fine family too. Your sister's children. Is that right?"

"Yes."

"My husband's sister was widowed in the war, and after she died, her son came to live with us. He was like our own son from the very start. I promise you, raising your nieces and nephew will be worth whatever sacrifices you have to make."

"It's no sacrifice."

"I know better, Luvena. You must have given up a great deal to care for them after their parents died." Shannon's expression was both kind and solemn. "There is always sacrifice involved when one loves another. Child or adult. Always. But as I said, it's worth it."

Luvena missed having someone to confide in, someone she could trust with her deepest secrets and most private thoughts. Her sister had filled that role in her life for as far back as she could remember. But Loretta was gone; Luvena felt so alone without her. If she could have stayed in Grand Coeur, she and Shannon would have become fast friends. She was sure of it.

As if reading Luvena's thoughts, Shannon asked in a near whisper, "Why aren't you staying?"

Because Clay doesn't want to marry me, and I must find a man who does. She swallowed the ache that rose in her throat.

Shannon's discernment continued. "You could change his mind, Luvena."

"No, I don't think so."

"Have you tried? Have you told him how you feel?"

How I feel? I'm not sure how I feel.

Perhaps Shannon would have said more, but they arrived at the Dubois home right then.

Luvena didn't know if she was glad or sorry for it.

❖

Dinner was a slightly chaotic event with so many children seated around the table, especially the two Dubois youngsters, but Clay couldn't help thinking this was how families were supposed to be. Not the chaos, in particular. He'd seen plenty of that as a boy growing up with four younger half brothers.

But the laughter, the smiles, the genuine affection evident on everyone's face.

Happy families. Lucky kids. The way Matthew and Shannon loved their children and nephew. The way Luvena loved her sister's children. Did they know how lucky they were?

"You're just like your father!" His mother's words echoed in his memory. *"You can't be trusted. Get out! Go!"*

Hurtful words, but also true ones. He remembered his brother Jacob as he'd looked on that Tuesday in April of 1861—split lip, missing tooth, blackened eyes, cut cheek, swollen jaw. Not the first time Jacob had come out on the losing end of a fight with Clay, but the last one. Four years later Jacob was dead.

Clay had allowed Luvena to think he left Illinois after the war because he hadn't wanted to work for his stepfather. The truth was, he hadn't been welcome there.

"You're just like your father!"

"Clay?" Reverend Adair broke into his thoughts. "Is something troubling you, son?"

Clay looked at his friend. "No, sir. My mind was wandering, I guess." Eager to escape the reverend's sharp gaze, he looked around the table and added in a louder voice, "Did Matthew tell you we've found our performer for the grand opening of the opera house? Thanks to Miss Abbott, I must add. The details were confirmed yesterday."

"Matthew didn't say a word to me." Shannon gave her husband a scolding glance down the length of the table, but it lost its force when she smiled. "Tell us more."

Clay obliged, giving them as many details as he could. Then he looked toward Luvena in a silent invitation for her to conclude the telling.

"Ada May was a friend of my sister, Loretta. She often attended parties and dances in our home. She and I even sang together once. That must have been terribly difficult for her, for I haven't her talent."

"Do you sing opera, Luvena?" Shannon asked.

"I did, years ago. Not professionally, of course. Just for my own pleasure."

"Perhaps you could sing something for us after dinner. We have a wonderful piano in the front parlor."

A blush colored her cheeks as she lowered her eyes. "I'm afraid I'm long out of practice."

Clay wanted to hear her sing. It surprised him how much he wanted it.

Shannon said, "It doesn't have to be opera. Sing anything you wish. A hymn perhaps. I could play for you. I used to play the organ at church, before the children were born."

Luvena's gaze lifted to meet Clay's.

"Please," he said softly.

In that moment, Luvena discovered a truth she hadn't known earlier in the morning. She didn't simply like Clay Birch. She wouldn't simply miss him. She'd fallen in love with him. She loved him, and there wasn't much she would deny him if it were in her power to give what he asked. Even when that something would open a wound in her heart. Still looking at him, she answered, "All right."

Clay grinned. "Thanks."

Love always involved sacrifice. Wasn't that what Shannon had said earlier? And Luvena loved Clay. More than their short acquaintance should have allowed. More than their circumstances should have allowed. She loved him, and yet—

Fight for him.

The breath caught in her chest as clarity washed through her. She'd allowed circumstances to determine the direction of her life. Oh, she'd tried to make good decisions for the sake of her nieces and nephew. She'd prayed for God's guidance. But had she fought for anything she wanted? No. Not in a long, long time.

But she was going to fight for this man.

CHAPTER ELEVEN

As evening approached, Clay stood on the newly rebuilt stage in the theater, looking toward the rows of seats where in a few weeks, God willing, a large audience would sit. Silence surrounded him, but in his head, he heard Luvena singing "Amazing Grace" in her beautiful, clear voice. Like the song of an angel.

Even now, hours later, the memory of it brought tears to his eyes. He knew the hymn. Had heard it many times, both before and after he'd come to faith. Why had it affected him so much more this time than ever before? Why did it still affect him, hours later, in some deep and secret corner of his heart? It seemed to Clay that God wanted to show him something, tell him something, and yet he wasn't able to understand what. The knowledge seemed just beyond his reach.

"Clay?"

His pulse quickened at the sound of his name, and he turned stage right. Dim light shrouded Luvena in the wing.

"May I ask you something?"

He cleared his throat. "Sure. I guess."

"Why must I go?" She took a couple of steps toward him.

It seemed a fair question, but one that was suddenly without an answer.

"Why must *we* go? You don't dislike the children. I've seen you with them."

Ah. He remembered now. Children. Those children were the reason she had to leave.

"You're so good to them. I don't believe it has anything to do with Grand Coeur not being a suitable place for them to grow up. Maybe it's still a rough gold town, as you warned in your first letter, but Shannon and Matthew have done all right raising their children here. And you believe it will get better. That's why you're investing yourself in this opera house. Because you believe in this town's future."

Reverend Adair had said almost the same things to him a week ago. Had the reverend and Luvena talked about him?

She took another step closer. "There's something you aren't telling me. It . . . it's something you've hidden in your heart. Maybe you haven't even told God what it is."

His jaw clenched, and it took effort to relax it.

"Please tell me the truth, Clay."

The truth. She'd traveled over twenty-six hundred miles by rail and by coach to get here. The least he owed her was the truth. Once she heard it, she'd be ready to leave.

"Let's go outside," he said. "It's stuffy in here."

Clay led the way in silence toward the back of the theater, past his office, and out the rear door. Twilight had fallen while he'd been inside, and the evening air had cooled. Music spilled from a saloon or bawdy house from somewhere down Main Street.

He helped her sit on the back stoop, then sat beside her. He thought she might say something to encourage him. She didn't.

"I don't remember much about my pa except for the size of his hands. They were really big. He had long fingers." He raised his right arm and bent his wrist to show his hand. "Like mine. And when he made a fist, it was rock hard. Like mine."

The music from the saloon fell still.

"He was an angry man, and he took most of that anger out on me. He broke my nose and my left arm when I was five. That's when my ma told him to get out and never come back unless he learned to hold his temper. He left. I never saw him again. He died of pneumonia that same winter."

Silently, she reached out and took hold of the hand he'd shown her, her skin warm against his.

He looked toward the sky. Stars had begun to appear in the darkening expanse. "I'm like my pa. I was an angry kid. I got into fights with my half brothers all the time. Especially with Jacob. It was like something shut off in my head when I got mad. I'd just start swinging until I couldn't swing anymore."

"Oh, Clay." The words came out on a breath.

"The last time I saw him, I beat on him hard. I was

twenty-two. He was only fifteen. I wanted to tell him I was sorry, but I didn't. He was my brother and I loved him, but instead of saying I was sorry, I just left. I went off and joined the army." He paused, then added, "War changes men."

Images flashed in his head. Faces of the soldiers he'd served with, fought with, laughed with, and cried with for four years. Some had died in his arms. Too many hadn't lived to see the end.

Softer now, he continued, "War changed me. I wanted to be done with fighting. I wanted to make amends with my brother. But my ma didn't want me to come home. Jacob had died in the war, and she blamed me for his death. She was certain I'd start brawling with one of my younger brothers if I was there again."

He glanced toward Luvena. There was enough light left to see tears streaking her cheeks. His chest tightened.

"She said I was just like my pa. She was probably right. I am like him."

"I don't believe that's true."

"You don't know."

She stared at him for a long time. "It was more than the war that changed you, Clay Birch. It was faith in God." Her voice softened. "'Therefore if any man be in Christ, he is a new creature: old things are passed away; behold, all things are become new.' That's what the Bible says about you."

Hope stirred in his chest. Hope and something more.

"I never knew the man you were before, Clay, the one you've just described to me. I only know the man who sits beside me now. The one with dreams for the future. The one who wants to make a difference for good in a world that can be very bad and sometimes ugly."

"Luvena, what if you're wrong? What if—"

"No. I'm right about this. I've seen you angry. Remember? The day you met us in Boise City. I've seen you angry and frustrated and anxious and worried, but even in those times, I have also seen you kind and caring and thoughtful. I've seen how you are with Ethan and Elsie and Merry. Always patient and giving. I've watched you with the workmen in the theater. I've listened to you talk and laugh with your friends. Good friends. People who've known you much longer than I. They would know if you were still that old Clay. But you're not."

"Miss Abbott—"

"I prefer it when you call me by my Christian name."

He couldn't help but oblige her. "Luvena."

"I have fallen in love with the man you are today, Clay Birch, and I don't want to marry anyone else. Perhaps we aren't what you wanted or expected, a wife with three children to be raised, but perhaps we're what you need. Please don't send us away."

He knew it then. He'd started giving his heart to Luvena Abbott from the moment she stepped off the stage in Boise, clad in a gray bonnet and gown, her hair as black as midnight, her wide eyes taking in her surroundings with both trepidation and courage. And not only to her. To those three children too. They were a family, and they were meant to be *his* family.

Darkness had obscured all but her shadow from view

by this time, but somehow his hands knew where to go. He cupped the sides of her head between his palms and turned her gently as he leaned forward. When their lips met, he realized in a flash that the poker game he'd won had given him far more than a broken-down hurdy-gurdy house. It had made him the richest man on earth.

Riches he would treasure for the rest of his life . . . beginning right now as he drew Luvena closer and deepened his kiss.

8 October 1870

Mr. Melvin Hitchcock
Proprietor, Hitching Post Mail-Order
Bride Catalogue

Dear Mr. Hitchcock,

A couple of weeks ago Luvena Abbott wrote to you, advising that someone in your employ tampered with the letters she and I exchanged prior to her arrival in Idaho Territory. At that time she requested an advertisement for a prospective husband be placed in your catalogue on her behalf. Please cancel that request. Miss Abbott and I were married this week.

Sir, you should know how very angry
I was when we discovered our letters had
been altered, hiding the fact that she was
the guardian for her nieces and nephew,
among other details. The deception seemed
a cruel joke since I had specifically
stated I did not want a woman with
children. And the fact that someone
at the Hitching Post paid the fare for
Mrs. Birch's three wards was even more
surprising.

My wife's niece reminded us that
the good Lord wasn't surprised about
the changes in our letters. Merry said
God knew and brought Luvena and the
children to Grand Coeur as part of His
plan. Seems that's one way God works. A
friend, Reverend Adair, showed me the
story of Joseph in the Bible. Lots worse
was done to him by his brothers than what
happened to us, but in the end he said, "Ye
thought evil against me, but God meant it
unto good."

I don't know if evil was the intent
behind the altered letters, but God meant
it for good. And so, although I don't think
your catalogue should make this a common
practice, I've got to say thanks for the part

you played in giving me this family I now know I was meant to have.

    Sincerely,
    Mr. Clay Birch
    Owner, Grand Coeur Opera House
    Grand Coeur, Idaho Territory

Winter Wedding Bells

Mary Connealy

Yea, though I walk through the valley of the shadow of death, I will fear no evil: for thou art with me; thy rod and thy staff they comfort me.

PSALM 23:4 KJV

DAVID'S AD IN THE *HITCHING POST MAIL-ORDER BRIDE CATALOGUE*:

Prosperous Wyoming widower with two sons needs a wife. I seek neither beauty nor wealth nor education. But must love children, accept ranch life, be willing to work hard.—David

MEGAN'S RESPONSE TO DAVID'S AD:

Dear David,

I helped raise my five younger brothers as my mother and father were ill and both died young. I know how to care for children. I am no great beauty, with no money to speak of, so I meet your needs in that way. I have only the barest schooling, but I read well and can cipher. I am a hardworking woman of thirty years. I keep house for others and would love my own home out of the city.

Megan McBride

DAVID'S THREE-PAGE RESPONSE TO MEGAN:

(Pg 1)

Dear Megan,

I must tell you about myself before you consider meeting me, let alone marrying me. I am, as I said, a prosperous rancher. We will live in comfort in a new house, built snug and tight against Wyoming winters. I have two sons, so your reference to little brothers is encouraging.

My sons are young yet, four and five. They are very lively and bright. There is no school within many miles of my ranch so what education they receive will be at home. You say you have only the barest schooling so I will handle that part of things to the extent I am able and, if you are willing, you can study with us. If you take to learning, perhaps you can stay ahead of Zachary and Benjamin with the goal of assuming responsibility for their education.

(Pg 2)

But here is the part that is hard to speak of, and yet impossible to avoid. I am very ill, Miss McBride. When I say I want a woman who loves children and accepts ranch life and is willing to work hard, it is because there is every chance that within a year of our marriage you will be widowed. If this is not acceptable to you, I understand. You would be one of

nearly thirty women who have responded to my letter seeking a mail-order bride, but who never wrote
back once they received these details. Something I
understand.

If we were to marry, I hope there would be respect
between us, but I do not expect affection or any type
of marital intimacy. That is not the kind of marriage
that would be wise for either of us. I would want no
additional children to be left fatherless. And I would
have no wish to engage your affections only to be torn
from your loving arms. You would be more nurse and
mother than wife in this marriage.

(Pg 3)

I have ranch hands so you will not be expected to
work outside. But I do want you to understand ranching so I would hope you will allow me to instruct
you. There are few enough women in the area that a
housekeeper is not possible. The work of running the
household and caring for the boys will be hard. If my
letter does not discourage you, I would like to meet
you. I am in Chicago but wish to return to my mountain home before winter settles in.

I am here with my sons to visit doctors. I have had
pneumonia, which has led to declined health. I am just
now feeling well enough to travel back to Wyoming
and am hoping a likely wife will be found to accom-
pany me.

Please respond if you'd like to meet. If not, I understand and will continue my search.

—David Laramie

Melvin Hitchcock of the *Hitching Post Mail-Order Bride Catalogue* looked at the pathetic excuse for a letter that came through his hands and shook his head. All that nonsense about David dying within the next year . . . why, that smacked of a man playing God. Laramie should be ashamed of himself. No woman would ever agree to marry such a pessimist. If he wanted the woman to agree to marry him, the letter needed one small change—Hitchcock threw out page two. Then he sent it on to Megan McBride.

CHAPTER ONE

MEGAN MCBRIDE STOOD SHIVERING OUTSIDE THE Tremont Hotel, buffeted by the cold November wind.

The doorman had refused to let her in. He'd told her to go around back to the servants' entrance. No amount of protest would convince the snooty man that she had any business—other than as a laborer—in their fancy hotel.

But she couldn't very well meet her new husband and his two young laddies if she was in the back of the hotel, now, could she? So here she stood waiting in the cold.

A church bell tolled from nearby, and just then a fine coach drew her attention as it rolled to a stop. The bell's tolling almost seemed like an announcement of the coach's arrival. Like wedding bells. Two little ones scrambled down. The boys were so close in size she'd have thought them twins if David's letter hadn't said they were four and five. Behind them emerged a finely dressed man.

He was a handsome man, and that was no blarney, but he looked gaunt for a fact. He'd spoken of pneumonia in his letter and one look convinced Megan he'd indeed been ill. His skin had an ashen color. A rancher, a man who spent most of his days outdoors, should be tanned even in November. Clothes hung on his tall frame as if he'd lost weight—a lot of it. His hair was well trimmed and his face clean shaven, but it looked to Megan as if all the tidying had been done lately. His face and neck looked scraped raw by a recent shave and haircut.

Sure and it had to be David Laramie—the two lively youngsters being the best clue.

Megan walked forward to meet them. The children, one was at best an inch taller than the other, laughed and shoved each other while the man's searching eyes rested on her and stopped. She'd described herself fairly it seemed, because he nodded in greeting from across the distance of the busy sidewalk.

"Miss McBride?" He removed his hat in a show of good manners and bad sense, since his head would now be cold.

As she opened her mouth, the smaller of the boys shouted in anger, "That's my hat!"

The cry drew Megan's attention in time to see the older boy reel back and fall beneath the wheels of their carriage just as it began to move.

"It's mine now!" The younger boy waved a woolen cap at his big brother and jeered.

"Stop the horses!" Mr. Laramie moved toward the coach quickly as if to dive for the child. "Ben!"

The carriage driver jerked the brake on his rig. "Whoa!"

It had just started rolling. The carriage skidded as the driver fought the reins. One horse reared and jerked the carriage forward. "Whoa!"

"Zachary, I'm gonna get you!" The older brother, almost under the wheels, ignored the danger and tried to dodge his father.

But Mr. Laramie's big hand caught the front of the boy's shirt. He hauled him out from under the heavy carriage.

Megan saw the littler boy, Zachary, run down the sidewalk, still laughing.

He dashed around the back of the carriage and straight into the street. Carriages, wagons, carts, and riders flowed from both directions. Zachary turned toward the rushing traffic. The boy, four years old, cried out in fear, tried to run back, but stumbled to his knees.

A pair of dappled gray draft horses drawing a heavy stagecoach thundered toward him.

The stage driver bellowed in horror as he sawed on the reins.

Megan charged forward, tackled the boy, and wrapped her body around him to protect him from certain death, but her speed forced her away from the sidewalk and its safety. She rolled to the middle of the hectic street.

An iron-shod hoof from one of the grays scraped her back. The blow knocked her out of the way of the stage but farther into the crush of traffic.

Despite the pain, she leapt to her feet. One wild look both directions told her horses came from her left and her right.

With no time to get back to the sidewalk, she grabbed the heavy leather harness of the passing horse, pulled herself onto its back, and dragged the lad up with her, sweeping him out of the way of the traffic. Her sore back and the boy's weight kept her from reaching the top of its tall back. She knew nothing of mounting a horse anyway. By the time she had a bit of balance, with her belly draped over the animal, the driver had slowed his team to a halt.

Furious yelling pounded at her. From the driver of the dappled gray horse and from all up and down the street as the traffic snarled.

Hands caught Megan's waist and pulled her from the horse's back. The boy came along with her because she wouldn't let him go. The world seemed to whirl a bit as she was lifted and rushed to the safety of the sidewalk.

Breathlessly, she looked at the man who had her and saw David Laramie, the man she was supposed to marry if this meeting went well. And so far it surely hadn't.

Zachary was torn from her arms.

"Mr. Laramie?" As she spoke, her left shoulder throbbed. She remembered the kick. A glancing blow, saints be praised.

"Zachary, are you all right?" Mr. Laramie dropped to his knees and inspected the boy, who was dirty but unharmed.

The traffic began flowing again.

"Yep, Pa. I'd've been fine if that lady hadn't knocked me down." The boy glared at her.

Megan didn't let it bother her overly. Zachary was a child and children weren't known for having the best judgment.

Sure and raising five rambunctious little brothers had taught her that.

"Hush." Mr. Laramie gave the boy a fierce hug. In the midst of that show of fatherly love—something Megan knew precious little about—Mr. Laramie's eyes lifted and he gave Megan a look of such gratitude, such understanding of what could have happened, that it almost brought tears to Megan's eyes.

"Are you all right?" he said to her then. "I saw you get kicked." David coughed and quickly covered his mouth. A deep, painful cough that shook his whole body.

"The kick was a gift from God. It knocked the both of us out of the way of the horse. I'll be fine. Shall we go in?" To give David a moment to get finished with his coughing fit, Megan reached for the older boy's hand with her left arm, checked the motion at the pain that sliced through her, then reached with her right. The tyke, five years old, his da had said in the letter, took it. Megan smiled. She had a knack for getting her way with boys.

David still hung on to Zachary, though he had his head turned aside while he coughed.

"It's sorry I am that I knocked you down, laddie." She brushed a smudge of grime off the little one's chin. "I got both of us fair covered with dirt. Next time I'll let that horse and stagecoach run right over you to spare us this untidiness."

Her sharp sass earned her a rueful smile from the boy. Mr. Laramie let him loose and stood. As he gained his feet he staggered slightly, and Megan's hand, her wounded left, shot out and steadied him. The man was still ailing from the pneumonia he'd mentioned in his letter. He clutched at his chest. Megan saw his jaw tighten and his lips go nearly white as if it took everything he had to keep a groan of pain inside. Megan's mother had died of pneumonia and she'd had two little brothers who caught it. Megan knew how deadly it could be and even if a body survived, it took awhile to shake the cough.

Grabbing him helped her ignore her arm. Though sore, she'd used it so she knew it wasn't badly injured. A little pain. Honestly, a lot of pain. But no real damage. Megan knew the difference well enough and she saw that difference in the agony David Laramie was trying to keep to himself.

After a few seconds, David's jaw relaxed. He glanced at the hand she used to steady him. A faint blush painted the man's cheeks and something flashed in his eyes, probably embarrassment for needing help. Megan knew a bit about how boys thought—another knack she'd learned in a hard school by raising her brothers. She'd not had too many dealings with men, but boys were just a younger version of them. And she knew men had their pride.

Megan looked down at the boy she held. She asked, "And can I be trusting you to stay at my side, laddie? No running off? No horseplay?"

The boy nodded as if he was quite terrified to disobey. Megan released the child, took a few moments to dust herself off. She straightened her bonnet, which had been knocked nearly off her head. Then she tidied Zachary with quick, efficient motions. Regaining Ben's hand, she said, "I'm ready to go in then. We can have our visit and decide if we'll be suited to one another, Mr. Laramie."

"You just saved my son's life," Mr. Laramie said with grim satisfaction. "I reckon we'll suit just fine. In fact, we'll suit well enough you oughta call me David."

CHAPTER TWO

THE MAN HAD HIS OWN TRAIN CAR.

Megan had been on a train once before when her family had moved from New York City to Chicago. They were crushed in like cattle, and Megan was told firmly by her mother to be grateful for the ride.

"Time to board." David's voice was firm, but Megan saw a slight tremble in his hands.

They'd married the day after they'd met. Megan, David, and the laddies were the only ones present at the little church David had found for them, save the parson and his wife who served as a witness. David had then taken them straight here to the train.

Ben and Zack clambered up the steps. David stepped aside to let Megan go ahead of him. As she passed him she arched a brow. "You have your own train car?"

David smiled. "No, it's not mine. But I made arrangements to use it."

"So you know someone who has his own train car? Know him well enough to borrow it?"

"I'm not feeling up to a long ride sitting up in a crowded train."

He rested a supporting hand on her lower back as she climbed up the steps.

Megan stepped onboard and gasped. A velvet couch, brass lamps. A table with four chairs to her right, the table laden with platters covered by domed metal lids for keeping food warm. Her stomach growled.

"We'll eat first." David pulled the door shut. She wondered if he'd heard her stomach.

He threw a latch, which blocked off a means of escape for the rowdy boys.

Megan said, "We've got them inside. They should be safe."

"You're a woman to look on the bright side. You need to get over that. My boys can find trouble anywhere." David's eyes flashed with amusement.

"Aye, but we'll keep a sharp eye out."

Ben, under the table, jumped up and banged his head. The domed platters all bounced. Ben's shout was more anger than pain, but he rubbed his head and climbed out more carefully before he charged toward a narrow aisle on the far end of the car, opened a door to the right side of the aisle, and vanished. Zack was on his heels.

"I'll go lock the door on the other end, then maybe we can relax while we eat." David went toward the escape route.

"To my right are bedrooms," David went on as if his boys disappeared all the time. He walked past Megan to the door that led to the front of the car and latched it as the train's whistle blew and they pulled out of the station. Megan held on tight until the train settled into a steady speed.

Raising his voice, David said, "Let's eat, boys." The boys raced out of the bedroom, shouting as always, and beat David to the table. Megan was a bit slower, and by the time she sat down, David was already scooping food onto the plates.

Megan settled onto the bench seat by Ben just as the boy grabbed a chicken leg. She said, "We should ask God to bless the food and our journey."

The boy froze.

Megan hated to stop them. They were all famished, her included. But this was the right moment to make her mothering preferences known, and in any household that she might run, prayer before a meal would be the way of things.

David nodded. "Let's bow our heads."

After saying a sincere but very brief grace, David went back to serving food and Megan hurried to help him lest Ben climb onto the table and dive straight into the bowl of mashed potatoes.

The meal was chicken with mashed potatoes and gravy, along with steaming hot creamed corn and a loaf of bread, already sliced. The last dome hid an apple pie with juice oozing out of slits in the crust.

Megan ate with as much enthusiasm as the menfolk.

The meal was gone within minutes. As the boys finished, David pulled a cord that Megan hadn't noticed before, then went to unlock the door to the rest of the train car closest to the bedrooms.

Zack climbed out of his seat. Ben ducked beneath the table and crawled past Megan's legs. Rolling her eyes at the boys' behavior, Megan began stacking plates.

"Leave that." David snagged Zack and lifted the lad. With a quick swipe with one of the heavy white napkins, David wiped gravy off the boy's chin.

"Can you bring Ben? It's nap time." David sounded so tired, Megan wondered if he wouldn't mind a nap himself. Megan could understand how tired a body could be at mid-day. She hadn't slept much the night before, mulling over marrying a stranger.

"I don't want a nap, Pa." Ben's complaints didn't match his heavy lids. Megan urged him from the couch and followed David into the first bedroom. The tiny room had one narrow bed. David settled Zack next to the wall, then turned to Ben. The boy, despite his protests, climbed straight in and was asleep before David had the covers straightened.

Megan backed out of the room—there was hardly space enough to turn around. As David followed her out, he rubbed his chest. She'd have to ask him more about his pneumonia. It took awhile to recover. The man needed to rest. But he'd been single-minded about getting on this train, so Megan had kept her opinions to herself.

A movement to her right drew her head around.

"Hello," Megan said.

A man with black skin, and wearing a crisp black suit coat, tipped his small hat and returned her greeting, then went back to clearing away the dishes. He must have entered while they'd been in the bedroom. She felt strange letting someone do that work for her, but no doubt the rich expected such things. And no one would be waiting on her once she got home to Wyoming, so she'd put up with it.

David locked the door after the waiter passed through. "I think I'll lie down for a while." He reached for the second bedroom door and swung it open.

"That sounds good. I'll catch a few winks myself."

David stopped in his tracks. "Uh . . . we maybe need to . . ." He turned to look at her. "I can sleep on the couch."

Megan craned her neck to see past him. This bed was a bit bigger than the one the boys were in, but only a bit.

Very close quarters for her to share with a stranger. But she'd taken her vows; she intended to keep them.

"No, go on in. A man and his wife are expected to share a bed." Megan's mother had discussed such things with her, in very general terms, before her passing. But Megan knew what was expected of a lawfully wedded wife—well, she didn't exactly *know*, but something was expected of her and she was prepared for whatever it was. She swallowed hard but forced herself to say, "I won't shirk from my wifely duty."

David took one more look at the couch, which was far too small to be used as a bed, then stepped inside. "I reckon we'll have to make do, Megan, but I want you to know I won't . . . what I mean is . . ." His Adam's apple bobbed as he swallowed hard. "There's no need for you to concern yourself on that account. I'll ask no . . . duty of you."

Megan had been worrying about it, worrying quite a bit. Especially because she had no real idea what it meant. It was the main reason she hadn't slept last night. "It might be best to wait until we are home."

"You needn't worry about it at home either. I don't expect that . . . that sort of thing, not ever." David sat on the bed.

Not sure exactly what he meant by "I don't expect that sort of thing," Megan watched as he bent to pull off his boots. One hard tug and he straightened, gasping, hand resting on his chest.

"What's the matter?" Megan took over removing his boots. Crouching, she tugged. It was stubborn so she took a better grip on the heeled boot. Megan had seen pictures of such boots in dime novels. They were probably more what he wore in his normal life than his suit.

With a strong second effort, she got the boot to slide off.

Reaching for the second boot, David caught her shoulder and she looked up at him. He seemed riveted on her face as if he were determined to read her every expression. "What's the matter is what I talked about in my letter. And that's the same reason there'll be no wifely duty expected of you. I don't want to leave you carrying a child. That's too much to ask."

Leave her? Carrying a child? Surely the boys were big

enough to walk, but if David's chest hurt and the boys needed to be carried, she'd manage.

"Do you intend to spend your time away from home then?" She shrugged off his grip and pulled on the other boot.

"No, I'm talking about after I die."

The boot chose that moment to come off. Megan tumbled back and fell against the wall. The room was narrow, thank heavens, or she'd've ended up on her backside.

"What kind of talk is that?"

"There's no sense ignoring it," David said. "We need to be honest about it as we go on. That's why I put it all in the letter. I couldn't marry a woman who wasn't able to accept that she'd soon be a widow."

Megan straightened, dropped the boot on her toe with a sharp thump. Squeaking with pain, she stayed upright when she wanted to sink to the floor. With sudden panic, she spun to her satchel and dug in it, producing the letter. "Where in this letter do you mention such nonsense as death?"

She slapped the letter against his chest. David flinched. She'd hurt him. That little bit of force caused him pain.

Looking from the letter to her and back, David pulled the two sheets of paper apart and studied them, front and back. "I . . . I sent . . ." Shaking his head, he lifted his eyes, horrified eyes, to her. "Th-Three pages. I sent three pages. One of them is missing. The second page is missing."

"And what does this missing page say, pray tell?" She clutched her hands together, wishing she had the strength to hold back the words she knew David was going to say.

"I'm dying, Megan. We talked about it. At lunch."

"Aye, we talked about your health. You said you'd had pneumonia."

"I said I had pneumonia . . . which I did. It weakened my lungs and heart. I have terrible chest pains. I can barely work. I can only sleep on one side because the side closest to my heart is too painful. If I cough, which I do far too much, it's agonizing. I came to Chicago to consult with a doctor. Dr. Filbert told me my heart was giving out." David paused, his eyes shifting back and forth between both of hers. "Megan, I have less than a year to live."

Light-headed, Megan turned and sat heavily on the bed beside David. "Less than a year?"

"Yes, that's why I've been searching for a wife who will be good to my children. That's why no one ever responded to my second letter . . . except you. I was clear in that letter—"

"On the page I didn't get," Megan interjected.

Nodding, David said, "Yes—that any woman I married needed to be willing, within a few months, to raise my boys alone."

"Because you'll be gone." Megan's voice was weak. She let her eyes fall shut and she flopped backward on the bed.

"Megan?" His voice was too close.

She looked. He'd reclined beside her, propped up by his left elbow. Turning to look in his blue eyes, Megan was suddenly swept by the sense that his eyes were too lively, too full of the fire of life to be dying.

Shaking her head, she refused to believe it was true. "I

watched my ma and pa die. The vitality left their eyes once there was no turning back from death. I see too much life in you to believe you're dying."

He rested one hand on her arm. "I fought it at first too, Megan. If you need time to adjust, I understand that. But we have a lot to do before . . . before . . ."

"You're too alive to accept a death sentence."

"I went to the top doctor in Chicago. In fact, I came here on the advice of the doctor in Medicine Bow when he didn't know what was causing my chest pains. I asked around and Dr. Filbert was the top man."

"The top man, is it? I'm telling you, David, your top man made a mistake."

His hand tightened on her arm. "We can't waste time lying to ourselves. We have a lot to do. The boys need to get used to you as their ma. You need to learn how to run the ranch. I've got a foreman but—"

"No! I need to focus on taking care of you and helping you get well. Planning on dying is a waste of time. No man knows the number of hours granted to him by the *real* top man, God. Why, Zack and I could have died yesterday under the wheels of a stagecoach. We won't live as if we're planning on your death. Yes, I'll be working on earning the lads' trust and learning the ways of ranch life, but not with the idea of carrying on without you. You're too alive, too young, too strong to believe such nonsense on the word of a doctor."

"The *top* doctor."

"Well, I say he's a twit."

For a moment, David's hand clutched hers so tightly it was painful, then he let go and sat up. Silence stretched. Megan couldn't think of what to say as his revelation soaked in. Her protest had been a reflex. But he'd been to a doctor. And he was clearly ill.

Maybe he really would die within the year. It took most of her energy to sit upright.

"I want to believe you, Megan." David massaged his chest, a motion Megan had seen him make a dozen times since they'd met. "If it weren't for my young'uns, I'd hope for the best and go on living without giving it much thought. Hoping the doc was wrong. I wouldn't have even come back east if not for the boys."

"Did the chest pains just come on suddenly? You said you had pneumonia."

"I broke a couple of ribs tangling with a longhorn. I ended up with pneumonia, a bad case of it. Near scared me to death thinking of dying and leaving the boys. Doc Sattler in Medicine Bow pulled me through. But that was clear last spring. After all this time, the pains in my chest are still terrible. Doc Sattler said it's either my lungs or my heart, no way for him to tell. He suggested I find a doctor with more skill."

Megan slipped her hand over his, tugging it away from his chest. David relaxed and wove his fingers through hers.

Lifting his eyes, he gave her a sad smile. "Coming back east would have been out of the question a few years ago, but with the train stopping at Medicine Bow, I decided to make the trip. I did a lot of research to find the best doctor. He's the man who gave me the bad news. Then I turned my attention to making plans for my sons. Until I got the doctor's report, I had no intention of marrying again. My wife, Pamela, was the love of my life, and I want no other wife."

Megan took that blow and did her best not to flinch. He wasn't paying attention to her anyway. He was looking into the past, thinking of his true love. Maybe even longing to be with her.

"I'd have been content to simply live on the ranch, raise my boys, and be otherwise alone with my memories. But I don't have that luxury. I reckon it'd be the honorable thing to let you go. We could get an annulment, I expect, especially if you tell a judge you didn't realize about my health. But, Megan"—his eyes turned fierce—"I need you. I need help. Will you help me?"

Megan couldn't look away. She'd imagined this wealthy man had somehow seen past her poor clothing and work-roughened hands, her flyaway fire-red hair and heavy Irish accent, her lack of education and polish—he'd seen past all of that and known she was lovable. But she'd been a fool.

Her parents had used her willingness to work hard to support the family while they'd idled. Her father had died of drink. Her mother had succumbed to pneumonia almost as if she was relieved to quit living. Her little brothers had, one by one, left home and found lives of their own, and forgot they had a big sister. But she'd foolishly hoped that this man had seen she was a good and decent person inside.

She'd had it all wrong. He just wanted someone to raise his

children. That, at least, would be a high honor if he found her worthy, because the man was a devoted father. But she couldn't even claim that. No one else had written back. His choices were her or no one. Which meant marrying her was an act of desperation. He'd scraped her off the bottom of the barrel.

For all that, her vows had been before man and God. No annulment would change the oath she'd sworn.

She had a few chest pains of her own as she hung up her foolish dreams and consigned herself to be what she'd always been, a nurse to the ailing and dying, a caretaker of children not her own, someone who cleaned and tended and served in other people's homes.

Taking a few firm breaths and steadying her voice lest it tremble, she finally was able to say firmly, "I'll not be asking you for an annulment, David. My vows were made. I'm a Christian woman who hates to see a child suffer. Even if I'd known the whole of it, I'd have still married you so your children could have someone to care for them."

She'd never know if that was true. But seeing that there'd be no chance to test the truth of it, she decided to go ahead and believe it.

"Thank you, Megan." A cough ripped through him and he clutched his chest.

Terror drove all her selfish thoughts from her head. What if he died right now, his young sons in the next room with only Megan, little more than a stranger, to care for them?

Jumping to her feet, Megan used her strong, hardworking hands to ease David onto his back, even as the coughing fit continued. She raised his feet to the bed and positioned a pillow behind his head to elevate him slightly. It had helped her mother a bit when her chest was aching.

Rushing out, she found a pitcher of water in the main room of the car. It was set in such a way that it wouldn't spill as the train chugged and swayed. She got water for David and rushed back to give him a few sips.

"Aye, 'tis a shame we're on the train. I could make you a likely cup of tea laced with honey that might ease your cough."

The water settled him. Megan sat down on the bed. David looked so fragile. But his eyes. She saw the life in them. Pain, yes. Worry, definitely. But bright, shining vitality.

Praying, she felt God whisper in her ear that she shouldn't treat David like a dying man. But rather she should go on as if he were only a sick man in need of tender care. That it felt like a word from the Almighty gave her hope and it was a task she was able to do.

With that whisper she let go of her fretting and was struck by the weight of her own long day and the sleepless night before and her battered body from being kicked by a horse.

"Move over with you, husband. We came in here because we both wanted a bit of a nap. No reason not to go ahead and sleep a bit while the lads are abed."

David pulled back the covers and slid sideways to make room for her. Unlacing, then toe-ing off her own half boots, she lay down and was surprised when David slid his arm under her shoulders and drew her to his side.

"We aren't going to be husband and wife in the way of

nighttime goings-on, Megan." His deep voice in her ear was an odd and stirring feeling. She nestled closer. "But in every other way, I will try to be the best husband to you I can. Let me hold you while we sleep."

It felt wonderful. Resting her head on his shoulder, she let herself be held. Not since her youngest brother had reached that inevitable age when he no longer allowed cuddling had she touched anyone except in passing, shoulders brushing on a busy street perhaps, nothing more.

Could a woman be hungry for a strong arm? Because lying with David fed her as surely as a feast.

She was a fool to let herself enjoy him. If she got used to having him in her life, the pain of losing him would be terrible.

Oh, she would care about him. That was the nature of simple human kindness. She could even love him as called by her Maker to love her neighbor, and—seeing as how they'd be sharing a house—he was the truest sort of neighbor.

But that was a far sight from falling in love. She dared not do that. She needed to remain separate from him, think of him as a patient under her care. Then when he died . . . if he died . . . her heart wouldn't be torn asunder.

He shifted and pulled her closer, and she wasn't sure she could protect her heart from loving him.

CHAPTER THREE

THE TRAIN CHUGGED ACROSS FOUR STATES. BIG STATES at that.

David was proving to be a quiet man—if one didn't count the coughing fits—and she didn't. They slept a night in each other's arms but nothing of marital prerogatives passed between them.

They entered a land of endless brown grass. They rode through stretches of snow too. She saw a huge herd of buffalo. Neither blizzard nor herd stopped the train, though she expected either could have done so.

Idleness didn't suit her, and she'd grown hardily sick of the world moving endlessly past her window to the music of a clackety, smoke-spouting train, when they finally reached Medicine Bow, Wyoming.

"I wired ahead to have one of the hands bring the wagon and team into town once I knew when the train'd be coming,"

David said. "If we hurry we can be at the ranch before sunset. I'd like to sleep under our own roof tonight."

He shouted orders to men working around the train's baggage cars, and they immediately loaded a wagon standing beside the tracks. A few more shouts from David and a man emerged from a livery stable leading a pair of well-fed brown horses, their coats thick with winter fur.

The weather was chilled but not painfully so despite a gusting wind.

As the back end of the wagon filled with crates, Megan began to worry that she'd need to walk alongside it. Well, no matter, she might prefer to move about for a change.

David found room for her on the high seat of his wagon. There was room for Ben, squeezed in between them. Zack was on her lap.

"It's glad I am for you boys being close," she said, hugging Zack tight. "It shelters me from the wind."

David smiled at her as he slapped the reins to keep the horses moving as they left town. "It's about an hour's drive to the ranch. We could make it far quicker riding horseback and we'll usually do that. Do you ride, Megan?"

"Never have I been astride a horse." She didn't mention leaping on that horse to save Zack. "There's much to learn about Wyoming and that's a fact."

Zack squirmed around to look at her in amazement. "You've never been on a horse? Pa had me riding right from the start."

"True enough." David guided the horses onto a road

frozen with ruts. "We moved out here when Ben was three and Zack just past two. I'd take both boys on my lap to ride into town for services on Sunday and we'd do the same if we needed to go for supplies, leading a packhorse."

"I'm willing to learn. You boys can be my teachers; how about that?"

Ben smiled sideways at her. Zack snuggled deeper onto her lap. Megan could see the day when the four of them would make a likely family.

"Was your ma good with horses, then?" she said to Ben. White breath puffed from Megan's mouth when she spoke, quickly whisked away by the wind. One of the horses tossed its head and the traces jingled like Christmas bells.

Ben said, "Ma never lived out here with us." He didn't sound very sad. He'd have been about three when his ma died. He probably couldn't remember her.

Megan expected David to pick up the story, but instead, he seemed to withdraw. Megan wasn't quite sure why. True, it was sad to bury a wife, but death came at a time of God's own choosing. Kicking against the truth only hurt your foot.

"So how did you end up back east, David? I can see you love it out here. What took you away to begin with?"

David shook his head and gave the boys a significant glance that told Megan this was a subject he wasn't willing to speak of in front of them. She scrambled around in her head for a new subject, but David's mood was so surprising that her mind went blank.

"We meant to move west but kept delaying it." David

seemed willing to speak of his wife now, rather than of what took him back east. So that meant leaving Wyoming was worse than losing his wife?

Megan sat silently.

"Pamela liked the East," David went on, his words cold as the ground. "She was born and raised in New York City. We met there, married there, and we lived there all through our marriage."

"New York City? Not Chicago?" Megan wondered if it was right to prod, but she wanted to know more about her husband and, though he begrudged talk of his wife, he was at least, finally, saying a bit. Perhaps she'd ask questions about him leaving Wyoming whenever she wanted to learn something else.

"Yep, I—I left the ranch for New York City when I was seventeen."

But why? Megan burned to know.

"I lived in New York until a couple of years ago. I came west when Pamela died. I want my boys to grow up in the clean air, with mountains around them and cattle to tend. It'll make men out of 'em."

Zack giggled. "I'm a man already, Pa."

With a quick chuck of Zack's chin, David said, "Reckon you are, son. You too, Ben."

David rested his gloved hand on Ben's head and rocked it a bit. Ben shoved at the hand in good-natured protest.

"You—you—" David fell silent and clutched his chest.

With a twist of terror, Megan knew she had to keep the boys from noticing their father's struggles. The reins began to slip through David's fingers and she reached over and took them. "I'll be havin' me first lesson on driving a wagon right now."

There might be a lot to driving a team, but as far as Megan could tell, the horses knew the way home and all David did was hold on. She could do that.

David gave her a hard look as he struggled to breathe.

"Can you drive a wagon?" Zack caught hold of the reins from where he sat on her lap. It didn't seem to affect the horses so she let him.

Barely able to tear her eyes from David, praying he wouldn't fall from the high seat, she kept her voice steady with considerable effort. "It seems that I can, and if not, it's time I learned, laddy."

With Zack helping hold the reins, she reached behind Ben's back and laid hands on her husband to pray while she distracted his sons and drove the team.

A sudden fit of coughing drew the boys' attention. Megan saw worry lines on Ben's face.

"You think you're getting pneumonia again, Pa?" Ben patted David on the knee.

With a hard shake of his head, David wrapped both arms across his chest as if he wanted to hold his body together through pure force. Megan saw agony etched across his face. Their eyes met, and he had to know what his face revealed because he lowered his head until his broad-brimmed hat shielded his expression. "Just a cough, boys. Not pneumonia."

The next cough cut off his words. Megan noticed a splash

of bright crimson blood on David's lips. Knowing he'd want her to protect his boys from worry, she snatched a handkerchief out of her sleeve and nudged David's arm. He looked and she touched her lips with the kerchief.

"Cover your mouth when you cough, David. That's just good manners." Trying to sound light, she tucked the kerchief in his hand and he swiped at his lip, saw the blood, then covered his mouth. The deep, painful cough sounded as if it tore at his chest and throat.

"Ben, would you like to help Zack and me hold the reins?" That distracted both boys. Megan prayed as they rode on down the grassy, rutted trail.

The land along their trail had open stretches broken by woodlands. The trees got thicker, the hills higher and more rock-studded, as they rode. They curved around a jagged bluff and the land opened into a beautiful valley, surrounded by trees and bluffs but rich with flat grassland.

"We're home!" Zack bounced in her arms.

Megan spied a lovely log cabin only a mile ahead. It was a single story high, with shuttered windows across the front. Smoke curled out of the chimney as if waving them home to warmth and comfort. It would be the largest home Megan had ever lived in.

The boys talked over top of each other as they pointed out a barn and several other outbuildings behind the house. There was enough thin daylight left so Megan could see corrals of sleek brown and black horses. Cattle dotted the vast, grassy valley beyond the buildings. Behind the corrals stretched a long building with a low porch and a hitching post out front. A man standing on the porch started toward them. Three more came out of what had to be a bunkhouse, pulling on heavy coats.

Megan wondered at this strange western world of horses and cattle and bunkhouses. She did indeed have a lot to learn. "Your home is beautiful, David."

"That's not my home. The foreman lives there." David squared his shoulders and sat straighter as they curved more fully into the canyon valley. A large, whitewashed house appeared, nearly tucked into the trees on the valley's north side. "That's my home."

Megan gasped. It was huge. Two full stories with an attic. Twice as long and twice as deep as the lovely cabin. There were glass windows. A porch with spindle railings ran across most of the front of the house. The roof had gables on the three sides Megan could see, and even in the dusk, stained-glass windows sparkled with color in those peaks.

"You live in a mansion." Megan needed to readjust her thinking about her husband's wealth.

"I grew up in the little house." David retrieved the reins, and Megan was happy to let them go, the boys less so. "My pa built it. We were heading for Oregon, but we . . . we turned aside and found us a home here."

The way he said it told her there was more there. Why had they turned aside from their previous destination? But right now that wasn't what she wanted to know.

"Why did you want the larger house?" Megan waited

in vain for her husband to respond. But his gaze was on the men ahead. Megan was grateful to see those who'd come out of the bunkhouse ambling toward the big house. They'd need help with their wagonload of supplies. David wasn't up to it and there were many crates. It was daunting to think of doing it alone, though if need be, she'd have managed.

There was no smoke curling out of the chimney—chimneys, Megan corrected herself.

David climbed down to talk with an older man with bushy white brows and a full white beard. She saw the old-timer note the bloody handkerchief David clutched.

Megan took each boy's hand and they went into the house. Mansion indeed.

Right inside the front door, which was in the center of the house, a wide hallway opened on the left and right to large rooms. On the left was quite the most elegant room Megan had ever seen. Couches that looked too delicate to bear weight. Finely made tables scattered about, all in matching dark wood. Two lamps sat on tables alongside the sofa. The lamps were of elegantly carved brass, topped with light blue glass chimneys. Megan wondered how two healthy young boys had avoided breaking those lamps.

To her right through broad doors was another large room, but this one looked less intimidating. Far fewer things to break in here. Far less to dust too. The walls were lined with enough books to make her squirm with pleasure. She had little schooling, but she read well enough and she dearly loved a good book. Her whole house growing up, with eight of them, would have fit into one of these large rooms.

Men toted crates into the house, so she moved farther in to clear their path. Beyond the fancy parlor, a hallway was half filled by a stairway. On farther was a bedroom and a ridiculously large dining room with a dusty table stretching ten feet long. Next a pantry closet. She might have missed that door if the men hadn't been carrying things into it. Past the pantry was the kitchen, which seemed to be the only room on this end. She peeked out a door and saw another big porch, this one enclosed. To one side was a flight of steps leading downward to a cellar.

Daunted from the work ahead of her to tend this monstrosity, Megan decided to get out from underfoot.

"Boys, is your bedroom upstairs?" She needed to get a fire going, but she wouldn't waste energy building one in that parlor.

"Yep! Come and see!" Ben dragged on her hand, but she was happy to be led. They dodged cowhands and went back toward the steps. As she turned to abandon the chaos down here, she saw David leaning against the front door. He looked near collapse.

The foreman stood beside him talking. Megan met the foreman's eyes, and he gave a tiny jerk of his head at David.

"You boys go on up. I'm going to speak with your da for just a moment. I want him to help with this tour." The boys ran up with an undo clatter of feet and a fair amount of shouting.

"Howdy, Mrs. Laramie. I'm Roper. Dave's foreman here on the Circle T. Welcome to Wyoming." The man tugged at the brim of his hat by way of greeting.

"'Tis nice to be here, Roper. It's pleased I'd be if you'd call me Megan. Are things in hand?" Megan assumed that the way the men worked, hard and fast, without asking David to help, meant they knew he was sick—though maybe not just how sick. She suspected Roper was used to handling things himself and would continue to do so.

"We have everything inside and most of it unpacked and shelved, boss. We'll get out soon'ez we can. Brought a pot of stew over from the bunkhouse. We'll have the fire going in the main fireplace before we leave. Lots of kindling stacked in the wood box in the kitchen that we'll refill when need be from the mighty big pile outside."

"Sure and it's a fine job you've done of welcoming us home, Roper. Thank you. David, will you come up with the boys and me? I want you to show me around."

David looked up, his eyes blazing. "You don't have to pretend I'm anything but useless."

Megan simply waited. If she didn't need to pretend, then she wouldn't. His temper faded but vivid life still flashed in his eyes. Megan couldn't believe he was dying, but he believed it sure enough. The only way to convince him differently was for him to stay alive, and there was no fast way to do that.

"All right." David's jaw tightened into a grim line. "Maybe bring me a meal in bed, Megan."

David was shaping up to be a bit of a stubborn ox. But

there was no point getting angry about it. Megan was torn. Part of her wanted to hug him and let him lean on her as they went upstairs. Part of her wanted to shake him until he admitted there was no failure in accepting help while he got well.

Thinking neither reaction was quite appropriate, she just stepped back, exchanged a worried glance with Roper, and let David lead. David went straight to the room closest to the top of the stairs. As Megan moved to follow, she found the door snapped shut in her face.

Four upstairs bedrooms, each large and airy and cold. A bit of heat started coming into the upstairs, so the men must have gotten a fire going in the kitchen.

The chimney was bare brick exposed in the boys' room. Megan felt sure that if she gained entrance to her husband's room—which she'd do or know the reason why—she'd find the other side of this warm brick fireplace heating his—that was to say *their*—room too.

Well, she could read a closed door well enough.

Leave me alone.

Find another place to sleep.

But a wife's place was by her husband at night. And he needed to eat too. For now she let the boys show her around, then they went downstairs and ate a hearty if flavorless stew with overcooked biscuits drenched in butter and honey, and milk.

Aye, and it was a fair home indeed. Ornery husband notwithstanding.

CHAPTER FOUR

Dave kept his backbone straight—mainly by nurturing his anger—until he got into his room. Then he nearly toppled over.

The ride home from the train station had nearly finished him.

Stripping down to his underdrawers, he was in bed before Megan and the boys got done making a fuss next door. He fell asleep to the sound of their talk and laughter.

His eyes opened to a soft knock on the door. Megan came in without being asked, carrying a tray of something steaming in a bowl. It smelled good but his bunkhouse cook was no genius. Still, being hungry helped make food seem tasty.

"We'll make do with this stew tonight, and grateful I am for it." Megan held the tray in one hand and a lantern in the other. She set it on the bedside table and only then did David realize just how dark it'd gotten. Megan must've been working a long time.

"But come the morning, I'll be taking charge of your kitchen and then we'll see about feeding this family." She sat down on the bed beside him. "Do you want help? I can spoon the stew if you've need of my assistance."

Busily, she adjusted his pillows so he sat nearly straight up, then she tucked a napkin into the collar of his woolen shirt.

Shaking off the grogginess of sleep, he asked, "What time is it? How long did I sleep?" Sitting straighter, he reached for the bowl. "I can manage."

He fought down a surge of irritation that he was so helpless, so useless. But it wasn't fair to Megan to be annoyed. She was caring for him. He tried to think of once in his life when Pamela had brought him food, served him in any way. They'd had a cook in New York and a maid. Pamela got served; she didn't do the serving. But she was delicate and beautiful and gracious. Dave was honored to be able to arrange for servants for her.

Megan McBride with her corkscrew curls and solid patch of freckles and work-worn hands was mighty different from Pamela.

Thank God for that.

He'd loved his Pamela something fierce. His wife had been stunningly beautiful, with a smile as bright as the noonday sun. Pamela was more than a bit spoiled, but so beautiful and kindhearted that men stood in line to spoil her.

Marrying her had been one of the finest things he'd ever done.

Megan was nothing like her. Megan was sturdy as a summer weed. Pretty enough in a very Irish sort of way. Quick thinking. A woman of action. She was all that he needed and nothing that touched his heart.

Pamela's pale elegance and expensive taste appealed to Dave. He'd wanted a fine wife to match the fine fortune he'd made in New York.

He'd always intended to go back to Wyoming. He'd left for a good reason, his quickness with a gun. There'd been men hunting him, wanting to make a name for themselves by killing a known man.

In New York, he'd built a fortune with the same ruthlessness and deadly accuracy he'd brought to a gunfight.

Then he'd met Pamela and had fallen in love. That love had freed him of his driving desire to gain wealth. He had enough, and wanted to focus on his wife and the sons who soon followed his marriage. He wanted to return to Wyoming to see his pa after more than fifteen years of separation.

Though returning to the West was always his dream, he'd known Pamela wouldn't like his pa's rough cabin, so he'd delayed while he'd had a nice ranch house built. Still, he'd put off returning to the West, knowing Pamela wouldn't do well there. The Wyoming winds would have blown her away the first winter.

Then his father died and he grieved deeply that he'd gone so long without returning. With Pa's death, his reason to hurry back was gone. He decided to forget the West and settle into New York City, though he'd never felt really at home there.

And then a runaway carriage had careened off the street and killed Pamela and five others, wiping away his single reason to stay in the East. He'd gone west with his boys, and for the last two years, he'd done well at the ranch, the boys dogging his footsteps and thriving in the sometimes harsh conditions.

And then he'd taken ill and come far too close to death. Little scared him, but he'd known real, solid fear of what would become of his sons. It brought him to Chicago where he'd gotten the doctor's grim death sentence. Then he'd turned his attention to the boys and finding a caregiver for them.

And now here sat pretty Megan with her servant's heart. He was a lucky man. Except for dying, of course.

"Are the boys asleep?" Dave dipped his spoon into the bowl of stew. The chunks of meat were few and far between, and what there was, tough and gristly. The only vegetable was potatoes and precious few of those. The gravy was gray and pasty. Whoever was cooking at the bunkhouse was doing a poor job of it. If he wasn't starving, he wouldn't eat it.

"Yes, we ate and they were asleep as soon as we'd walked upstairs, the poor lads. It's been a long journey home for them."

Filling his empty belly with the stew, David forced himself to keep eating after the worst edge of his hunger had passed.

"So, do you have trouble keeping cowhands?"

David looked up from the awful stew in surprise. Then he laughed. "We've got an old-timer named Tex who's been here since before I came back west. He's got achy joints and he's not up to riding herd, but it shames him to not work, so years ago Roper made him the cook." Dave kept eating, determined to fill his stomach. "But it's clear he's got no great gift for the job. And no, I don't have trouble keeping cowpokes, but I pay really good wages."

"I'm wondering, David, would you mind if I gave a few lessons to your cook?"

"So, you think you're a good cook, huh?" Dave found he liked her company more than he thought possible.

"I'm a fair to middling cook. I can feed you much better than this." She nodded at the bowl.

"You've my permission then to talk to him, and good luck to you."

As his belly filled, his exhaustion began to get the better of him. Dave set the bowl aside. "I think that's enough for now. I'll get to sleep then. Have you gotten settled for the night? I had the men set linens in the bedroom across the hall and had your satchel put in there."

It was all Dave wanted to say about sleeping arrangements.

"A wife's place is beside her husband in bed." Megan gathered up the dishes, then tucked the blankets around Dave's chin in a way that made him feel like a child. As she worked in her efficient, quiet way, she talked. "I'll be sleeping here with you. Besides, this chimney warms your room and the boys', but not the other two rooms. I've no wish to lie in a cold bed, and I'd need to light the parlor fire to get any heat. I've no wish to waste the wood your men worked so hard to chop. Now, I'll tend to these dishes. Get to sleep, and we'll face the new day together come morning."

She didn't wait for him to give her leave. He knew it was best if she didn't. He'd liked holding her close on the train ride. Liked it too much. Being close made maintaining a distance more difficult. And he *had* to maintain a distance. Megan could stubbornly refuse to accept his impending death, but Dave felt the pain in his chest. He could hear his heart pounding. He felt it struggle, felt it crush at his chest as it beat heavily.

Before he could insist, though, and start another difficult conversation about her being realistic, she'd turned the lantern off and swished out of the room.

❀

Megan woke wound up tight in blankets. She tried to free her arms and realized she was cuddled up next to David. It was his arms that held her, not a blanket. Her eyes flickered open and it was full daylight. Her head rested on his shoulder as she wondered how long she'd slept. She listened a moment to see if the boys were busy tearing the house down. There was only silence.

Wishing to let David sleep, she eased one arm free.

"Good morning, wife." His sleep-graveled voice tickled her ear.

Megan smiled and lifted her head to enjoy being near him. They'd slept side by side on the train too, in a smaller bed. But they'd never snuggled up like this.

"Good morning, David. I've lazed the morning away, it seems. Time to be up and about."

He seemed to focus on her smile with undue interest. Then slowly, smoothly, he lowered his head and kissed her.

Her first kiss. It was warm and gentle and she found a surprising pleasure in it. How could a kiss be felt all through a woman's body? It made no sense, yet at the same time it was undeniable.

David raised himself up on his left arm—the one wrapped behind her neck. Without loosening his grip, he was over her, the kiss deeper, his head slanted as if he wanted to be closer, which didn't seem possible.

Just as David shifted his weight to press down on her more fully, the bedroom door flew open.

"Pa, it's morning! Get up! We're hungry, Ma!"

David moved away from her fast, but his arm was wrapped around her and he dragged her on top of him. Their eyes met. She saw dismay dawning in his gaze. She wasn't sure why he was dismayed, but she found herself annoyed at it. Hadn't he enjoyed their kiss?

Before she could ask what he was thinking, the boys pounced, Zack on top of Megan's back. Ben on his knees, bouncing on the bed beside them.

"Time to get up." Megan decided talking about what had just happened was probably not a good idea with the boys here. She rolled over, careful not to dump Zack on the floor, then she left the bed. Fetching her only dress besides the one she'd worn on the train, she said, "I'll dress in the other room, then we'll see about breakfast."

Snapping the door shut a bit too hard, she was dressed and had pancake batter mixed up before the boys could finish pestering their father.

CHAPTER FIVE

"YOU'VE GOT TO SAVE THE MEN IN THE BUNKHOUSE. YOU can start Tex's cooking lessons right away." Dave tried his best not to just bolt down the whole plate of fried potatoes, steaming fried eggs, and crisp bacon. He'd already done that with his first serving, and the boys were eating so fast they didn't have time to squabble. He hadn't had food like this since . . . well, never. He could barely remember his ma's cooking, but it seemed she'd been a decent hand at it. But after she died, he and his pa had lived off the land even after they got the ranch up and running. Venison and raccoon, trout and pheasant. They'd managed a few potatoes, but gardening wasn't a skill they worked at. Mostly they ate whatever they could hunt.

Megan laughed and began clearing plates nearly licked clean. Even the boys had been unusually silent, eating every bit. She set small bowls of her steaming peach cobbler in front of each of them. "I'll try and think of a way to give him some advice without bruising his manly feelings."

"You can stomp on his feelings with hobnail boots if you want to. Reckon Tex'll put up with anything from a woman who can cook like this."

Dave finished the meal with gusto and rose from the table. "I need to go out and talk with the men, but before I do, I want you to see what I bought for you. There's fabric and I found some ready-made clothes that I think will fit you. There is material for the boys too. Take a few hours to settle in, then we'll talk ranching."

Dave caught her wrist as she reached to scoop water out of the steaming wells on the side of the stove. "Leave that."

She giggled as he dragged her behind him and he tried to remember ever insisting Pamela do what he wanted. It had never happened. He'd spent his life pampering her.

"Where are we going?" Zack asked.

Dave looked at the boy over his shoulder. "You'll see."

He found the crates right where he'd told Roper to leave them, the tops already pried loose. Plunging his hand deep into the biggest crate, he pulled out a fistful of wool and calico. "You can make clothes for yourself and the boys with this."

"David, I only need fabric for a dress or two and wool for a coat. You've bought enough for me to dress the whole state of Wyoming."

"Since there aren't many women in Wyoming, that might well be the truth." Dave flashed her a smile, digging for the coat he'd packed. She met his smile with one of her own, the first full smile since the boys had interrupted them that morning. What had come over him? What was he thinking to let himself turn to his wife in that way? He'd assured her he wouldn't. Then when he had a weak moment, she'd just kissed him right back.

He needed her help. They both needed to be vigilant so no more children would come along. The ache in his chest might have eased after a long night's sleep, a relaxed morning, and a good, hearty meal, but he was dying and he couldn't leave more of a burden behind for Megan in the form of a new baby. Though he'd relish the sight of Megan fat with his baby. He'd love to watch his sons grow up and have children of their own someday. These thoughts caught in his throat until he feared there were shameful tears in his eyes, so he turned briskly to the next crate.

"Boys, there are plenty of things in here for you too. Ready-made clothes for all of us."

With a shout of excitement they helped dig through the box.

"Here's a warm coat for you. I'm sorry I didn't have it out for the ride home yesterday. I didn't think of it when they were crating things up back in Chicago."

With a gasp, Megan reached for it. The coat was long and thick, made of black wool with soft black mink around the neck and cuffs. Shiny, oversized jet-black buttons lined the front. "I've never had such as this. It's too beautiful to wear." Even the boys seemed in awe of it.

"You get cold enough, you'll wear it. But for around the ranch there's a buckskin jacket hanging by the kitchen door;

it's sturdier than this. There should be boots for all of you in here somewhere too, and gloves. I bought you a couple of riding skirts and some warm blouses. I'll leave you to sorting it."

Before he could go, Megan wrapped her arms around his neck and kissed him right in front of the boys. "Thank you so much, David. Sure and it's a fine thing to have such a kind and generous husband. It's far too much, and I'd make you take every bit of it back if we hadn't left Chicago far behind."

With a smile, Dave said, "Why do you think I didn't show it to you until now?"

Laughing, Megan kissed him again. The boys put up a cry of protest at the kissing. Zack shoved between them. Ben fell over on a soft pile of fabric, holding his throat, pretending to gag.

Megan plunked her hands on her slender hips and turned to the boys in mock severity, her eyes sparkling with humor. "You both need to be thanking your da for all this bounty. Now go ahead."

"We don't have to kiss him on the lips, do we?" Ben asked with dread echoing in his voice.

Dave chuckled. "Nope, but I'd take a hug."

Both boys hurled themselves at him. It hurt his chest, but Dave kept his face clear of that. Then he looked up at Megan and knew he hadn't done a good enough job at masking his pain.

The boys let go and went back to digging in the crates.

Dave headed outside, glad his boys were distracted enough that they didn't notice him start to cough.

MARY CONNEALY

❀

"Megan, can you and the boys come out?"

The tearing pain in Dave's chest should have forced him back into the house and into bed. Instead, it made him almost desperate to teach her ranching. She needed to know horseflesh and when the cattle were ready for market. He had to get the books out to show her the ranch's accounts and how to manage his investments back east. She should be taught to saddle her own horse. She also needed to— Dave quit adding to the list before he started banging his head on the barn wall.

First things first. They were going for a ride.

The boys came dashing out, still pulling their coats on, shouting as always. Dave looked at Roper. "I think the horses and cattle are actually calmer because they've had to get used to the noise. My rowdy boys are training them to overlook a ruckus."

Roper smiled.

Dave knew he'd run wild on the ranch as a kid when his pa settled here when he was eight. Of course his wild ways had nearly led to his own death, but that was because he was so fast with a gun. In fact, he'd been told he was as fast and accurate as anyone heard tell of. He wasn't sure why he could handle a gun like he did, but it might've been because deep inside he still felt the rage from finding his mother murdered.

Ma's death had turned them aside from their journey to Oregon and left them in a wilderness. Then Dave's rage had

338

led to trouble, and that trouble had driven him back east away from his pa and the Wyoming land he loved.

He still thought of those days and the hard way his ma had died, and he wondered how he could have done anything different.

Now he was back on his pa's ranch, but once he'd gotten back east, he'd changed his name from Stewart to Laramie, the fort near his home. He brought his new name west with him, and to the world, it was believed he'd bought this ranch, not inherited it. No one was left from those days, not a single hand on the ranch knew him as anyone but David Laramie.

That, plus the peace of the West, plus the passage of time, should be enough to keep gunmen from coming, hunting a reputation. The West was getting purely civilized these days. Pamela might've even liked it.

Megan stepped outside wearing the buckskin jacket he'd told her about. She had on the black riding skirt he'd bought. The wind, which never seemed to stop blowing, buffeted her as she pulled on gloves.

She was even wearing her new boots and the black, flat-topped hat he'd gotten for her. Head to toe she wore items he'd provided. Seeing it gave him enough satisfaction to ignore the ache in his chest. Her tidy little skirt kept him going when he wanted to fold up and rest.

Roper had the horses saddled and the boys were already boosted up. His sons were decent riders, though Dave wasn't close to trusting them to ride alone. But with the old cowhand to keep an eye out, Dave could attend to Megan.

"Let's mount up."

Megan stopped dead in her tracks, her eyes wide as she looked from Dave to the sleepy, sway-backed old mare at his side. The hardest part of riding Old Blue was keeping her awake. Second hardest, keeping her moving. This was the horse his boys had learned on. Megan was halfway done putting on her second glove; she didn't give it another yank to finish putting it on.

"I thought you were going to—to show me around." She turned her gaze from Dave and focused on the horse as if the beast had reared up on her back legs and was flashing her hooves in the air right at Megan's head.

The blue roan stood, nose drooped nearly to the ground, her weight on three legs. Dave thought he might hear her snoring.

Dave went to Megan and gently but relentlessly towed her over to the mare. He looked to see if her boot heels left a line cut in the ground.

"Now, you put your left foot in the stirrup." Dave pointed at it in case she had no idea what a stirrup was.

Megan didn't move. Her glove was still only half on.

He finished dressing her—which was to say he pulled her glove the rest of the way on—then took both of her shoulders and forced her to face him and look away from Old Blue, who might be renamed Tornado if Megan got her way.

Finally, after only one small shake of her shoulders . . . or two . . . Megan looked away from the horse and into his eyes.

"Now, you put your left foot in the—"

"I've some baking to do, David." Megan smiled, but it was as fake a smile as he'd ever seen. Her skin, where it wasn't brown with freckles, was milk white. Her eyes were so wide open he could see white all the way around her blue irises.

Her gloves were on though.

"Wouldn't you like a nice pie for supper?"

Bribery. It should've been beneath her. And yet, pie sounded really good. David resisted temptation. "Quit stalling. We can have a short ride and then you can bake for the rest of the day."

She swallowed as if she had a lump of last night's lousy stew meat still stuck in her throat. Then she squared her little shoulders and jerked her chin. "All right." She turned to the horse, staring straight at the saddle, and reached for the saddle horn. Dave decided not to get his hopes up just yet. Learning the terms for mounting a horse, like *stirrup* and *reins*, could come later, as well as the details of swinging up.

"I'm going to give you a boost." He thought it best to warn her, since she seemed apt to startle easily. He caught her by the waist and hoisted. She lay over the horse's back on her belly, much as she'd mounted that horse back in Chicago. He plucked her very pretty right ankle and swung it over the horse's rump to get her settled. The horse didn't bother to lift her head.

Dave tried to put the reins in her hands and, since she had a death grip on the saddle horn, he had to slip them into her gloves and hope she held on.

He led Blue toward where his own horse waited. Megan

gasped and hung on tighter, which wasn't possible, but some-how she did it. She also clung with her legs, which might've had the effect of kicking Blue. Luckily, Blue either didn't notice or had no intention of speeding up under any circumstances.

Dave mounted up. His chest ached as if the horse had kicked him. He hoped Megan was too terrified to notice. "Let's ride."

That got her to quit staring at her clinging hands and turn to him. With a sigh, he reached down, fetched the reins from her, and took a step. Megan squeaked loud enough that Dave's horse would have danced sideways if he didn't have the stallion under firm control. Blue's ears came forward, so the old beast was at least alive.

Dave led his sturdy little wife out of the ranch yard, walk-ing at a pace that was only the least bit above a full stop.

Teaching Megan to ride looked to be a task for a man anticipating a long, long life.

"So now that I know how to ride, what will you be teaching me tomorrow?" She certainly hoped she knew enough to be done, because the riding lessons were terrifying.

David gave her a long look but didn't answer. Instead, he passed through the kitchen, and she heard him clomping up the steps.

"Supper will be in an hour!" she called after him.

He grunted but didn't respond. Smiling, Megan felt keen satisfaction at how well she'd done. Why, she was good enough at riding, she doubted another lesson was necessary. She prayed fervently it would be so.

She rolled out the piecrust while the boys played under the kitchen table and contemplated something she had confidence in.

Cooking.

It was a whole hour before David came back down. His

eyes were a bit puffy as if he'd been sleeping. He settled into his place at the head of the table, rubbed his chest, and said, "Let's bow our heads."

Then her menfolk dug into the meal. David seemed pleased with it and showed a good appetite.

Once they were stuffed, the boys went up to their room to play and David disappeared into the front of the house. She'd barely stepped foot in either front room—the day had been full enough without turning her attention there. He closed the pocket doors on the library and occasionally she heard him coughing.

After the kitchen was tidy and the boys tucked into bed, she turned to what David needed. She'd spent her last pennies in Chicago buying the makings for the concoction that had helped her little brother mend after his pneumonia. She made a strong cup of tea, laced with honey, ginger, willow bark, and cayenne pepper. She let it steep a bit while she prepared a poultice for his chest and a few other little tricks she had learned from an old doctor who was willing to treat the very poor.

When it was all ready, she went into the living room to find David asleep in a comfortable stuffed chair with a book open on his lap.

"Here now, David." Keeping her voice low, she gently caught his wrist and coaxed him awake.

He didn't respond at first and fear caught in her throat. What if he was dead? She saw the rise and fall of his chest and knew he wasn't, but it might happen. If not now, then one of these times. His heart would quietly stop beating. She'd come into a room expecting that he was sleeping, only to find he'd died.

Tears burned at the very thought. Megan knew only too well what a dead body felt like. She'd prepared her mother's body for burial. She could still feel that hard, cold flesh. David was warm. His pulse beat in his wrists. He shifted a bit as she talked to him, and finally, slowly, his head came up.

To cover her worry she turned to focus on the cup of tea she'd fixed for him. "I want you to drink this. It's full of things that will make you feel better." She lifted the tea to his lips.

He roused enough that he took the cup and sipped it, then shuddered. "What is in this?" His brow furrowed and he stared at the cup.

"Just drink it down. And I've got a plaster for your chest."

David downed the tea on a single swallow, grimacing. He set the cup aside. "Megan, I don't mind taking any medicine you have or any treatment you've concocted. But to think you can save me—that's false hope, little lass." He rested one open palm on her cheek.

Megan met his eyes, wondering if a man who believed himself to be dying would give up the fight to live. She needed to give him reason to hope.

"Let's go upstairs. I want you lying down when I put the poultice on. It's bedtime anyway."

"So I need to wake up so I can go to sleep?" David laughed, but there was a touch of bitterness in it. "I slept half the morning away. I had an afternoon nap. Now it's bedtime. I have a schedule like an infant."

"Just you hush, David Laramie. A man who's been sick needs rest. All I see when I look at you is a full-grown man, that's all." She did her best to glare that truth into him. "You know my mother died of pneumonia."

"I believe you mentioned that."

"Did I mention that my brothers didn't die? They were very sick but I pulled them through. I learned a lot about the disease, and I talked with a doctor many times about how to treat it. He said there can be pain after the pneumonia, sometimes for a long time. And the cough can go on for months. Now, I don't care what your fancy doctor told you."

"The best doctor in Chicago by all accounts."

"I'd put an old doctor from a poor neighborhood, a man who's seen most everything, against a fancy doctor who's only treated healthy rich people any day. I want you to plan to live to an old age. And part of that planning is to do whatever I say when it comes to treating you."

"Whatever you say?" David smiled. "I'm not surprised you want to run things, Meg."

"When it comes to the sickroom, I've got more knowledge than you." She did her best to be stern, but he'd called her Meg. She liked it and it took a fair amount of will to go on scolding the sweet, stubborn man. "If it comes to putting reins on a horse, then I'll bow to your superior knowledge."

Their eyes locked for far too long. No indeed, there was nothing childlike about her handsome husband.

"I'm sorry about your ma, Megan. How old were you when she died?"

346

"I was fifteen. Da had been gone for three years but he was a drinker with a bad temper. Things got better when he was gone. There was more money too, because he always drank up whatever I earned."

"You worked at a job when you were twelve?" David caught her hand and tugged until she sat in the fancy stuffed chair beside his.

"I started working when I was seven or eight. I ran errands for the general store. Then I got a job at a carpet mill and did that most of my growing-up years."

"I've heard of those places. They're dangerous."

"They're loud and hot. The hours are long. The pay is miserly and, yes, they're dangerous. I saw children die, tangled up in the machinery. I did my best to keep my little brothers from having to work in a mill."

"There were five, weren't there? Little brothers, I mean." David was still holding her hand. It felt wonderful.

"Yes. Sean, Donal, Conor, Killian, and Brendon. The youngest, Brendon, was born after Da died." She could remember the last time she hugged little Brendon, the morning of his first day of school. He'd hugged her back when she'd sent him off in the morning. When he'd come home, he'd pushed her away, embarrassed. Too old to let a big sister hug him, he said. The other boys had each done the same in turn and she had been able to shrug off their growing-up airs. But there'd been other, younger brothers to hug and she hadn't minded much. But when Brendon had done it, her heart had hurt for days.

"And none of them had to work while you slaved away in a carpet mill?" Dave's fingers tightened.

"It was something I could do for them. I didn't mind. I felt as if I was saving their lives." She smiled. "I was quite the hero."

Lifting her hand, David kissed her fingers, woven between his own. "Then you cleaned houses?"

"I've worked a lot of jobs, but lately, yes, I cleaned houses. It was a much preferable job."

"And where are your brothers now? You've barely spoken of them. Do you miss them? Do you want to go back east to visit them?"

"They've spread out all over." It lifted her heart to add proudly, "All five of them graduated from high school. None of them took to the bottle like Da. They're fine men."

"It's clear that you love them. If you want to go see them, we can do it. The train makes that possible."

"I wouldn't know where to go look for most of them to visit. I haven't seen a one of them in years."

"So you sacrificed your entire childhood and young adulthood for them, and they don't even let you know where they're living?" Color rose up David's neck along with the indignation in his voice. "None of them offered to take you in and support you after all those years of brutally hard work while they went off to school?"

"Hush," Megan scolded. "Their loyalty is to their wives and that's as it should be." Megan smiled, but she felt the weight of turning up the corners of her mouth. "No sense thinking on sad things, is there? It does no good."

"Megan, do you think you can be content out here? Wyoming is a harsh land. It's not for some folks."

Because his anger was so unlike him, she watched him closely, knowing this question was important. "It's beautiful. And so quiet. The roar of the city liked to knock away my ears. I can't imagine how you brought yourself to leave this place."

Something flashed in his eyes. Regret maybe.

"How could you leave it? How could you exchange this peace and quiet for the city?"

The look David gave her was a long one. If she hadn't been holding his hand, she'd have never felt him trembling. "You want to know why I left, really?"

The reason had to be terrible, she realized. Megan hesitated. "If you want to tell it."

There was silence between them, broken only by the crackling of the fire. David lifted her hand to his lips and just held it there, kissing her hand, almost as if he were trying to stop the words that he needed to say.

"No one knows this, Meg. I probably shouldn't tell you. My life, what I left behind out here, is well and truly over and it would be best if it stayed forgotten." At last he met her eyes. "You have to swear to never repeat this to another soul." He paused. "Are you sure you want to know?"

She wasn't sure at all, but it seemed that he needed to speak of it. "You can trust me with your secrets."

"I know I can." His eyes seemed to burn with the longing to trust. At last he spoke quietly. "My ma and pa and I came west with a wagon train in 1843. One of the early trains to cross the Oregon Trail and not a big one, only about ten wagons."

"I can't imagine crossing this whole country in a wagon, the train took long enough."

David quirked a smile. "The train took days. Our journey took months. Pa was so tired of it he'd considered many times leaving the group and finding a place to settle. And then one morning I rode out with Pa to hunt. He let me come along. We'd scout the trail ahead and hunt for the wagon train. Pa was teaching me to read sign."

"Read sign?" Megan interrupted.

"Yes, like to recognize an antelope track or a mountain lion print. He was teaching me to hunt and skin. All the things a boy needs to survive in the West. I loved every minute of it, and I'd gotten to be a fair shot and had brought down food to bring to the family's fire." He breathed in and out slowly.

Megan didn't break the silence.

"Then one day we came riding back into the camp, late in the day, with enough food for everyone to get a piece of meat and . . . and . . ." David let go of her and ran both hands over his face as if he wanted to wipe the memory away. "The wagon train had been attacked. Burned. The horses and supplies stolen. Everyone was dead. Man, woman, and child, all dead. Including my ma and two little sisters."

"Were they attacked by Indians?"

"Pa said no." David uncovered his face and looked into the fire as if he were staring into the past. "He could read Indian sign. He said it was outlaws who wanted to make it look like Indians. He didn't tell me that until a long time later. When it happened he barely spoke a word while he buried everyone. It took a long time. Pa scouted around and found this canyon and we settled here, long before there was anyone else in the area."

"And when you were grown up, you left because of the memories of losing your ma and sisters?"

"No." David pulled his faraway stare from the fire and faced her.

And she knew this was the important part.

"I left because as soon as I was old enough, I started guarding the Oregon Trail. My pa told me what really happened to my family and it made me mad enough to kill. I was quiet about it, but the band of outlaws preyed on people along the trail and I hated it. Hated them."

"Guarding it, how?"

"I was a good shot, a great shot. Fast and accurate. Nothing scared me or made me back up. I think I hurt so bad over my ma and sisters I didn't care if I lived or died, and that made it easy for me to face danger."

"When did you start doing this? You were too young when you first settled here."

"It was years later. We heard about another train being attacked and I was raging mad at the Indians I thought had done it. Pa said he didn't want to see me hate like that so he told me what really happened with Ma. About the time I turned sixteen, I stumbled on men planning to attack a wagon train and I . . . I stopped them."

Megan knew he meant he'd killed them. She shuddered at his bleak tone.

"It felt good. The wagon trains came through regularly. I'd tell Pa I was going hunting or trapping, which was common enough. Staying out overnight, even for several days, wasn't unusual. Then I'd guard the trains until they left the area or the men threatening them were all dead."

A chill rushed down Megan's spine at the cold tone of his voice.

"They called me the . . . the . . ." David shook his head and looked at her. "I shouldn't tell you. It's better you don't know. I only wish the whole thing would be forgotten."

"They called you what?"

He swallowed hard. "The O. T. Rider. Oregon Trail Rider. No one connected me to Pa until one day a man rode into our ranch. He'd tracked me somehow. We shot it out and I won. Pa saw the duel, so I had to explain. Pa had heard of the O. T. Rider but he'd never imagined it might be me. But he saw me draw on that man and knew I was deadly with a gun. And we both knew that if one man found me, others would.

"Pa told me to run, change my name. Stay away until everyone forgot who the O. T. Rider was. I did. I knew living that way could kill me. Someday, someone would come along who was faster—someone always does. But I hadn't figured guarding that trail might get my pa killed. He gave me what money he had and I rode east all the way to the ocean. I turned Pa's meager stake into a fortune. I wasn't a man you'd have admired back then, Meggie. But then I met Pamela. I married her and had two wonderful children and found the Lord. I became a man I could respect. I'd been away long enough that I could come back here. I've always felt like this was my true home."

"The O. T. Rider." Megan shook her head. "I'm married to a fabled gunman, and all he does is buy me clothes, compliment my cooking, and love his boys soundly."

"And teach you to ride. Don't forget that, Meg."

"That horse is a menace. I can't help it if he's hard to ride."

"It's a mare, a gentle mare."

"Hah! That beast has a wicked gleam in his eye. I don't trust him."

David laughed. She was amazed he could laugh after sharing the darkest part of his life. "Let's go up to bed."

Megan reached her hand down for him and he took it, rising to stand without letting her bear much weight.

"The tea was good. It soothed my throat a bit and the coughing has eased. I like it. Except for the taste."

"Go on up. I'll get you another cup while you change for bed and I'll fetch the poultice."

David smiled. Megan couldn't resist smiling back. He bent over and rested his lips on hers, as if matching their smiles together.

"I'll get into bed and wait for you, Dr. Megan."

With mock severity, Megan said, "Just see that you do."

Laughing, David led her out of the room, then turned and headed upstairs.

CHAPTER SEVEN

THE DAYS FELL INTO A PATTERN AS THANKSGIVING approached.

Megan trying to get the house in order.

David fussing at her to learn ranching.

Boys screaming and wrestling, running wild inside and out.

Good food.

A pattern marked by terror as David shooed her outside to ride that awful blue horse again and again.

"Why can't I just ride in your wagon?" Megan almost fell off the other side of the horse as she mounted, but David caught her. The horse had a bad habit of putting his head down, which made his back slope toward the front. Only clinging to the saddle horn kept Megan from sliding straight down the horse's neck and onto the ground. The horse was just being plain spiteful.

"There are places out here a wagon can't go. And a horse can travel much faster than a wagon." David patted the unruly critter.

Megan wished he'd quit, lest the horse become upset. "But I don't want to go faster."

"Well then, you've picked the right horse. This old mare won't go one bit too fast."

Megan wondered what a mare was and wondered if it was where the word *nightmare* came from.

She should probably ask, but David was sure to answer, and that could go on a long time and get very boring, all without making a lick of sense.

David's cough seemed a touch better as long as Megan poured tea into him steadily. He'd taken to having a cup many times a day and his chest pains seemed to ease for several hours afterward.

The ranch cook, Tex, had brought Megan a turkey for Thanksgiving, all cleaned and ready to roast. Tex's cooking had gotten some better since Megan had taken to advising him, which had made her very popular with the cowhands.

The turkey was huge, and Megan contrived quite a feast for the family. She sent pies made from dried apples out to the bunkhouse too, which raised her even higher in the eyes of David's men.

After the boys had been tucked into bed for the night, Megan and David left their room and in the hallway outside their own bedroom door, Megan asked, "You're feeling better, aren't you?"

He rubbed one open hand on his chest. "I really am. Do you think it's possible I've beat this thing?"

Megan touched his cheek. "It's God's most generous Thanksgiving blessing." She kissed him.

He kissed her back with much more enthusiasm than she'd expected. "Lying next to you every night, especially now that I'm feeling better, is tough."

Frowning, Megan said, "Do you want me to get out? I don't—"

A rusty laugh cut her off. "What I want has nothing to do with you getting out, Meggie." His expression grew very serious as he pulled her close. "It's wrong of me to . . . to be . . . with you in the night."

"I'm not going anywhere. I've made that perfectly plain." Megan lifted her chin so David would know every ounce of stubbornness she possessed. "I've told you that a wife's place is beside her husb—"

He cut her off with another kiss. Without lifting his lips away, he pushed open their door. "If I'm getting well, and you're in my bed to stay, lass, I'm not going to be able to resist showing you more about being a wife."

"We aren't going to go over the ranch accounts again, are we?" Megan let herself be pulled inside the room.

"No, this is something brand new." He shut the door with a firm click. "It's a part of married life I think we're both going to enjoy."

Then he stopped her next question with a kiss.

She found this lesson far superior to any she'd known before.

❊

"If you're going to live, why do I have to ride this blasted horse?" Megan hissed at Dave as the boys rode off with Roper.

"We've got a nice day on our hands. No sense wasting it." As Dave boosted his little wife into the saddle, he inhaled deeply with almost no pain.

He watched her trim form settle in. She was getting better. Or he might be substituting hope for common sense.

It was the first day of winter and uncommonly mild. His cowhands were scurrying around checking the cattle, making sure the animals had access to water and prairie hay.

As he mulled over whether to let Megan hold the reins herself—most likely Old Blue wouldn't move if Dave wasn't leading her—five cowhands rode into the yard. They'd gone to town for supplies and ended up staying four days while a blizzard blew itself through the area, followed by the unusually warm weather. They'd finally managed to get home.

"Unpack the horses and leave the supplies I ordered in the house." Dave hated giving orders for the men to do work he couldn't do. It made him feel worthless. He was healing. He could help, he thought, as a hard cough tore at his chest and stopped him from offering.

All the men but one rode on to the house. The eldest of

the bunch, newly hired, swung down off his mount. "We had to make a few changes in the supplies. Hope they suit you, boss."

The new cowhand gave a quick rundown, all of it fine, then suddenly was seized by a fit of coughing worse than Dave's.

Dave stepped back so fast he almost tripped over his feet. Megan gasped and threw herself off her horse. The cowpoke had his head down coughing and didn't notice their reactions.

When the coughing ended, he shook his head. "Reckon I caught a cold in town."

Two nights later David started running a fever.

※

Megan had fought for her mother's life. And that of her little brother. Now David, already fragile, had a cold and Megan prepared for battle.

Megan didn't get the cold. She never got sick. But the boys did, and the coughing and sneezing abounded.

Megan prayed for complete healing as if every bit of David's health rested in the hands of the Almighty. At the same time she worked as if it was all up to her. She thought God supported her in that approach to life.

The lads healed up quickly with no ill effect. And David right along with them.

When the cold finally eased away, David said, as he ate chicken soup for the tenth time in a week, "I think I'm going to beat this cold without it getting into my chest."

Megan smiled. "Maybe I can finally make something else for a meal then."

"Would you please, Ma?" Ben did his share of fussing, but the hardy stew, brimming with onions and carrots and potatoes besides the thick noodles and big chunks of chicken, got scooped up and gobbled down fast.

"Can't we fry the chicken next time?" Zack added.

David smiled at her and shrugged. "It's delicious soup, Meg." He inhaled the warm, savory smell of it. "But I reckon we're ready for a change."

"As am I." Megan laughed. "So all three of you are well? It's glad of it, I am."

Rubbing on his chest, as he did so often, David said, "I feel better even than I felt before I got sick. I think staying to bed for the last few days—"

"You didn't do that as well as I wanted." Megan jabbed a very bossy finger at him.

"—and eating your soup," he went on.

"Eating it and eating it and eating it." Ben talked around a mouthful of biscuit.

"—drinking your medicinal tea," David added.

"There's tea for all of you after supper. No shirking on medicine until I'm satisfied that you're all safe as a mouse in a malt heap."

"All of that has helped." David turned back to his chicken stew with a sigh. "I think I'm going to be fine, not just from this cold, but from what was ailing me before. And it's thanks to you, Meggie."

"In time for Christmas too." Megan's satisfaction ran deep.

The boys filled their bellies with her stew, biscuits and honey, lots of milk, and a peach pie.

Megan couldn't stop herself from smiling as she watched her men feast.

"In fact, I'm feeling well enough that tomorrow I'm going to teach you how to feed the livestock and saddle a horse." He smirked at her, knowing just how well she liked her ranching lessons.

CHAPTER EIGHT

On Christmas, Dave felt more himself than he had since he'd tangled with that longhorn last spring.

At day's end, the boys tucked in bed, David and Megan sat before the fire in the parlor, watching the logs crackle and blaze. It was their special way of celebrating Christmas, just the two of them. Dave took the last sip of his tea and let the warmth ease into his bones.

"Why did you build such a large house, David?"

Maybe it was the warmth and the fact that he was drowsy and feeling the thrill of good health, but for the first time Dave could talk freely about Pamela.

"My first wife was born and raised in the city. She was used to civilization, a social whirl, and a fine home."

Megan smiled as she looked over her head at the high ceiling. "So you were trying to give her one of the three out here?"

A crack of laughter surprised him. Never, since her death,

had he come close to thinking or talking about his wife and found any urge to laugh. "I reckon that's exactly what I had in mind. I always wanted to come back west. Pamela didn't want to leave her mother or her friends. I knew they were building the railroad, and I had it in my head that we'd come when we could ride the train all the way. I even told her she'd be able to come back east to visit easily."

"Easily? We were days on that train and that was only to Chicago."

"Well, *easily* compared to riding a covered wagon."

"And I suppose if you have your own car it's fairly comfortable." Megan leaned her head on his shoulder. "Though not as comfortable as staying at home."

He felt the weight of it, the relaxed closeness, and realized he'd never felt this with Pamela. He'd been so determined to cherish her. Spoil her. Anything to make her happy. She'd reveled in the lavish parties and the glittering balls. She'd delighted in the theater in New York City and dinners in fine restaurants. She loved to shop and there was always a new bit of jewelry catching her eye or a gown that she simply had to have. And he'd been delighted to provide them for her.

But never had she sat quietly by the fire, exhausted after a long but lovely day, her weary head on his shoulder. Dave had respected Megan ever since she saved Zack's life. He'd been fond of her ever since she'd kept the boys quiet on the train so he could sleep. He was attracted to her wholesome beauty and loved holding her and sharing passion with her in the night.

Only now, at this moment as she rested her weary head

and enjoyed peace and quiet before a crackling fire, did he realize he loved her.

"I should have gotten you a Christmas present, Meg. You made something for me and got nothing in return. I'm sorry." He turned, expecting to see some trace of hurt in her eyes.

Instead, she raised her head off his shoulder and smiled until she nearly glowed. "You're well. 'Tis true, isn't it?"

"It's true. But don't change the subject. Can you forgive me for not getting you a gift?"

"You got me the most wonderful gift of all—you're healed." Megan stretched up and kissed him generously. "Beyond that—well, I just can't imagine what I'd even want."

Dave rested one open palm on her cheek, caressing the glorious freckles. Enjoying the blue eyes sparking in the firelight. "There is a gift I'd like to give you, such as it is."

"You don't need to get me anything." She sounded stern and honest, which only made Dave want to give her the gift more.

He inhaled slowly, wanting her to be fully aware of how true his words were. At last he spoke. "I want to give you the gift of my love, Megan Laramie."

A tiny gasp escaped her lips. He caught the gasp with his mouth and returned her kiss full measure. He was a long time going on. "Getting you for my wife is the best thing that ever happened to me. Will you accept the gift of my love?"

"Oh yes, David. I accept it and return it completely."

Dave didn't know he was waiting to hear that until he did. Relief swept through him like a Wyoming windstorm. He kissed her deeply and pulled her hard against him. Her arms came around his neck. He pressed her down on the sofa until they lay together.

The fire burned low. The smell of the crackling wood surrounded them. A log split and fell, sending sparks dancing upward. The wind howled outside, but it couldn't reach them as they shared their warmth within sturdy walls.

It was a peaceful, holy night.

"Everything is going to be perfect," Megan whispered between kisses. "I feel it in my bones."

CHAPTER NINE

But Megan's brain wasn't located in her bones, now, was it?

David's lessons on ranching continued at an almost desperate pace, as if he expected to die any moment. He still clutched his chest, though when she asked about it he would catch himself and shake his head.

"I know I'm fine. I'm sure of it. But any little twinge sets me to worrying. I'll get over it."

The tenth time in a week she found David holding his hand against his chest, looking into the distance, she finally took action.

A little talk with Roper. A few arrangements, then wait for the first nice day to present itself . . . which took over a month. February third. Spring was still a long way off, but the day was clear; the wind wasn't bitter. And Megan was losing her mind.

"Sure and 'tis a beauty of a day, David. I'd like for us to take a trip to town if we could."

David looked up from his breakfast, surprised. "Town, why?"

She'd considered claiming to be out of flour or sugar or needles. But those would be lies and she wasn't a liar.

"Because I'd like to talk to the doctor. Roper told me there's a new doctor in town and he's a good one."

"D-Doctor?" David took such a nervous glance at her middle, she knew exactly what he was thinking.

Laughing, Megan waved two hands at him. "No, not for that."

Although she had to admit it wasn't altogether impossible. But the notion of having a doctor involved in something as natural as having a baby, should one ever come, was foolish.

"I want you to go."

"Why? I'm fine. I don't need a doctor."

"True enough and that's exactly why I want you to see him. To tell you you're fine. I see you worry, and it's because of that Chicago doctor. I want someone to reassure you."

The boys picked that moment to come clamoring into the kitchen, still in their nightshirts, demanding breakfast. Nothing more got said about town until the boys had cleaned their plates.

Later, as Megan guided the boys out of the kitchen to get them dressed, she looked over her shoulder at David. "Get your warmest coat on. Roper is going to mind the boys while we're gone. He's bringing the horses around now."

"The horses?" David sat up straight. "You're going to ride a horse all the way to town?"

"I've been practicing, haven't I?" And she'd gotten pretty good.

"You'll fall off and break your neck."

The boys had run ahead. She knew they were capable of dressing themselves so Megan stayed to have this out. "We're going, and that's that. I'll be back with my coat on in two shakes."

"I don't think—"

"David Laramie." Her tone was too sharp, but she couldn't help it. He was so stubborn. "We're going or I'll send Roper to town to fetch the doctor out. But you are going to see a doctor however it has to be arranged."

"I don't need a doctor."

"I see the worry in your eyes. You're willing to hope that you're well but you can't let go of your fretting, and what's more, I don't blame you. It's a sword hanging over your head and I want to have done with it."

"The doctor in Chicago said—"

"Fine!" Megan cut him off. She charged for the back door as Roper led the horses up. "You're going to have to ride to town for the doctor," she told the foreman. "David won't go."

Roper nodded and turned to lead one horse back to the barn.

"No, bring them back." David came up behind her. "I'll go."

She could feel his irritation, his hot breath felt rather like an angry bull breathing down her neck.

But she was getting her way, so she didn't fuss.

✤

"We have to ride hard to get to town and back, the weather can change suddenly and we'll be trapped away from the boys." Dave looked at his stubborn wife clinging to her saddle horn. He'd put her on a livelier horse than Old Blue, one Megan had ridden a few times.

If they took Blue they wouldn't get to town until after the spring thaw.

"It's a long ride in and home. The weather may not hold." Dave was in the mood to torment his wife just a little. He took her reins. "Hold on tight. We're going to trot."

But not gallop. Dave knew she'd never survive that.

They set a steady pace and Megan was hanging on well, when they rounded the last of the rugged hills. One look at the snow-packed trail and Dave pulled both horses to an abrupt halt. He snagged Megan before she could go flying off her mount.

"What's—"

"Hush." Dave hissed the word at her. "This way." He whirled his horse, still hanging on to Megan, and rode behind a stand of aspens. "Get down."

He didn't wait for her to obey him. He dragged her off her horse. Tied both animals to the meager shelter and whipped his rifle out of the boot on his saddle. "Stay behind me."

"What is it?" Megan whispered.

Dave pointed. "Up there." He barely breathed the words as he pointed to a massive oak tree with branches that stretched across the trail.

A thin gasp told him Megan had seen the mountain lion lying on the low branch, waiting to pounce on anything that came down this trail.

"I'll clear her out."

"Her?" Megan leaned forward until her front was pressed against his back. Her warmth and strength made him smile even while he was shaken from how close they'd come to being a meal for a lion.

"Shh!" Dave found he enjoyed bossing Megan around. It wasn't an admirable quality, but that didn't stop him from smiling as he took aim.

One blast, the branch splintered under her front legs and the lion leapt to its feet. With a snarl, the lion coiled its muscles and looked straight at David as if to attack. Dave fired a fast line of bullets across the branch inches below where the cat stood. Bark splattered the critter with every shot. Dave sprayed the old girl without hurting her. He hadn't done much shooting for a long time, but he still had that almost eerie speed and accuracy. He traced a line of bullets all the way to her tail, taking pleasure in how naturally the skill came and how confident he was that he wouldn't harm the cat.

Finally, in an almost human scream, the mountain lion whirled away and vanished from sight.

"Let's get out of here before she comes back."

"You could tell it was a girl?"

"Yes, a mama with babies in a den around here some-where." He could see that she was nursing young ones. Dave hadn't realized how much he'd missed life in the West. He'd learned so much before he'd been driven away, and now he was back and he had a wife he loved and sons who filled his heart with pride. He was going to live. In that instant he knew it, as well as any man can know a thing like that.

"If we were closer to home, I might've killed her to protect the cattle and my hands, and because there's good eatin' on a big cat like that. But this far from the ranch there's no sense shooting her and leaving her babies orphaned." The thought of his own boys almost being orphaned had stayed his hand.

"That's how good a shot you were when you were the O. T. Rider, wasn't it?"

"Yep. I was too good and too willing to pull the trigger."

Megan stared at that line of bullet holes for a long time, then she tossed her hair and said, "I reckon you oughta teach me to shoot."

David controlled a shudder to think of Megan with a gun. "Just as soon as you've learned to ride." That'd give him a long, long time.

"I'm a fine rider now so we can start target practice tomorrow." She gave him a chipper little pat on the back as they returned to their horses.

He'd need to figure out a way to keep her busy or she'd fill all their backsides full of buckshot. Climbing back into their saddles, Dave took Megan's reins, then kicked his horse into a gallop.

Megan, the master horsewoman, squeaked as she clung to her saddle and galloped alongside him.

CHAPTER TEN

Somehow Megan had expected a young man, but the word *new* just meant new to the area, apparently.

Dr. Sirpless had a tidy white moustache, a clean black suit on his small frame, and a gruff, no-nonsense attitude.

"Take another deep breath." The man listened to David's chest while Megan stood off to the side, praying.

Finally the doctor heard enough. "Who'd you say told you your heart was giving out?"

"Doctor Filbert. I couldn't get over my chest pains, and I was told he was the top doctor in Chicago. I—"

"Doctor Filbert, you say? Norman Filbert? Tall, stout, wears a monocle."

"My doctor had a monocle."

"And practices out of a flashy office in the tallest building in Chicago?"

"Well, that sounds like him. It was a tall building for sure. I didn't get his first name. But I was told he was the top—"

"The man's a quacksalver."

Dave's eyes narrowed. "A quack-what?"

"A quacksalver. A fraud."

"Oh no. I saw his college diploma framed right on his wall."

"Of course you saw it. He's a real doctor, just a poor excuse for one. He's told so many people they're dying they ought to name a section of the Chicago cemetery after him. Except no one'd be in it. He's wrong most of the time."

"B-B-But then, why was I told he was the top doctor?"

A rude snort came to that question. "Who told you?" The doctor paused for just a second, then held up a hand. "Wait, I'll answer my own question. It was a rich Chicago socialite, right?"

"Well, I suppose that describes her. But more than one person said it."

"He prescribes snake oil to rich old women. Not that he doesn't get a few men to take it too. He convinces them they're dying and they need his snake oil to delay their deaths. He's an outright fraud. But he's got devoted followers in the richest part of Chicago, so no one can make him close his doors."

"He never tried to sell me any medicine."

"Were you supposed to go to a follow-up visit?"

"Yes, but he made it sound so hopeless, I didn't go back. I started getting my affairs in order instead."

"If you'd gone back he'd have given you an elixir he invented himself. It's about eighty percent whiskey. And you'd have felt mighty good after you drank it." The doctor added, "You've got pleurisy, son."

Megan broke in. "What's that?"

"It's an ailment of the lungs. An unusual side effect of pneumonia. It can be dangerous, but yours isn't. You say the pain has ebbed?"

"Yes. I feel much better and keep improving, but I keep hearing Dr. Filbert's voice saying I'm dying."

"Well, you need to get over it because you're fine. Sometimes a body that's had pneumonia is a little more apt to get it again. Their lungs are weak. If you find yourself troubled by it next winter, you might want to consider pulling up stakes for a warmer climate. Texas or Arizona. But you're going to be fine."

"Fine? Really?" David's shoulders squared. Life blazed from his eyes.

Megan laughed for joy, then abruptly stopped. Her head felt a bit fuzzy with all that relief. Her legs wobbled and the room lurched. She reached for the table. David caught her just as her knees gave out. She was only vaguely aware of being laid down on the table.

The doctor fussed over her and asked her a few questions that made no sense before helping her sit up. She was a bit disgruntled to be the patient instead of David.

"Foolishness to faint over such good news," Megan muttered.

"Stop getting your affairs in order and start enjoying life. Including that baby you've got on the way." Dr. Sirpless jabbed a finger at Megan's midsection.

Megan looked down at her stomach, then up at the doctor, then over at David. "Baby?"

"Really, there's a baby?" A smile broke out on David's face. "You're sure?"

"I am indeed sure. I've been doing this for a long time." The doctor smiled and slapped David on the back so hard he almost stumbled into Megan on the examining table. "Now, get on home and forget Norman Filbert. I think I'll sit down and write another letter to Chicago. They need to be warned not to bury any of that idiot's patients just on Filbert's say-so."

A few moments later Megan found herself on the sidewalk with David. They walked silently down the street for a few seconds, then Megan turned to David just as he turned to her. He moved toward her just as she moved toward him. She threw her arms around him. He laughed, lifted her off her feet, and swung her in a circle.

Setting her down, he pulled back to look her in the eye.

He sobered and pulled a kerchief from his pocket. "Why the tears?"

"They're happy tears, David. Joyous tears."

"Oh, good. I thought maybe you were crying because you just realized you were stuck with me for life."

Megan gasped in outrage just as David started laughing. Then Megan joined in. David hauled her toward the horses tied to the hitching post. "Let's get on home."

As he reached to untie his horse, the building across the street caught Dave's eye. "Wait. Before we go, I want to do something."

He grabbed Megan's hand and she came along, laughing,

as if she were almost giddy from all the good news as he crossed the dirt street and went into the church across from the doctor's office.

Inside were a few rows of rustic benches. At the front was a platform with an altar made of rough-cut wood.

David kept moving until he stood in front of that altar, then he turned to face Megan.

"What is it you want, David?" Her smile was so generous. So kind. She was happy. And it was because he was going to live. He couldn't remember when anything had touched him more.

"Do you remember our wedding day?"

Megan made a rude scoffing sound. "It was only a few months ago. Sure and I'm not likely to forget something so important."

"Well, pretty little Megan, do you remember the vows you took—for better or worse, richer or poorer, in sickness and in health as long as we both shall live?"

"I made all those promises before God and man and meant every one of them."

"As did I. But when I said 'for better or for worse,' I thought things were going to be much worse. When I said 'for richer or for poorer,' I knew the money was there for the richer part but was mighty afraid you were making a poor bargain. And when I said 'in sickness and in health,' I was consigning myself to death and you to the hard work of caring for me through it. And when I said 'as long as we both shall live,' I thought I was making a six-month promise with a wild chance at a year."

"There's nothing wrong with any of those promises, David. Just because things will work out much better than we hoped, it doesn't change the power of that oath."

"Yes, but I want to say them again. I want to say them with joy, with hope for a long life and a future shared that may well last until our old age."

Megan smiled.

"So you'll do it? You'll take these vows again with me?"

Her smile turned into a laugh. "I would be honored to repeat my vows with you." Megan leaned forward and kissed him.

"I wish the boys had come, though I didn't dare bring them. At our first wedding I felt like you were taking all your vows with only motherhood in mind. I didn't plan to be around long and I believed that you knew that."

"Hush, it's a sad thing to speak of at such a happy moment." Megan pressed her fingers against his lips.

David said, "No, it *was* sad when we were first married, but today is the most joyful day of my life. A new chance at life. A woman I love in my arms. A baby on the way. I want to take joyful vows. Today they will mean something different and wonderful."

Another lingering kiss delayed the moment, but finally David raised his head, his eyes locked on hers. "In sickness and in health."

Megan echoed him and they kissed again.

And so it went as each vow came from their hearts, until their promises were made and their love declared before the

Lord in His holy church. When they were finished, Dave rested one hand on their child. He could almost cover her whole belly with one of his big hands.

The door to the church swung open and an elderly man stepped in. He seemed to understand their wish for privacy because he said, "I'm the parson here, but don't mind me, folks." He gave them a gentle smile and turned aside. As they faced each other, from high overhead, bells began to peal.

"He rings those bells every morning and night at the same time," Dave whispered, kissing her forehead. "But tonight they are wedding bells."

The crystal-clear song of the bell declared their love and happiness to the whole town.

"I love you, Megan Laramie."

"And I you, David Laramie."

They turned, and as if this were a formal ceremony in fine dress with the pews full of family and friends, David wound her hand through his elbow.

"'Tis not proper that our child should attend our wedding, husband. It's best the wee one never knows of this."

David laughed. "Let's go home."

Side by side, arm in arm, with reason at last to hope they were beginning a long, healthy, joyful marriage, they marched out together to the sound of winter wedding bells.

Reading Group Guide

And Then Came Spring

1. Mary-Jo's most prized possessions were a deck of cards and her Singer sewing machine. One represented the past; the other her hopes for the future. How did those playing cards keep her from embracing God's plan and giving her heart fully to Tom?

2. Mary-Jo blamed luck for everything good and bad that happened. What do you think was the biggest influence in helping her learn to put her faith in God and His wondrous grace?

3. Tom had some preconceived ideas about mail-order brides in general and Mary-Jo in particular. He was soon to learn the error of his ways. Have you ever judged someone negatively in advance, only to change your mind in a positive way later?

An Ever After Summer

1. After only dreaming of a different life, Ellie is handed the opportunity to actually change her life. Dreaming and stepping out on faith and taking action are two very different things. Ellie felt the Lord by her side and committed herself to take action. Have you ever dared to step out in faith and change your life?

2. Lem told Mathew to "Quit thinking about what you don't have and start thinking about what you have." Many people miss blessings in their lives because they are looking back instead of forward. Discuss this with the group. What does the Bible tell us about looking back?

3. Despite his fears Mathew fell in love with Ellie. What was he afraid of? He wasn't as ready as Ellie was to trust the Lord. What changed his mind? Have you ever been fearful of trusting God? Discuss this with the group.

Autumn's Angel

1. On page 245, Merry says that God wasn't surprised by the altered letters. Are you able to trust God, even when circumstances seem so wrong? Can you see that when the enemy means to do evil, God can mean it for good? Share when that has been true in your life.

2. On page 276, Shannon says that love always involves sacrifice. Do you agree? Why or why not?

3. On page 283, Luvena reminds Clay that he is a new creation in Christ. What old things has God made new in your life?

Winter Wedding Bells

1. The trip from Chicago to Wyoming on a train was considered an almost miraculous improvement and yet it took days in uncomfortable conditions. Talk about the difference between the hardships of pioneer days versus hardships now.

2. A poor medical diagnosis given by an influential "doctor to the upper classes" sent David's life into a tailspin. Megan accused David of not trusting his life to God. Do we do that today? Put our faith in science over God?

3. Megan and David's marriage was a complete marriage of convenience. Two strangers married a day after they met. But their commitment was freely given and they found a way to make their marriage work under difficult circumstances. How much differently do people treat their marriage vows today than they did back then?

An Interview with the Authors

Behind the Scenes with Your Favorite Matchmakers

AMI MCCONNELL, EDITOR: Your readers and I are interested in how this collection came together. Can you tell us about how the four of you met?

MARGARET BROWNLEY: I first met Robin years ago when she was president of Romance Writers of America and I was on the board. Mary is partly responsible for my switching from secular to inspirational fiction. Her *Petticoat Ranch* caught my eye, and it had everything I love in a story. I had the pleasure of first meeting Debra during a book signing at the Anaheim Convention Center. That huge auditorium was filled with five hundred writers, and Debra just happened to be sitting across the aisle from me. I took that as a good sign.

DEBRA CLOPTON: Yes, that was amazing to find you sitting there in that huge room, Margaret. I was so glad to meet you, and it was meant to be. I'd met Robin in 2003, when my first book, *The Trouble with Lacy Brown*, was up for the Golden Heart, and she was there to present the RITA award. I met Mary soon after on a bus heading to the Denver airport from the ACFW conference—"Hey, Deb," she said, then added something witty, and she's been cracking me up ever since. When my agent asked me if I had time to be a part of this novella group, I jumped at the chance . . . I know a good thing when I see it. And this has been nothing but a good thing!

ROBIN LEE HATCHER: Absolutely, Debra, it's been a good thing! One of my favorite writing activities is brainstorming with other writers. Brainstorming with you gals has been double the fun because you're all amusing, witty women. I love how our conference calls have been filled with laughter. Better yet, working with you has brought me three new friends to treasure.

MARY CONNEALY: I remember that bus ride, Debra. You were so Texan! With such a great Texas accent. (I know what you're thinking, *I don't have an accent.* YOU have an accent!) You're a perfect fit for our *A Bride for All Seasons* collection. I remember when we started brainstorming this book, and honestly, we just had to start from nothing, right?

Robin seems to be the brains of the organization, although it is Margaret who figured out how to do a conference call. Just getting the call dialed right is pretty hi-tech for me. Then when we were talking, all I could add to the mix was, "Mine's gonna be a cowboy." Not real helpful.

Margaret, you really started writing what you're writing because of me? That's a little annoying, honestly, because you seem to be doing it *better* than me, which hardly seems fair.

Brainstorming with you ladies has been as much fun as I've ever had. It's just amazing how we can bounce ideas off each other and veer off this way and that and end up far from where we started. I need you all to help me brainstorm my regular books.

MARGARET: Better than you? Mary, surely you jest. Speaking of that first conference call, I remember it well; we settled pretty quickly on the "mail-order bride" idea. We decided to give each bride a season, and I chose spring. That's because I don't do weather well. My first historical novel was a family saga spanning fifty years, and not once in all that time did a single cloud mar my fictional sky. In California, the only seasons we know are baseball, football, and basketball.

DEBRA: If I remember right, we each grabbed our favorite season. In Texas, you never know what's going to happen during the long summer months, so it offers lots of plot problems to throw at my hero and heroine.

ROBIN: Where I live in southwest Idaho, we have over three hundred days of clear sunshine every year so I totally understand your no-clouds comment, Margaret. But Idaho does have four distinct seasons, and I do love autumn. So Debra's right about that.

One of the things I loved so much was seeing how the idea of having the owner of the catalogue creatively edit customers' letters played out in each of the stories. First Mary shared her idea, and I remember thinking, *I wish I'd thought of that.* And then someone else shared, and I wished I thought of that too. I was convinced I would never come up with anything Hitch could do for (to?) my characters. Am I the only one who suffers "brain freeze" when I see, hear, or read the creativity of other authors?

MARY: Robin, this is so true about the brain freeze. One of you would suggest something and I was just amazed at the way a writer's mind works. Who came up with Hitch and the *Hitching Post* (our mail-order catalogue company), anyway? Robin, it seems like it was you, but I really can't remember. When someone said it, it felt like, *of course* that's what we'll call it. It was such a perfect fit. But it all evolved in great brainstorming style.

MARGARET: Actually, the *Hitching Post* idea had been sitting in my computer for quite some time, but it never went anywhere. That's because it was only a seed. It needed the four of us working together for the idea to fully blossom. Personally, I think we should put our minds together and work on the economy next.

DEBRA: I don't know about that, Margaret! But I *loved* Hitch and his *Hitching Post* from the moment you suggested him in the brainstorming session! Matchmaking characters who cause trouble are my favorite, and he did it with such good-hearted intentions. And my entire Mule Hollow series is based around the "Matchmaking Posse," so it fit. Plus, I had two matchmakers of *my own* about four years ago, when two friends who knew both Chuck and me talked us into a blind date. Neither of us was dating or had been on a blind date before and we were both leery of them. But I was a young widow and had been alone for six years and felt God leading me to say yes. Chuck felt God's lead also—so we agreed to the date! Most nerve-wracking thing I've ever experienced. I was hyperventilating when I opened the front door! We hit it off instantly and have been happily married for a couple of years now. So, I'm not a mail-order bride, but I loved Hitch, in part because one of my matchmakers was a six-foot-four man :).

ROBIN: Jerry and I met poolside at my apartment complex on 8/8/88. Long story short, I asked him to let me know when I'd swum laps for fifteen minutes so I didn't have to bother to look at the clock (hard to see from in the pool). I swam and I swam. Finally I asked, "Isn't fifteen minutes up yet?" "No, not yet," he answered with a grin. After that exchange was repeated a few times, I knew I'd been had. By about an extra ten minutes worth of laps.

I guess Jerry's brothers kind of played matchmaker for us (and one of them is six foot four as well, Debra). After Jerry took me home to meet the family in the fall, they pulled him aside and told him he'd better not let this one get away or they'd give him what for. (Did I mention I liked his brothers from the start?) Poor guy. I'm not sure he knew what hit him from then on.

MARY: Wow, how did this little conversation turn to husbands? My husband is a farmer and rancher in Nebraska. He's my high school sweetheart, and we just celebrated our thirty-sixth anniversary. My husband is from a family of seven sons, and we've got four daughters. Much of the comedy in my books comes from watching My Cowboy try to figure out the girls. He adores them, and at times they drive him crazy with their tears and the nonstop chatter and all the giggling. My first book, *Petticoat Ranch*, is about a mountain man who's never been around women, who winds up married to a widow with four daughters. He is plunged into this confusing, charming, terrifying, all-girl world. A lot of the comedy from all my books, the way the women and men misunderstand each other, comes from watching my husband react to our girls.

MARGARET: Your husbands all have my deepest sympathies (especially Mary's). Any man brave enough to marry a woman who dreams up tall handsome cowboys for a living should have his head examined. Speaking of which, my husband is six foot six and even taller in his cowboy hat. We met in church, which seems rather dull, except I was engaged to someone else at the time. A sensible, logical, left-brained type, he's mystified to be married to a woman who knows how to travel across country in a covered wagon but can't figure out how to put gas in the car.

DEBRA: I love all of your how-I-met-my-husband stories! Hearing others' real-life beginnings is one of my favorite pastimes. My novella, *An Ever After Summer*, was my first historical love story, and I loved coming up with my characters' backstories and showing God's love to my characters. Y'all were so helpful walking me through the research process, and when I was lost as a goose on the Internet and coming up with *nothing*, I would ask and y'all were like the fastest guns in the West shooting me the answer or telling me where to go!

ROBIN: After more than thirty years of writing, I have the strangest information, especially of an historical nature, tucked away in my brain. Glad someone appreciates the info, Debra. Jerry has said I sometimes talk like I'm a hundred and fifty or two hundred years old. When he and I were first dating, the book on my coffee table was *The Cholera Years*. He should have had a clue about what being with a writer meant from my choice of reading material. But, lest I seem a complete relic, I also read *People* and *Entertainment Weekly*. Nothing like pop culture to snap me out of an historical fog!

MARY: I would love a copy of *The Cholera Years*, Robin. I tried to give one of my fictional towns a cholera epidemic and it was just all wrong. So frustrating. I needed a disease and settled on scarlet fever to wipe out a crowd of people, but I wanted a cholera outbreak badly and just couldn't make it work. Uh . . . that doesn't sound strange, by any chance, does it?

MARGARET: That particular book isn't on my coffee table, but the search history on my computer would make a great witness for the prosecution. Before the sheriff pounds on my door, I better run; I have a stagecoach to catch (oops, there's that historical fog Robin mentioned). One thing remains clear: we couldn't have written this book without the support and enthusiasm of our editor, Ami McConnell, and the entire Thomas Nelson gang. The best part? The four of us get to do it all over again—with a second collection!

DEBRA: For this next go-round I've already started collecting research books—so, girls, y'all have hooked me. And yes, as Margaret said, we couldn't have written this book without the fantastic support of our editor, Ami McConnell, and the awesome team at Thomas Nelson—thank you all so much. And, girls, I'm thrilled that we get to do another anthology together. I can't wait to get started!

ROBIN: How could any of us not adore an editor who says she is "impressed" with our "fantastic" ideas for the next collection? Seriously, it's been such a treat to work with Ami and everyone at Thomas Nelson. I count myself very fortunate.

MARY: Thomas Nelson has made this such a fun book for the four of us. We've managed to be ourselves in our own novellas while tying the four stories together in a way that makes a really fun collection. Ami, thank you for all your help. You've got a great gift, and I appreciate you sharing it with us.

AMI: You ladies are wonderful, and this has been so fun! But I'm going to have to close the interview now because you need to get back to writing. After all, we're now looking forward to your next collection, *Four Weddings and a Kiss*!

About the Authors

New York Times best-selling author Margaret Brownley has penned more than twenty-five historical and contemporary novels. Her books have won numerous awards, including Reader's Choice. She has published the Rocky Creek series, and *A Lady Like Sarah* was a Romance Writers of America RITA finalist. Happily married to her real-life hero, Margaret and her husband have three grown children and live in Southern California.

Debra Clopton is a multi-award-winning novelist who was first published in 2005 and has more than twenty-two novels to her credit. Along with her writing, Debra helps her husband teach the youth at their local Cowboy Church. Debra is the author of the acclaimed Mule Hollow Matchmaker series, the place readers tell her they wish were real. Her goal is to shine a light toward God while she entertains readers with her words.

BEST-SELLING NOVELIST ROBIN LEE HATCHER IS KNOWN for her heartwarming and emotionally charged stories of faith, courage, and love. The winner of the Christy Award for Excellence in Christian Fiction, the RITA Award for Best Inspirational Romance, the Carol Award, two *Romantic Times* Career Achievement Awards, and the RWA Lifetime Achievement Award, Robin is the author of more than sixty-five novels.

MARY CONNEALY WRITES ROMANTIC COMEDY WITH COW-boys. She is a Carol Award winner, and a Rita, Christy, and Inspirational Reader's Choice finalist. She is the author of the best-selling Kincaid Brides series: *Out of Control, In Too Deep, Over the Edge*; Lassoed in Texas trilogy; Montana Marriages trilogy; and Sophie's Daughters trilogy. Mary is married to a Nebraska rancher and has four grown daughters and two spectacular grandchildren.